King

75

Will Shakespeare and His America

Will Shakespeare and His America

by NANCY WEBB and
JEAN FRANCIS WEBB

Illustrated by EMIL WEISS

New York THE VIKING PRESS

Library of Congress catalog card number: 64-21479

Acknowledgment is made with thanks to Brandt & Brandt
for permission to quote on page 13 from *Western Star*
by Stephen Vincent Benét, published by Holt, Rinehart
& Winston, Inc. Copyright 1943 by Rosemary Carr
Benét.

For Lucinda, who
loved "the quick,
hot sting of words,
the bite of mind on
mind"

Since the curtain could not have risen upon much of this account of Will Shakespeare's adventures on American stages without the generous guidance and help of George Freedley, Curator of the Theatre Collection of the New York Public Library, the grateful authors hope that he will not be unwilling to take a bow.

Contents

8 *Contents*

Will Shakespeare and His America

Shottery
Anne Hathaway's Birthplace

1. The Yankee Swan

And one man in his time, he wrote, *plays many parts. . . .*

The line was not intended by its author as specifically autobiographical. Will Shakespeare was not even writing specifically of those Englishmen who, in his own lifetime, were exploring and settling a wide New World across the ocean.

Yet he was suggesting the one great characteristic which he and the hardy generations who would create America held in common: adaptability.

An ability to adjust himself to constantly changing circumstances is a pioneer's first requisite. He must be prepared to survive within environments unfamiliar, even unimagined. He must adopt, as his own, ways of life previously unknown. He must take unto himself strange customs, alien ideologies, foreign climates and agricultures and economic theories and religious tenets and social mores. He must be able, as Americans say, to roll with the punches.

Since the days of America's earliest beginnings, such adaptability has always of necessity been part of her national character. No other nation in history was ever called upon to meet such widely varying conditions in so compressed a period of time. We have gone from log cabins to skyscrapers, from huddled communities along one ocean's rim to the straddling of a wide continent, from physical hardships to luxuriant abundance, from colonial dependency to political world leadership, from Indian wars to the threshold of international peace, from forest trails to interplanetary rockets, all in less than four centuries. A people unable to adapt swiftly would have collapsed before even a fraction of such rapid and mighty changes.

As with America, so with William Shakespeare of Stratford-on-Avon in England's Warwickshire. The earliest English colonists on American soil, or nearly the earliest, brought with them from home a full familiarity with the playwright Shakespeare. And as the land they gentled and made their own progressed from stage to stage of its development, the playwright progressed with them—changing to fit the temper of each new time, speaking with an altered accent to each new generation, always and invariably an integral part of their daily living, yet always himself.

Stephen Vincent Benét says in *Western Star,* that:

> Those who came were resolved to be Englishmen,
> Gone to the world's end, but English every one,
> And they ate the white corn-kernels, parched in the sun,
> And they knew it not, but they'd not be English again. . . .

If this was true of those early adventurers, then surely it was equally true of the literary Englishman they had transported into their wilderness.

They tamed their forests and they built their cities and they bridged their continent. And almost from the first, Shakespeare was a part of it. He was read by candlelight as a revered philosopher in New England's earliest cultured homes. He was presented as a "moral dialogue" in Puritan communities enforcing the strictest bans against immoral theatre. He was set upon the first stages of Carolina and Virginia by actors who crossed the ocean with his prompt copies in their trunks. He provided the material for political broadsides in the struggle for liberty. He beguiled the Father of His Country, George Washington, and the voice of its conscience, Abraham Lincoln. He drew eager frontier audiences to river showboats and log-walled theatres. He was in the vanguard of the wild stampede to California's gold fields. He adapted himself to American-developed media unthought of in his time—to motion pictures, to radio, to television. He was part of America's first telecast to outer space.

And having been and done all this (and infinitely more that was American!), whatever part of him had grown into the fabric of this newer country than his own "would not be

English again." It was Will Shakespeare, Yankee. William Shakespeare, citizen of the United States.

John Shakespeare's son was English; English, blood and bone. His father's people for generations before him had played a sturdy part in Warwickshire history. In the village of Stratford, at various times, John Shakespeare was established as a glover, a wool dealer, a seller of cattle, and as a holder of public offices. First elected as one of the community's official ale-tasters, he was advanced to constable and then to bailiff, alderman, chamberlain and at last—in 1569, when his son Will was five years old—to the highest local office his fellow townsmen could bestow upon him. He became High Bailiff.

John's wife, Mary, came of sound English stock as well. In nearby Smithfield, her father—Robert Arden, Esquire—had been, until a year before Mary's marriage, the head of a land-holding family so venerable as to derive its name from the Forest of Arden. As seventh daughter of the squire, she had brought her husband considerable property—good, substantial, English property.

Yet English Will, even in his very young days, must sometimes have dreamed himself free of rural England. In those days when he was climbing the tile-roofed outdoor staircase by which pupils reached the classrooms of Stratford's free school—an ancient school founded under Edward IV—he probably indulged in frequent fantasies. And these very likely featured the intrepid figure of himself as an adventurer and explorer in the wide New World across the Atlantic.

His times were times when people talked avidly of Sir Francis Drake's amazing circumnavigation of the globe; of Sir Martin Frobisher's daring searches for a northwest passage to India. *A Discourse of a Discovery for a New Passage to Cataia* was a book which schoolboys (along with their elders) were gulping down whole. Englishmen were discussing at intimate range the contemporary exploits of John Hawkins, privateer extraordinary; his raids on the Portuguese western traders, his flaming adventure against the Spaniards in the Gulf of Mexico at Vera Cruz. The New World was an all-consuming interest. Studying his "small Latin and less Greek" at Stratford, Will Shakespeare could no more have escaped the fever of his era than twentieth-century youth can escape a fascination with space exploration.

During his final years at the school (the last of which saw him serving as assistant teacher to the junior boys) and during the years immediately following (when he was employed in the office of one of Stratford's seven attorneys-at-law), one great new enterprise in the Americas was following hard upon the heels of another.

In 1582, at the age of eighteen, Will married Anne Hathaway from Shottery, a short mile away, and became a family man. In the very next year, Sir Humphrey Gilbert voyaged to Newfoundland and founded there the first English colony of the New World. A year and a few months more, and Walter Raleigh was establishing another colony at Roanoke in what is now Virginia.

Will Shakespeare might have been chained by circumstances and responsibilities to familiar Warwickshire. But since he had an imagination—and it is doubtful that anyone questioned young Will's!—it would have been natural for him to set out in daydreams with Thomas Cavendish upon a circling of the earth, to see for himself these new marvels men prattled of.

By 1586, when Will was twenty-two, the lure of far places at least had grown strong enough to draw him from Stratford to bustling, thriving London. He left home to try his fortune with a company of play-actors. Various actors of the company, including the great Burbage (who one day would become the first Hamlet, the first Richard III, and Romeo, and Macbeth, and Shylock, and Othello), were neighbors from Stratford or the nearby region. In Warwickshire he had already written his *Venus and Adonis* and *Lucrece*. His marriage to Anne was not so happy as to anchor him at her side, and there were two other matters that troubled him. His father had recently been suffering financial misfortunes. Worse still, Will was in trouble with the influential Sir Thomas Lucy because of the poaching of a deer from Lucy forests. Perhaps what drew all these considerations together in a clear decision was the prevailing restlessness of the times. The urge was on him to be up and away, seeking new worlds to conquer even though these might not be the fabled New World itself.

A mere two years after his first arrival in London, England experienced panic and then riotous triumph as the "invincible" Spanish Armada closed in upon her for a kill, and was, instead, itself broken and scattered. This overwhelming victory, making Queen Elizabeth the undoubted mistress of the westward seas, determined once and for all that the New World was to be Anglo-Saxon rather than Spanish. New expeditions seemed to be setting sail on every favorable tide. Returning voyagers penned volumes about their travels that were widely circulated and eagerly read. The two most popular literary forms of the period were the plays of the dramatists and the accounts of exploration and travel. It is interesting to speculate about the extent to which discoveries in the new

America may have influenced the career of young William Shakespeare. For they vastly stimulated the public imagination, lifted old mental limitations, and inspired a general spirit of receptiveness to fresh ideas.

In the years following the defeat of the Armada, Will was an established figure at London's prominent Blackfriars' Theatre. He was active there as an actor, an owner, and most of all as a facile writer who was expert at altering older pieces of drama to fit the special needs of his own company of players. London already knew him as a playwright of distinction. His *Comedy of Errors,* his *Titus Andronicus* and *Love's Labour's Lost* and *Two Gentlemen of Verona,* had become established successes. Within an astonishingly few years thereafter, he was chief adviser and dramatic author for the Lord Chamberlain's Company—the theatrical cream of its time. He was, in fact, Ben Jonson's "Sweet Swan of Avon"—the term *swan* being then a reference to Apollo's assuming the form of the bird, a usual accolade for outstanding poets. Vergil was "the Mantuan Swan," Homer, "the Swan of Meander," and Will had earned his own feathers. Now New World heroes, Sir Walter Raleigh among them, were his intimates. He could learn from them at first hand of the marvels they had beheld.

Each day, the Thames became more and more crowded with vessels departing for, or returning from, the infant colonies in America. Businessmen were expanding their trade across the ocean. Prosperity and optimism were in the air. And London was the center, the heart, of immense activity. Its newest theatre had been fittingly christened the Globe.

Small wonder that into the noble plays which a maturing Will produced there should begin to creep references to this virgin land on which the interest of the day was focused. He was not deterred by the fact that many of the plays were set in periods of time long antedating man's acceptance of the fact that the world was otherwise than flat, or that fabulous new continents might lie beyond the Ocean Sea. He was writing poetry, not formal history. Anachronisms did not disturb him or his audiences. His characters were apt to be quite conversant with the New World, though they might be supposed to have lived long before the discoveries of Columbus, Vespucius, or Magellan.

Only once, to be sure, did Will actually use the name of the land inevitably so much on his mind. It was in *A Comedy of Errors,* a play set in "the ancient city of Ephesus," that Dromio of Syracuse was made to say, in describing a certain kitchen wench, "She is spherical, like a globe. I could find out countries in her." Having located several such, Dromio then was asked: "Where America, the Indies?" His answer: "O, Sir, upon her nose, all o'er embellished with rubies, carbuncles, sapphires. . . ." The allusion sprang from a mind accustomed to picture a land overflowing with uncounted riches—America! The first map ever to show a region called "America" was one drawn by Leonardo da Vinci and dated 1512–1515. In all, twelve Shakespearean plays—chiefly, the comedies—contain references to America and its current exploration.

"The Indies"—by which Will meant the West Indies—were introduced into half a dozen of the plays, regardless of the supposed periods of their action. Thus, a courtier in *Henry VIII* said of Anne Bullen, "Our king has all the Indies in his arms, And more, and richer. . . ." Shylock in *The Merchant of Venice* remarked upon "an argosy bound to Tripolis, another to the Indies." Falstaff, in *The Merry Wives of Windsor,* torn between the charms of Mistress Ford and Mistress

Page, declared, "They shall be my East and West Indies, and I will trade to them both." Orlando, in *As You Like It,* penned to his beloved a vow that "From the east to western Inde, No jewel is like Rosalinde."

As with the New World itself, so was Will Shakespeare familiar with the peculiar treasures of this realm. The newly discovered potato was a much-discussed luxury of the day, a novelty par excellence. It had remained entirely unknown to the European world until Hawkins and Raleigh brought it home from America when Will himself was just approaching his twenties. Yet many a Shakespearean character was gifted with an astonishing foreknowledge of the vegetable. In the reign of Henry IV, Falstaff could say, "Let the sky rain Potatoes." In the Grecian camp before Troy, "the devil luxury" could be described by Thersites as possessing a "fat rump and potato finger," just as though a potato were the prized gourmet treat to Troy that it had become to Elizabeth's England.

It was not merely the physical adventure of the discoveries and the sea battles, the rumored riches and the derring-do, that stirred Will Shakespeare to absorbing interest in the New World. Even more dazzling than these, no doubt, was the new breed of adventuresome political philosophy which was going into the colonization of that far-distant America.

The liberal-minded Earl of Southampton was Will's personal patron. And others equally important in the Virginia Company (formed to colonize that area of the New World, once Raleigh had claimed it and named it for Elizabeth, the Virgin Queen) were also his friends. Sir Edwin Sandys, Richard Hooker, and the Earl of Pembroke—he listened to them all. They discussed with him the future they envisioned for this vast, strange land. These were the men who were introducing into the charters of forming colonies their own concepts of equality and personal freedom; of due process of law and the rights of representative assembly; of goverment by the consent of the governed. They were the men who truly laid the cornerstones of America's future liberty. Will listened to their talk of "the well-ordered state where merit shall govern, and not the favoritism of kings or their fabled divinity." He was profoundly influenced by it. All through his works may be found evidences of his sympathy with their liberal convictions; convictions which in Will's day were startling and radical.

He could not guess, of course, that men of generations still unborn—men to be named Benjamin Franklin, Patrick Henry, Thomas Jefferson, Samuel and John Adams—would be as greatly moved by this philosophy as was he himself, nor that the ideals he personally heard expounded would one day form the basis for a document to be called the Declaration of Independence.

He could, however, stroll beside the Thames and view the masts of ships in which those adventuresome colonists were setting out in pursuit of much the same dreams he was writing into poetry. And who can say what part of him sailed with them?

Small wonder, then, that he should eventually come to the composition of more than brief lines and scenes drawn from the prevailing New World fever of his age. It was all but inevitable that Will Shakespeare should write a full play based upon his preoccupation with this great new America.

2. A Play about the New World

When capable Sir Thomas Gates was sent out from England in the year 1609 to assume the governorship of prospering Virginia, a party of some five hundred hopeful new colonists sailed with him. Gates's full-rigged flagship, the three-hundred-ton *Sea Venture,* moved out from port at the head of a worthy fleet of "seven good ships and two pinnaces." Aboard her, in addition to Sir Thomas, were 150 souls. They included Sir George Somers, Admiral of the Seas, and his Vice-Admiral, Captain Christopher Newport. More important still, the *Sea Venture* was transporting to an infant colony the newly granted Virginia Charter—as well as critically needed supplies of food and goods.

Along with their hopes and aspirations, few of the emigrating company could have failed to take with them memories of the plays of Will Shakespeare. Elizabethan England was devoted to the theatre, and the humblest Londoner stood often in the pit to watch the great Richard Burbage enact the roles written down by his even greater neighbor from Stratford. Scarcely half a dozen years earlier, *Othello* had been first played before the Queen herself. More recently yet, *Macbeth* had become the new popular favorite. The colonists could not have escaped awareness of Master Shakespeare, nor he, with his close relationship to the Virginia Company's Earl of Southampton, an awareness of them. Whether or not he actually watched as Sir Thomas's fleet took the tide, certainly his thoughts and speculations must have followed them.

The expedition failed to live up to the glowing purposes of those who had undertaken it. While it still lay far short of Virginia, a savage typhoon—"a dreadful storme and hideous" —scattered the fleet. Although the rest of the buffeted vessels eventually fought through to their destination on the mainland of America, the *Sea Venture* herself was driven toward the little-known but much-feared coast of Bermuda. Listing sharply, more than half-sunk, she had been bailed continuously for three days and nights by her exhausted crew before land was sighted. On the orders of Sir George Somers, she was intentionally headed for the reef and run aground.

Then, while jagged underwater outcroppings held her in position, her longboat was launched and the whole of the ship's company, men, women, and children, were ferried ashore. After the human cargo came the rest of it—provisions and goods, personal possessions and supplies, even a good portion of the ship's rigging and iron and timbers, all to be piled along the beach safe in from the tides. Only as the salvage work neared its completion did the *Sea Venture* writhe free of the submerged reefs which gripped her, and, sliding off into deep water, sink from the sight of those on the shore.

During the following nine months the castaways cut and trimmed the island's native cedar into planks, and built with salvaged nails and rigging two smaller pinnaces fit to carry them to their original objective, Jamestown on the Virginia shore.

When first reports of the disaster returned to England, talk of the storm and the shipwreck eclipsed all other topics. Bermuda had borne an evil name with navigators because of her treacherous reefs since the shipwreck of the Spaniard, Juan Bermudez, who discovered the island group. Henry May, the first English victim of the undersea barrier, christened the scene of his shipwreck late in 1591, Isle of Devils, "for the number of black hogs that all the men did shun as hell and perdition." Each writer of the day to discuss the islands thereafter merely added to their unsavory reputation. In his *History of Virginia,* Captain John Smith described Bermuda as "to all seamen no less terrible than an enchanted den of furies and devils, the most dangerous, unfortunate and forlorne place in the world."

The scene of the *Sea Venture*'s misfortune thus already offered a mysterious and sinister image to the public mind; an image to enhance greatly the factual reports which presently began to make the full story known. Promptly upon Governor Gates's arrival in his appointed colony, there was published "by advice of the Councell of Virginia" a pamphlet, entitled *A True Declaration of the estate of the Colonie in Virginia,* which officially absolved Gates of responsibility for the disaster. This pamphlet made available to Will Shakespeare, back in England, a full account of the storm and wreck.

He had other sources of information, less official but perhaps more graphic. Upon returning to London, one of the shipwrecked—a certain Silvester Jourdan—published, in October 1610, his own version of the disaster. Gate's own secretary, William Strachey, later to become recorder of the Council of Virginia, had already written during the previous July a letter to "an excellent lady" in England, describing the events. Although this letter was promptly suppressed by the authorities (because of its candid reports on governmental abuses, starvation, epidemics, misfortunes with unfriendly savages, mutinies, and other happenings not thought to be encouraging to prospective colonists), much evidence still exists to indicate that it came into Shakespeare's hands long before its eventual publication. A tradition survives in the Strachey family that upon William Strachey's return to England in 1611 he personally furnished new details of the wreck to Shakespeare by word of mouth.

It was almost inevitable that such an event, set against such a background, should profoundly stir the poet's imagination. And it is far from surprising that out of his imaginings a new play should emerge. He called it *The Tempest*. It was first performed at Whitehall on November 1, 1611, only a few months after Sir Thomas Gates (who had returned to England to purchase cattle) sailed again for Virginia.

The very title suggested the relationship of the play to the disaster of the *Sea Venture,* and this suggestion was immediately strengthened by the play's opening with storm and shipwreck and an eerie enchanted isle. Descriptions of the New World which were current in England at the time obviously provided models for Shakespeare's landscapes, birds, and flowers. These would have indicated Bermuda as his actual setting, even had he not caused Ariel to speak in so many words of "the still-vexed Bermoothes." The concept of Ariel was probably based upon William Strachey's account of a mysterious "little round light, like a faint Starre," which Sir George Somers had sighted while on watch during the *Sea Venture*'s final struggle with the sea.

The naming of its principal characters is further evidence of the play's New World genesis. Richard Eden's *History of Travayle in the West and East Indies,* in Elizabethan times a master work on the subject, contained them all—Fernando de Soto for Ferdinand, Gonzalo Jiménez de Quesada for Gonzalo, Antonio Pérez for Antonio, and so on.

Certainly Caliban was a native American—Shakespeare's single attempt at such a characterization. His name is merely a variation of "cannibal." The voyagers and explorers of Elizabethan days unanimously reported that devils and Indians and cannibals were to be found in the exotic New World. Caliban himself is made to stress the point of his origin by referring to "my dam's god, Setebos," and by exclaiming, "O Setebos, these be brave spirits indeed!" Setebos was the devil-god of the Patagonians who occupied the whole southern half of the South American continent. Richard Eden had fully described him for Shakespeare and other avid readers of the age.

Three and a half centuries after Will Shakespeare had been laid to rest in the chancel of his own parish church, there occurred a postscript to the disaster of the *Sea Venture*—and so, in a sense, to the plot of *The Tempest*—which certainly would have captured his active imagination.

One of the original ship's company was a young man of twenty named George Yeardley, later knighted and appointed Governor of Virginia. During the summer of 1958, one of Yeardley's latter-day descendants, Edmund Downing, was stationed in Bermuda as a civilian employee of the United States naval station there. Downing had taken to diving from his launch, the *Yachet,* in stubborn search for the vanished ship upon which his ancestor had arrived in the New World. Although the *Sea Venture* had lain undisturbed for centuries, and her very existence was regarded less as fact than as legend by many Bermudians, Downing had pressed his search all along the island coast throughout the summer. Months of failure had not discouraged him.

On the afternoon of October 18, the American got into his rubber diving suit as he had done so many times before, adjusted the air hose attached to his face mask, and went over the *Yachet's* side and down the ladder. At the point where the *Yachet* was anchored, the reef lay three-quarters of a mile offshore, and the sandy bottom was thirty-five feet below the launch's keel. Almost as soon as Downing began to prowl along the ocean floor he sighted piles of flint such as had been used for ballast in the ships of the sixteenth and seventeenth centuries. Then, dead ahead in the shimmering water, he made out the configuration of two jutting coral walls some seven yards apart. In the sand between them, he could see the dim shape of a keel and the ribs of a ship—obviously, even at that first glance, a very old ship indeed.

Excitement seized him as he studied his find, for he had not come upon it altogether by accident. A friend in Bermuda had suggested that this was a likely place for the *Sea Venture* to have gone down, since it was almost the only formation in the reef where a vessel might have been wedged and held motionless, as ancient records reported the lost flagship to have been. The bow of the ship's skeleton was pointed dead toward a sandy beach to the south of St. Catherine's Fort; a favorable place for landing a longboat. And the depth was close to Ariel's "full fathom five" of the wreck Shakespeare had described in *The Tempest*.

During the weeks following Downing's discovery, the possibility that he had indeed at last come upon the *Sea Venture* became stronger. As long salvage operations went on, artifacts from the skeleton wreck were brought up to the sunlight they had not seen for over three centuries—a pottery vase warped from its original shape by encrustations of coral, a large cannon, a six-inch pewter spoon, a Bellarmine stone jug, and numerous ancient cannon balls. The operations attracted so much attention that an expert was flown to Bermuda from the Smithsonian Institution in Washington to study the finds. He pronounced the objects he examined, every one, to date from the general period of the *Sea Venture*'s disaster.

Meanwhile, a retired Canadian engineer had become interested and had taken it upon himself to check another aspect of the mystery—what the *Sea Venture* had looked like. An exhaustive hunt for information on this point had already revealed that no plans of the vessel were still in existence. Diligent research had yielded up only two facts, that the *Sea Venture* was built in Suffolk, England, between the years 1603 and 1609; and that she was "an English shippe of 300 tonnes."

For the Canadian, with his expert's knowledge, this meager information was enough. Since all ships of the period were constructed on the same formula, he had needed to know only the *Sea Venture*'s tonnage before beginning to construct a scale model. He worked on a standard rule for early seventeenth-century shipbuilding—that the distance between the forward tip of the keel and the "king timber" (located at a vessel's center of buoyancy) must be exactly one-third of the keel's total length. If the keel's length were known, then measurements for the remainder of the structure could be computed. These dimensions were immutably fixed by the length of the keel.

The distance between the ancient wreck's king timber and the forward tip of her keel—22½ feet—indicated an original keel length of 75 feet, of which the forward 54 feet still remained. Using the established ratio—a depth dimension of 15 feet, a beam of 26½ feet, a deck length of 100 feet—the engineer was able to determine that the remains of the wreck duplicated the *Sea Venture*'s original measurements almost precisely. This, added to the wreck's position, wedged into the reef in exact accord with contemporary accounts; the fact that no other ship of her period had gone down anywhere nearby; and the evidence of undoubted English construction in the salvaged scraps of the wreck, convinced naval experts that the *Sea Venture* had been found.

Will Shakespeare would have been delighted by the drama, the adventure, the detective work, combined in this sequel to his play about the New World. To that world's misfortune, he survived by only five years the first production of *The Tempest*. Had he lived longer, and wearied of his self-imposed retirement, who can say what further "American" master-pieces he might have written? What other comedies or tragedies concerning the distant land to which he, in common with all Englishmen of his time, felt closely allied?

3. Rise of Curtain

In view of the influence he was to exert over all future American theatre, it would be pleasant to be able to claim for Will Shakespeare the authorship of the first theatrical venture in the New World. Unfortunately, this is not possible. It took Master Will a hundred years and more to duplicate his London "on-stage" success in the growing colonies.

America's first theatrical performance (in Europe's understanding of theatre) was probably given in Mexico about 1519, the date of the Spanish Conquest. In the English-held regions along the Atlantic seacoast, such activities did not begin until much later, yet as early as 1602, in Virginia, the officially prepared Daily Prayer referred to "Papists and Players . . . the scum and dregs of the earth." Actors were held in such low esteem that they were debarred from the growing settlements, a circumstance which resulted, back home in England, in vengeful stage parodies against the colonists. It goes without saying that, to be singled out for discrimination, players must already have existed in the New World.

The earliest theatrical performance on record in the northern part of the New World was not in English, but in French; not in one of England's colonies, but in King Louis's Canada. But it was the forerunner of a form of American entertainment that was to become popular after a passage of centuries—it was an "aqua show." It was called *Neptune's Theatre* and was written and staged at Port Royal in Acadia (now Nova Scotia) in 1606, the year Will Shakespeare wrote *Macbeth* and fourteen years before the *Mayflower* arrived at Cape Cod. The performance was intended as a celebration of the return of the governor, who had been off with Samuel de Champlain, the "Father of New France," exploring the coastline of the Cape, but the "jovial spectacle" served the dual purpose of maintaining morale among the soldiers left behind at the fort by the expedition.

When the Governor's barque dropped anchor offshore, an astonishing armada moved out upon the water to meet the returning adventurers. White beard and blue robe flying in the wind, trident and gold crown gleaming, King Neptune himself stood in the leading barge. Following him came canoes manned by Tritons and "savages." Each one in turn delivered an oration of welcome, and when the performance was ended the Governor invited all comers to a hearty feast inside the "Habitation." Champlain wrote appreciatively in his *Voyages* of the "sundry jollities for our entertainment."

French Canada appears to have been more hospitable to the theatre than her English neighbors to the south. On September 10, 1640, "in honor of the new-born Dauphin," actors presented a tragicomedy which so impressed one spectator, Paul Le Jeune, that he wrote: "I would not have believed that so handsome apparel and so good actors could be found in Kébec." A secondary purpose of this entertainment seems to have been to impress Christian piety upon the pagan Indians. Le Jeune continued, "We had the soul of an unbeliever pursued by two demons, who finally hurled it into a hell which vomited forth flames." And he expressed considerable gratification that at least one of the "savages" reported horrendous dreams after viewing this exhibition.

By the close of 1646, a Canadian performance of a play called *The Sit* was being talked of in the English colonies to the south. It is likely that the drama was actually Pierre Corneille's *Le Cid,* and by 1651, Corneille's other works were being staged in Quebec. Toward the end of the century, when Count Frontenac's young officers were amusing themselves by staging classic dramas, the French colonies were well on their way toward theatrical sophistication.

Dramatic enterprise among the English emigrants developed more slowly. The first definite record of a play performed by British colonists is dated 1665. In the frontier settlement of Accomac, in Virginia, certain daring villagers defied both the late August heat and a puritanical local attitude toward acting by staging a playlet called *Ye Bear and Ye Cubbe.* The law promptly swooped down on them and remanded them to court, "in those habiliments that they then acted in," to "give a draught of such verses and other speeches which were then acted by them." For reasons best known to himself, the magistrate found the accused players not guilty. Indeed, the plaintiff was directed to assume all costs of the action. But the temporary plight of the amateur actors is evidence of the public attitude of the day toward theatre.

Twenty-two years later, in 1687, this official disapproval had not decreased. In Boston, Increase Mather was decrying the fact that "there is much discourse of beginning Stage-Plays in New England." He emphasized the sad state of morals in a community which could even contemplate such abasement by sternly reminding his fellow townsmen that, "The last year, Promiscuous Dancing was openly practiced." After still another two decades, in 1709, New York City (then a bustling community of 4436 souls, including slaves) enacted a law prohibiting "play acting and prize fighting" as injurious to public morals.

There were, to be sure, occasional exceptions to the blanket condemnation. Williamsburg, the capital city of Virginia, was one of these. In July of 1718 a contract was recorded between William Levingston, "merchant," and Charles Stagg and his wife Mary, "actors," agreeing to erect a theatre in Williamsburg and provide actors, scenery, and music out of England, "for the enacting of comedies and tragedies in said city." By the next November, Levingston had taken title of three half-acre lots in Williamsburg, put up several buildings (one of which was a theatre) and laid out a bowling green. But such cultural undertakings were rare in the extreme. For the most part, to act a play was to bring down the thunder of the pulpit and the reprimand of the law.

Probably the first professional actor ever to set foot upon Colonial soil was Anthony ("Tony") Aston, black-sheep son of an English lawyer, who played a comedy called *The Fool's Opera; or, The Taste of the Age* in the colonies no later than 1705. An autobiographical sketch printed in London about 1731 contains this engaging self-description:

My merry hearts, you are to know me as a gentleman, lawyer, poet, actor, soldier, sailor, exciseman, publican in England, Scotland, Ireland, New York, East and West Jersey, Maryland (Virginia on both sides Cheesapeek), North and South Carolina, South Florida, Bahamas, Jamaica, Hispaniola, and often a coaster by all the same.

Of his family, Aston blithely added:

As for my relations every where, I don't care a groat for 'em, which is just the price they set on me.

A veteran of theatres in Ireland and elsewhere, Aston arrived in America about 1701. He wrote that he was landed "after many vicissitudes at Charles Town [Charleston, South Carolina], full of lice, shame, poverty, nakedness and hunger —turned player and poet, and wrote one play on the subject of the country." This statement not only dates its writer as probably the earliest actor to perform here, but also as the first known playwright to wield his pen in the English colonies in North America.

Heading northward for New York, Aston still was not rid of his "vicissitudes." He records that, almost within sight of New York harbor, the ship which was bringing him from the Carolinas encountered a storm which blew it clear to the Virginia Capes. It took him a considerably longer time to reach his destination "by way of Elizabeth Town." He describes that winter (1703–1704) as being given over to "acting, writing, courting, fighting." At the end of the cold weather, "my kind Captain Davies, in his sloop built at Rhode, gave me free passage for Virginia." By August of the year following, he was back home in London and married to "a Bartholemew-fair lady," his pioneering on the stages of the colonies safely at an end.

The gay, pleasure-loving community of Charleston, which had given Tony Aston his original welcome, was swifter than most others in the New World to accept theatregoing as a pleasant part of life. On a January evening in 1735 a tragedy called *The Orphan; or, The Unhappy Marriage* was "attempted" in no less a place than the Council Chamber. The play was so well received that the actors repeated it four days later and wound up playing a three-months' season in the city. In May of that year, there was a movement toward making the performance of dramas more regular: "All gentlemen that are disposed to encourage the exhibition of Plays next winter may see the subscription list at Mr. Shepheard's, and any persons who are desirous of having a share in the Performance thereof, upon application to Mr. Shepheard, shall receive a satisfactory answer."

By February 1739, Charleston's dancing master, Henry Holt, went to New York, to fit out an auditorium of sorts, called the Long Room Holt, and present to the public *The Adventures of Harlequin and Scaramouch; or, The Spaniard Tricked*. New York appears to have been receptive. Included in the poems of one Archibald Home, Esquire, was a prologue for "the second opening of the theatre at New York, Anno 1739." That there had been a *first* opening is shown by his lines:

Encouraged by the Indulgence you have shown,
Again we strive to entertain the Town,
This generous Town which nursed our Infant Stage,
And cast a shelter o'er its Tender Age,
Its young attempts beyond their merits praised.

Except for infrequent clerical or legal warnings of moral danger in their midst, the people of those early times were not well informed about theatrical matters. References to the stage in their daily newspapers were all but nonexistent. But there must have been some theatrical activity because in an early issue of the *New York Gazette* an advertisement offered for sale "a negro girl about sixteen years of age, has had the smallpox and is fit for town or country." Potential buyers were instructed to seek out a Mr. George Talbot, who might be found "next door to the Play House."

This "Play House"—so far as records indicate, the first to entertain New York's public—occupied a large room in the upper floor of a building near the junction of Maiden Lane and Pearl Street, boasting a stage platform and seats to accommodate some four hundred spectators. It opened on December 6, 1732, with a comedy titled *The Recruiting Officer*. The owner, the Honorable Rip Van Damm, thus became godfather to an art form—or a business—destined to loom large in the infant city's future, and the quality of the cast may be guessed at from a published announcement that "the part of Northby [will be] acted by the ingenious Mr. Thomas Heady, barber and Peruque maker to His Honor."

So at last, with theatre beginning to shrug off the opprobrium which had retarded its American beginnings, it was time for Will Shakespeare to emerge from the wings.

The honor of first producing his work in the New World

rests—as far as is known—with the Dock Street theatre in Charleston. One of the earliest theatres to be erected in the colonies, the Dock Street offered its first public performance on February 17, 1736. Only a year later, it presented the first recorded American production of a Shakespeare play— *Richard III*. It is interesting that this cradle of American theatre continued its career into the second half of the twentieth century when it was still operation at the corner of Church and Queen (formerly Dock) Streets, owned by the city of Charleston, restored, and the home of two active local theatre groups.

Once having made the long leap across the Atlantic, Master Will was not slow in spreading his influence up and down a rapidly populating seacoast. On Monday, March 5, 1749, he at last arrived on the island of Manhattan.

In New York, a new theatre—considered in its day impressive—had been built in Nassau Street. It occupied a two-story gabled structure and its stage was raised five feet off a rough, earthen floor. To right and left of this stage, two paper screens were set up to serve as wings. Along its front ranged the footlights—six wax candles. Overhead hung a "chandelier" —a barrel hoop with more dripping candles impaled on its rim. A crude green curtain was suspended from the rafters, and most of the scenery and properties were produced from the trunks of each temporary manager. The theatre did possess pieces of drop background of its own, which could be made to pass for a forest, a castle, or a mountaintop. There was even an orchestra—drummers, horn players, and one musician with a German flute.

It was announced that a company of players, recently arrived from the far more cosmopolitan Philadelphia, had leased this playhouse with an intention "to perform as long as the season lasts, provided they meet with suitable Encouragement," and would first appear in "The Historical Tragedy of *King Richard III*." The broadsides published to attract the public (hopefully, a public prepared to spend five shillings for a seat in the pit, or three shillings for one in the gallery) had a wealth of provocative detail. The play, it was proclaimed, was "wrote originally by Shakespeare, and alter'd by Colley Cibber, Esq.: In this play is contain'd The Death of King Henry VI, the artful Acquisition of the Crown by King Richard, the Murder of the Princes in the Tower; the Landing of the Earl of Richmond, and the Battle of Bosworth Field." By this time, New York stretched as far northward as Warren and Hester Streets, housing a population of close to ten thousand in its 1834 dwellings. Evidently its "chaise-boxes, chairs and kitereen boxes" arrived at the theatre door in encouraging numbers, for *Richard III* was soon repeated and shared a bill with a farce entitled *The Mock Doctor*.

For all its success, the new theatre must have given less than complete satisfaction for the season of 1750–51 was ushered in by announcements that "the Play House is now floor'd and made very warm." As winter drew nearer, a new inducement was added: "Gentlemen and Ladies may cause their stoves [foot warmers] to be brought." New Yorkers might now enjoy their Shakespeare in comparative comfort.

One Robert Upton was then both manager and star of the company at the Nassau Street theatre. He had come from England as advance agent for a company owned by William Hallam. But upon arriving in New York, he found that thriving young town so hungry for theatrical entertainment that—

to Hallam's rage—he joined forces with two indifferent actors named Murray and Kean to try a season on his own.

From the Nassau Street, in December 1751, Upton took space in the *Post-Boy* to inform the public that, "By His Excellency's Permission . . . will be presented by a new Company of Comedians, a Tragedy, call'd OTHELLO, MOOR OF VENICE; to which will be added, a Dramatick Entertainment, wrote by the celebrated Mr. Garrick, called LETHE." New York thus was treated to its first *Othello* and its second Shakespeare play. Apparently, for all its historic significance, the treat was artistically insufficient. By January 17, the *Post-Boy* was relaying the sad intelligence that "Mr. Upton (to his great Disappointment) not meeting with Encouragement enough to support the Company for the Season, intends to shorten it." After that single season, no more was heard of the upstart Upton.

The ventures at the Nassau Street, for all their bravery, actually were little more than a curtain raiser. In June 1752, when the English ship *Charming Sally* arrived off Yorktown in Virginia, true first-class theatre came down the gangplank and set foot upon American soil for the first time. The company of actors aboard was headed by Lewis Hallam, Sr., brother of William. Both were of a family favorably known to the stages of London. Throughout the long voyage, Hallam had conducted daily rehearsals on the open deck. His company were letter-perfect in their parts and ready to offer Americans —"Colonials," then—Shakespeare as Europe had seen him played.

Charming Sally

4. The Fabulous Hallams

The arrival of the Hallam company in Virginia, and its prompt acceptance there, shattered long-established precedents.

From the first settlement of the colony, immigration of such folk as actors had been sternly prohibited. This ban had deeply angered the performers in London, for the stage of Elizabeth I and the early Stuarts was woefully overcrowded. Doubtless many hopeful eyes turned westward, and were resentful of the legal barriers that stood in the way of theatrical careers in the New World.

The proprietor of one of the second-rank nonpatent theatres in mid-century London was a veteran actor-manager, William Hallam. The intense competition of the time had all but bankrupted him, and as a last-ditch measure to recoup mounting losses he took advantage of a relaxed Colonial embargo to assemble a company of fifteen players and put them aboard the *Charming Sally* bound for Virginia. His brother Lewis, who was in charge of the company, was also to act the chief roles, with his wife as leading lady. With them were shipped out a few nondescript trunkloads of play scripts and costumes, an assortment of standard properties, a minimum of necessary scenery. Thus was launched the first really significant theatrical mission to America.

The finances of the company, quite typical of their time, are interesting to consider. All actual profits were divided between the Hallam brothers. But each individual member of the organization held a specified number of participating shares, in direct proportion to which was determined how much of the receipts he was entitled to receive in exchange for his services. This custom was the origin of the once-familiar theatrical term, "stock company." In the years following the American Revolution, the system was abandoned. A company's manager took all the shares, along with all the risks of loss, and his actors—as in present times—performed for a weekly salary.

The repertoire of the Hallam company, diligently rehearsed on deck each day of the *Charming Sally*'s voyage, consisted entirely of Shakespearean or Restoration dramas. Landed safely at Yorktown, the company proceeded directly to their destination, Virginia's handsome capital at Williamsburg. And here (although other more or less professional troupes had already offered their haphazard performances up and down the land) for the first time in America a professional company entertained its public in a building expressly built as a theatre.

The opening bill—on September 15, 1752—was *The Merchant of Venice*. Only one incident marred an otherwise highly successful debut. Twelve-year-old Lewis Hallam, Jr., son of the company's two stars, was making his first stage appearance in the one-line role of Portia's servant. Overwhelmed by sudden and awful stage fright, the boy burst into loud sobs and fled into the wings. It was a curious beginning to the career of the king of Colonial theatre which, in later years, the younger Lewis was to become.

The company's first year proved most encouraging, and its financial yield must have cheered brother William, back in London. By the summer of 1753, they were ready to expand the venture and Lewis Hallam, Sr., went to New York City to make arrangements for a season there. He encountered a major difficulty in obtaining the necessary license to appear at all because the overly colorful behavior of certain of the Murray-Kean-Upton actors, who had preceded him, had prejudiced city officials. But Hallam overcame this by printing appeals in the newspapers imploring the citizens to help him, which they did by expressing a wholehearted desire for a season of plays.

Then a new theatre had to be built for the company to play in. But this too was accomplished, and on September 17, 1753 the Hallams opened their first New York engagement with a schedule (then considered ambitious) of three performances a week. By November, they were playing *Richard III* with a popular farce called *The Devil to Pay* as its afterpiece. On January 14, for the first time in New York, *King Lear* was performed. Shakespeare himself might have been puzzled to recognize his lofty tragedy, for the version used was an adaptation by Nahum Tate, which disfigured the original by superimposing on it a "happy ending with general tinsel of language." This was the same script used by the great Garrick in London when he made his vast reputation in the role, and the taste of the day found it more acceptable than the noble original.

That first New York season of the Hallam company continued for four months. On January 28, they presented *Romeo and Juliet* for the first time in the city, the fourth of Shakespeare's plays to be produced there. As with *King Lear, Romeo and Juliet* was revamped to suit the preferences of audiences, with a happy ending in which Juliet awoke before Romeo had taken his own life.

The success of the Hallam troupe notwithstanding, playgoing was still far from being completely accepted by the society of America's mid-eighteenth century. Hallam's ticket window was sufficiently busy to warrant his inserting in his public announcements the suggestion that "Ladies engaging seats in the boxes are advised to send their servants early on the day of the performance to hold them and prevent trouble and disappointment." But the theatres themselves were anything but luxurious.

For the most part, they were crude structures like barns and even painted the now familiar "barn red." They were lighted by oil lamps or candles, and when candles were in use, they were set out in such a way that members of the audience might trim them when necessary. It was quite the accepted procedure for a spectator to climb onto the stage before a love scene or a tragic episode and diminish the light to a soft glow appropriate to the action. The houses were still virtually unheated, a sad discomfort in cold winter weather, and patrons were still advised to bring along their own foot warmers. Announcements were made from the stage, "respectfully requesting" audience to refrain from spitting on the communal stove.

Nor had long-standing prejudice against the playhouse as a seat of licentiousness and evil by any means been abolished. In comparatively sophisticated Philadelphia, for example, a hospital had virtuously refused to accept funds raised for it by a benefit performance. So at the close of his season Hallam packed off his company by boat to Jamaica, where attitudes were more like those of London. From 1754 until 1758, the colonies were again without professional theatre.

When the Hallam company returned at last, in 1758, there had been wrought important changes in it. Lewis Hallam himself had died in Jamaica. The actor who had played his second leads, David Douglass, had married the widow and taken over the starring roles. Lewis Hallam, Jr., by then a handsome young man of eighteen and quite recovered from any fear of audiences, had worked up in the company to leading man.

Douglass discovered that the old theatre in New York had been turned to other uses and was no longer available. Undaunted, he built a new one on Cruger's Wharf by the waterfront. This project was well under way before he took the trouble to apply for official permission, and piqued authorities promptly denied it. Stubborn Douglass refused to concede defeat. He announced the opening of "An Histrionic Academy" on the premises. Officialdom correctly recognized this as a ruse to circumvent their authority, and forbade the opening. Records of the day do not indicate how peace was eventually negotiated, but on December 28, the company was permitted to open for a season of thirteen nights. *Othello* was an attraction of the run, and *Richard III* was its closing bill. The somewhat battered Douglass-Hallam entourage then took itself off to Philadelphia.

The City of Brotherly Love, however, was not entirely prepared to open its arms to the returning thespians. Sober Quaker citizens attempted to obtain an injunction forbidding the company to play. A magistrate named Allen refused the request. Judge Allen's wife herself attended the opening performance—and three days later, suddenly died. The Quakers piously pointed to this sad occurrence as proof of the prompt retribution to be visited upon sinners. Nevertheless, the company received its permanent license to perform and remained in the city for a proper season of almost six months.

It was a poor time for theatre on many counts. The French and Indian Wars were at their height. The daily rumors of battles, raids, scalpings, and burnings could outstrip for excitement anything that was compressed on a cramped stage. Seizing upon this distraction of public attention, Pennsylvania's lawmakers established a fine of five hundred pounds to be levied against any individual found guilty of erecting a theatre or of offering for sale tickets to any exhibition of play-acting. The King's Council promptly set aside this enactment; yet it serves to illustrate the temper of the times in many high quarters.

When Douglass returned with his actors for a new Manhattan season, this time careful to obtain official sanction, he built a new playhouse in Chapel Street. There was more than the usual opposition in the press. A paper called *Parker's Gazette* was especially voluble on the subject. In its columns, almost hysterical letters were exchanged between a "Philodemus" who regarded play-acting as a work of Satan and an "Amanda" who held it to be laudable art.

The theatre was built, and its doors opened on November 18, 1761. Eight evenings later, young Lewis Hallam treated the city to its first *Hamlet;* both play and star were warmly received. On January 25, Douglass himself starred as *Othello* in a much-advertised performance "for the Benefit of such Poor Families as are not provided for by the Publick." The ticket office took in 114 pounds, 10 shillings—and this time the money was not refused by its intended recipients. Douglass had made a strong bid to secure public approval of his actors.

Still, there was no further production of Shakespeare in New York—actually, no theatrical season of any sort—until Douglass once more returned in 1767 to build the historic John Street Theatre. By then, he had appeared in Newport, Rhode Island, to offer with his troupe the first professional theatrical production ever to brave Puritan New England. So closed was the public mind in that area to the very idea of theatre that Douglass's *Othello* was publicized as "A Series of Moral Dialogues, in Five Parts, Depicting the Evils of Jealousy and other Bad Passions, and Proving that Happiness can only Spring from the Pursuit of Virtue." Moreover, he sugar-coated the even temporary presence of a theatre by calling it, as in New York, "An Histrionic Academy." Thus he adapted to the moralistic demands of the colonies a ruse already employed elsewhere by such English stars as the "Divine" Sarah Siddons and John Philip Kemble.

In New York, at least, the word "theatre" was now permissible. Although worthy burghers might still look askance at acting "gipsies," the favor of the English governors kept them from being arrested as vagabonds. A manager who knew what was good for him never forgot to include in his announcements the all-important line, "By permission of His Excellency the Governor"; nor to end them with a patriotic *Vivant Rex et Regina.*

Under such protection, the theatre in John Street was completed. An ugly wooden structure, painted red, it stood about sixty feet back from the street, on the north side and near its juncture with Broadway. A covered walk of rough wooden planks led from pavement to entrance doors. Inside, there were two tiers of boxes as well as a pit and a gallery—seating accommodation which would net some eight hundred dollars at the prevailing ticket prices. The stage was more ample than any other yet seen in the town. A popular restaurant now occupies the site, and on its walls are preserved proud memorials of that long-ago theatre.

Once opened by Douglass, on December 7, 1767, the theatre remained in operation until 1774, when a resolution by Congress ordered all "frivolous" playhouses throughout the rebelling colonies to be closed. That first season of the John Street's glory was also a triumph for Will Shakespeare. *Richard III, Hamlet,* and *King Lear* all were successfully revived. A new leading lady, engagingly billed as Miss Cheer (and said to have been the best actress the town had yet seen) was a great success as Juliet. *Henry IV, Part I* and *The Merchant of Venice* were given their first New York productions. *Cymbe-*

line, "as alter'd by Mr. Garrick," also made its local debut. And somewhat later in the year, another Garrick-Shakespeare collaboration (if that is the word) was introduced as an afterpiece. The farce, titled *Catherine and Petruchio*, was jigsawed together out of scraps of *The Taming of the Shrew*. Perhaps most interesting of all was New York's first presentation of *Macbeth*, which was done in a popular eighteenth-century version complete with singing witches.

A highlight of the season occurred on December 14 (*Richard III* was the bill), when distinguished visitors sat out front. A deputation of Cherokee Chieftains had arrived in New York on a visit of state. General Moore, in command of the local garrison, was concerned for their entertainment. Announcement of the performance said that it was being presented "by command of His Excellency the General For the Entertainment of the TEN INDIAN WARRIORS that arrived here last Friday, from South Carolina, among whom are the famous Chiefs, called Attakullakulla, or the Little Carpenter, the Great Warrior of Estatoe and the Raven Ring." Excitement over the event ran high. *Holt's Journal,* a few days later, described the evening in detail:

> The Expectation of seeing the Indian Chiefs at the Play, on Monday Night, occasioned a great Concourse of People, the House was crowded, and it is said great Numbers were obliged to go away for want of Room. The Indians regarded the Play with Seriousness and Attention, but it cannot be supposed that they were sufficiently acquainted with the language to understand the Plot and Design, and enter into the Spirit of the Author, their Countenances and Behavior were rather expressive of Surprise and Curiosity, than any other Passions.

When that first John Street season ended on June 28, 1768

(after an unprecedented run of fifty-one recorded performances), ten different Shakespeare plays had been included
in the repertory. In all, thirty-eight plays and thirty-one after-
pieces had been offered. Douglass had further illustrated his
business acumen by rechristening his troupe. Discarding its
former title of The Company of Comedians From London,
he substituted The American Company—to fit it better to the
increasingly independent spirit of the times. The closing night,
which once again offered its proceeds to charity, was hailed
by the much-read *Mercury* in glowing terms:

> This is the Second Play the Company have given this Season
> to public Uses; which, with their unblamable Conduct during their
> Residence here, and the Entertainment the Town has received
> from their Performances, has greatly increas'd the Number of their
> Friends, and considerably Obviated many Objections hitherto
> made against Theatrical Representations in this City.

Theatre in the New World was at last beginning to find its
place. Even so, Douglass was compelled, in the same issue
which carried this encomium, to insert a notice indicating how
tentative that status still was. He advertised: "A Pistole Reward WILL be given to whoever can discover the Person who
was so very rude to throw Eggs from the Gallery, upon the
Stage last Monday, by which the Cloathes of some Ladies and
Gentlemen in the Boxes were spoiled, and the Performance
in some Measure Interrupted." A *pistole* was not a weapon
but a Spanish coin then in wide circulation throughout the
colonies. It had a value of approximately $3.80.

As early as this opening season of the John Street, one
special public problem arose that has never been solved, and
remains to plague audiences in the twentieth century. In 1768,
the traffic jam at curtain time had already begun. David

Douglass manfully attempted to cope with it in his published announcements: "To prevent accident by carriages meeting, it is requested that those coming to the House may enter John Street from Broadway, and returning from thence down John Street into Nassau Street, or forward to that known by the name of Cart and Horse Street, as may be most convenient."

Now, suddenly, play-acting achieved social status. British garrison officers, brought to Fort George by the war against the French and Indians, began to amuse themselves and the town by appearing in a wide variety of farces and dramas. Even Shakespeare did not awe these military gentlemen. A Major Moncrieff of the Engineers ventured to portray *Othello* at the John Street in 1769. No account of his performance indicates that David Douglass's eminence in the part was in particular danger of eclipse. Over in Elizabethtown, New Jersey, a young school boy named Alexander Hamilton composed a prologue and an epilogue to embellish a play staged by officers of troops bivouacked nearby. Acting was not merely tolerated, but the vogue.

And Will Shakespeare amply demonstrated his talent for survival in a frontier society. He could succeed on his own terms where these were permissible, but could also become a "moral dialogue" if this better suited the temper of his audience. He could survive adulteration into a comic afterpiece, alteration from tragic to happy endings, musical interpolations, crude staging, indifferent acting talents—and still have something to say to a gradually emerging Colonial play public.

In short, he had shown how truly he possessed that first great requisite of the frontiersman—adaptability.

5. An Audience in Arms

The American Company was back in New York again for a second good season in 1769, opening with a "comedy" which surprisingly enough turned out to be Shakespeare's far from comical *King John*. The season included all the Shakespearean favorites made popular by Douglass and by the younger Lewis Hallam. It prospered from January until June.

In the summer of 1772 the city's new center of amusement, Vauxhall Gardens, announced the opening of its own tribute to an adopted son of the colonies. "A very great Variety of Wax Figures as large as life, also entirely new dressed, and that in the most elegant as well as genteel Taste. Amongst other curious Representations, one Room contains that of the Banquet in MACBETH, with the appearance of BANQUO'S Ghost, and a large Gallery filled with Spectators." Obviously the Colonial public was by now quite familiar with Master Will's works.

But events of an importance transcending theatrical matters were beginning to dominate the attention of Colonials from Canada to the Carolinas. The decade had witnessed a restless loosening of Mother England's apron strings. The theatre itself held timidly aloof from the mounting political excitements, relying upon the established classics and proving itself anything but radical in nature. But its audience was working up to a revolutionary frenzy. Theatre was still considered to be an English institution, and an excited public was almost bound to react against it.

Passage of the Stamp Act precipitated the first acts of violence against English-born players. Still, Douglass and his "American Company" opened in a third New York season April 1773, for what was to prove the popular manager-star's last American run. New York had a population of 21,863, some 3000 of them slaves, but the remainder were at least a potential audience. The new season presented a trio of novelties, two of them Shakespeare-inspired. For the first time, *The Tempest; or, The Enchanted Isle,* his play about America, was offered in the New World. It was not the simon-pure original, to be sure, but the Davenant-Dryden perversion of it. This introduced such extraneous characters as Hippolito, "the man who never saw a woman"; a second daughter for Prospero, called Dorinda; a lumpy monster known as Sycorax; and two comic sailors who went by the names of Mustachio and Ventoso.

The second novelty was the bill for the closing night, New York's first view of the masterpiece of another eminent English playwright—Oliver Goldsmith's brand-new comedy, *She Stoops to Conquer*.

And a third innovation was the soaring rise of America's first "matinee goddess." She was the company's chief ingénue, Miss Sarah Hallam, and Shakespeare had provided her with her ideal role. As Imogene in *Cymbeline* she so enthralled her audiences that the great artist, Charles Willson Peale, painted her in the role and the *Maryland Gazette* reviewed her performance in flowery verse:

> Around her see the Graces play,
> See Venus' wanton doves;
> And in her eye's pellucid ray
> See little laughing loves.
>
> Ye Gods! 'Tis Cytherea's face;
> 'Tis Dian's faultless form;
> But hers alone the nameless grace
> That every heart can charm.

When that season of the American Company was ended, so —for the next twelve years—was any true professional theatre in America. On October 24, 1774, the Continental Congress enacted a resolution exhorting all Patriots to give up their public amusements—"Horse Racing, and all kinds of Gaming, Cock Fighting, Exhibitions of Shews, Plays and other expensive Diversions"—and bend their full efforts to the struggle for independence. Before flight might become impossible, the Douglass-Hallam troupe, as well as most other English stage folk, bowed to the inevitable and removed themselves to the West Indies "in consequence to the popular commotions, and probability of hostilities commencing with the Mother Country."

They departed with little time to spare. Theatre had become so suspect by the Patriot cause that in May 1776 veterans of the Stamp-Act protests, who styled themselves the Sons of Liberty, fell upon the Chapel Street theatre while a performance was in progress and literally tore the building down. A large portion of the populace regarded it as offensive "that such Entertainment should be Exhibited at this Time of public Distress, when great Numbers of poor People can scarce find the Means of subsistance." The Sons of Liberty enthusiastically translated this sentiment into direct action. A public account of the riot asserted that those of the unlucky audience

were best off who got out first, either by jumping out of Windows or making their way through the Doors, as the lights were soon extinguished, and both Inside and Outside soon torn to pieces and burnt by Persons unknown . . . to the Satisfaction of Many in this distressed Time. . . . A Boy unhappily had his Skull fractured, his Recovery doubtful; others lost their Caps, Hats, Wigs, Cardinals and Cloaks, Tails of Smocks torn off (thro' Mistake) in the Hurry.

In proper Boston, too, theatre was soon subject to violence. A group of British officers quartered in the city had so openly expressed contempt for the unenforceable edict of the Continental Congress as to rehearse and present a drama called *The Blockade of Boston*. It was credited to the deft pen of General "Gentleman Johnny" Burgoyne. During a performance of the play at Faneuil Hall, presumably attended chiefly by British sympathizers, a uniformed sergeant dashed on stage shouting: "The Yankees are attacking our works on Bunker Hill!" The audience, much amused, were applauding this unexpected embellishment to the play when General William Howe himself appeared on the stage and bellowed: "Officers, to your alarm posts!"

Among the onlookers was one Timothy Newell, who confided to his diary that there followed then "much fainting, fright and confusion." Officers hurrying to their duties vaulted to the stage across the orchestra pit, "at great damage to the fiddles." Their Tory ladies had to find their ways home through the dark streets unescorted—to the glee of Patriot dames peering down from their windows.

A fuller report of the incident formed the basis for one of the earliest satirical plays to be written in America—and the first by a woman. Mrs. Mercy Warren, whose husband, General Joseph Warren, had given good account of himself in battle, wittily twisted Burgoyne's original title to *The Block-heads; or, The Affrighted Officers,* and stung her hapless red-coated subjects with salty mockery.

With the large-scale engagements contesting Bunker and Breed's Hills and their dominance of Boston harbor, war was on in earnest. And real theatre everywhere was at a temporary end. The ravishing Sarah Hallam, who for some reason had not gone to Jamaica with the rest of her family company, went into premature retirement from the stage. Decades later, the *William and Mary Quarterly* was to sum up thus the placid remainder of her life: "Sarah Hallam, the beautiful actress, lived afterwards for many years in Williamsburg, where she taught dancing and had a fashionable boarding school for young ladies." As late as 1839, the matrons of Brouton Church in the town were holding their weekly prayer meetings in Miss Sarah's modest parlors.

With Miss Hallam, the rest of the professional stage had faded away. In New York City, during that summer of 1776, a grimmer orchestra had replaced the playhouse musicians. Canon thundered from Brooklyn Heights. Muskets cracked in Harlem and over on nearby Long Island. By September, when Howe took possession of the town, American Patriots had abandoned it. Only six days after his entry, a third of the city went up in flames and the blocks lying to the south and west of Trinity Church became blackened tangles of rubble.

Amid the ruins, wretched survivors improvised miserable canvas tents. Out in the river, the sinister hulk of the infamous prison ship *Jersey* rode at anchor. She was to loom there for seven years in Wallabout Bay, with twelve hundred or more Patriots jammed into space intended for only four hundred— a reeking hell of pestilence from which lifeless bodies were daily dumped upon the Brooklyn shore.

In Crown Street, almost as grim, was the Sugar House— turned into a jail—where on hot evenings every window was "filled with [Patriot] heads, thrust one above another—to catch a portion of the blessed air of Heaven." It was an unpromising climate indeed for the enjoyment of concerts or plays.

But even now, Shakespeare was not forgotten, and his work indirectly became a weapon in the hands of American patriots. That weapon was parody, which requires for its effectiveness a speech or poem or passage so widely recognizable that a sharp point may be made by burlesquing it. Shakespeare, so familiar to readers and audiences alike, proved ideal for the purpose.

As early as the wrangling over unjust taxation by England, in 1770, the *Massachusetts Spy* in Boston ran a parody which began, "Be taxt or not be taxt—that is the question," and went on:

> Whether 'tis nobler in our minds to suffer
> The sleights and cunning of deceitful statesmen
> Or to petition 'gainst illegal taxes
> And by opposing, end them?

Throughout the war, such Shakespearean parodies were to appear in print all up and down the seaboard—now in New York, now in Baltimore, now in Charleston. The very fact that Shakespeare's verse was so frequently the model for parody shows clearly how well known it was to the public at large. For without a knowledge of the original, the clever distortion would have lost its bite.

The war grew more desperate, but after all, the country was half Tory, loyal to the Crown of England. Within weeks of New York's great fire, Tory belles were strolling with young officers along the city's Mall, to the spirited strains of military bands. General Howe had not been headquartered on Manhattan Island four full months before the John Street theatre reopened. Its bills were a series of performances by military amateurs—a series only to end with the Occupation itself, in 1883. *Tom Thumb* was presented first "for the Charitable Purpose of relieving the Widows and Orphans of Sailors and Soldiers who have fallen in support of the Constitutional Rights of Great Britain in America."

The Hallams might have found cause for professional

criticism of some of those casts, but a touch of distinction was bestowed upon several by the dapper presence of Major John André, later to be hanged by Patriot captors as the war's most notorious British spy. But the actresses available—who were paid from two to four guineas each appearance—were "such as had followed the drum," a drab lot of young women who were at best indifferent performers. John André, who was very talented with a paintbrush, made scenery for the later plays of the series, which apparently was sorely needed, for it was recorded of the earlier ones that while the costuming was elegant, the scenery was wretched.

By the time Sir Henry Clinton followed Howe to command in the city, the John Street Theatre had been rechristened the Theatre Royal. Sir Henry's arrival coincided with the return of Will Shakespeare to the New York stage. Almost at once Major Moncrieff was repeating his earlier *Othello;* and *Richard III* followed soon afterward. It was reported that His Majesty's officers "performed to a very crouded [*sic*] Audience with universal Applause." To be sure, there were outbursts of rude noise in the gallery where the "less desirable" citizens congregated. But the glittering aristocracy in the boxes took no notice, and the devoted performers on the stage were not discouraged.

Most of America's existing theatres were in British hands, but the rebellious Colonials—ignoring the interdiction of their own Congress—did not wholly ignore Shakespeare on stage. In Portsmouth, New Hampshire, where facilities for a true Shakespearean production were lacking, they managed to put on an *Epilogue to Coriolanus* written by Jonathan M. Sewell. And when spring at last ended the tormenting winter at Valley Forge in Pennsylvania, General Washington and his lady attended an army-acted production of Joseph Addison's 1713 tragedy *Cato,* which, if not true Shakespeare had at least been written by a man influenced by Master Will.

The King's loyal defenders in New York were by then well established as the principal theatre of the city. Their chief difficulty seems to have been a wartime inability to obtain scripts for the ambitious dramas they wished to produce. On December 22, 1779, the Theatre Royal published this hopeful appeal: "The Managers of the Theatre, understanding that a Gentleman purchased a set of Garrick's works from Mr. Robertson, Printer, will be much obliged to that Gentleman, if he will . . . lend them the particular Volume that contains the comedy of CATHERINE AND PETRUCHIO." Unadulterated Shakespeare seems to have been more readily obtainable, perhaps because the plays could be found in every gentleman's private library. The army's fifth season featured *Henry IV.* *Macbeth* was announced ("in the fourth Act will be introduced the original Dance of the Witches")—but was postponed from its intended opening date and perhaps was never actually played.

Old bills for the expenses of those army productions still survive. Some items on them carry a military rather than a Shakespearean flavor. "5⅛ gallons of old Rhum" and "a Quaker Cask of Sherry" had not been considered essential theatrical properties by the Hallams, or by their contemporaries or predecessors.

The Occupation was drawing to an end, and in the autumn of 1781, Lord Cornwallis was defeated at Yorktown. The following August the second-rank but popular actor John Henry—more popular now, because he had refused to come back earlier to play for the British—returned to New York after engagements at Philadelphia and Annapolis. His first postwar appearance was in a monody titled *Shadows of Shakespeare; or, Shakespeare's Characters Paying Homage to Garrick.*

Macbeth was back on the boards by mid-September, with or without dancing witches, performed in competition with the city's first drama on a totally American subject—*The Conquest of Canada,* with "Characters by Gentlemen of the Army." But for those British "Gentlemen of the Army," the footlights were dimming. Within a few weeks, the defeated soldiers had sailed away. America's stages, for good or ill, were back in civilian hands.

6. The General and the Genius

As the rumbles of war receded, professional theatre came creeping back to America's young cities, but it encountered, at first, a discouragingly widespread opposition. The public, binding up its wounds, simply was not yet ready for entertainment. The wartime laws passed by their Congress against "shews" carried over in the consciences of loyal citizens. Theatre was somehow "English," and as such to be avoided by men suddenly calling themselves Americans.

The immediate American future of actors and playhouses —and, therefore, of their particular deity, William Shakespeare—hung in a delicate balance. It was weighted toward the side of prompt acceptance by a staunch friend unconnected with the stage. His name was George Washington, and long before his rise to national prominence he had commenced a love affair with the theatre which was to last his lifetime.

Other leaders of the newly formed nation were far from unaware of the Swan of Avon. To many of them, he was a particular idol. John Adams and Thomas Jefferson, to name but two, had from earliest manhood revered Shakespeare's works. But to both of them, this homage was a matter quite separate from the stage. They *read* him, not as a dramatist but almost as an Old Testament prophet whose wisdom about the business of living had been distilled into noble (and readily quotable) verse. To them, Shakespeare's writing had only by chance cast itself in a dramatic form. Its author was a moralist and a philosopher; nothing so trivial as a journeyman of theatrical entertainments.

John Adams was Massachusetts born and Harvard educated. Three generations of his family had prospered in the colonies, so, not surprisingly, lawyer John was early arrayed on the side of the foes of British privilege. In almost his earliest public protest against the Mother Country's mistreatment, he had compared it to Lady Macbeth's unmaternal attitudes; thus indicating how much a part of his serious thought were the personages of Shakespeare's invention.

In this, he was little different from most other Americans of similar background and training. He knew Shakespeare by heart. He could pluck telling passages from their context and use them effectively in his own speeches and essays. Frequently, he so assumed their familiarity that he did not trouble to credit his source with chapter and verse. Yet John Adams was no theatregoer. He was seldom within the walls of a playhouse. Rarely did he see performed the Shakespeare he read so avidly.

Similarly, with Thomas Jefferson, Shakespeare was a hero of the library. During his student days at William and Mary College in Williamsburg, young Jefferson began keeping a small leatherbound notebook in which he transcribed favorite quotations from the masters. And in it, Shakespeare comes off well even by comparison with the Greeks and Romans and with Milton. Evidence of Jefferson's lifelong reverence for Shakespeare, as a great moral commentator on life rather than as a writer of dramas intended for performance, is a letter he dispatched from Monticello a few years before the outbreak of Revolutionary hostilities. An acquaintance with fifty pounds sterling to invest in a personal library had begged Jefferson's advice in the matter. The reply, thoughtfully considered, of course included the works of Shakespeare. And Jefferson was careful to explain that this noble fiction was created to instill "the principles and practices of virtue" more tellingly than "all the dry volumes of ethics and divinity ever written." In his view, the playwright mattered little; the moralist much. One learned disgust for villainy from *Richard III* and *Macbeth;* honor (by inference) from the Falstaff who would "have none of it"; stamina from assertions in *Troilus and Cressida* that the only "true proof of Virtue" lay in misfortunes, and in *Coriolanus* that extremity was the trier of men's souls. One learned a child's duty toward his parent from *King Lear*. But one learned these things by reading Shakespeare, by pondering him in solitude or in classroom study; not by attendance at frivolous theatres.

George Washington was a different sort of man entirely. Luckily for the early theatres of the Republic, luckily for plays in the living form for which Shakespeare himself had created them, Washington was an enthusiastic playgoer. And it was he, the idol of the day, who set the fashions. It was his example that molded the public taste.

The young Washington was no bookish student, as were so many of his eminent contemporaries, but was a typical man of action. He had been brought up as a member of the fox-hunting, posset-drinking, card-playing aristocracy of Colonial Virginia. He was an out-of-doors man, with little interest in classical study. Engineering, surveying, soldiering, the management of a prosperous plantation—these things he took seriously. For his relaxation, he wanted gaiety and activity. It is recorded that all his life he would happily ride many miles to attend a cotillion. He enjoyed concerts, although he once wrote ruefully, "I can neither sing one of the songs, nor raise a single note on any instrument." And part of this life, a part he particularly relished, was attendance at the theatre.

He may have seen his first play while accompanying his half brother Lawrence to Barbados in the year 1751. But two days later he was stricken with the smallpox and went to the theatre no more that season. When he returned to Virginia he was detailed as a military aide at Fredericksburg, where theatrical activity was all but unknown.

But luck was with him. The Hallams had arrived in Williamsburg only a brief while earlier. In the management of his company, the elder Lewis Hallam was guided by two chief business principles. He first saw that, in order to prosper, a company of players should establish itself wherever politics was centered—hence that first long season of eleven months at Williamsburg. His second belief was that players must travel wherever great estates and social life existed, or to other gatherings of the public where there was money to be spent. Hence, the company's interest in prospering centers such as Annapolis and New York City, and their awareness of even temporary gathering places.

In May 1752, having for reasons unknown appeared at a nearby community with the unlikely name of Hobb's Hole, the Hallams arrived in Fredericksburg at the season of its June Fair. Washington's half brother Samuel advanced the eager young aide the sum of one shilling and three pence to buy himself a gallery seat.

After this second exposure, Washington was hopelessly theatre mad. The Virginia of which he was a part was theatre-minded. Performances, by the Hallams and others, were frequent. In Washington's ledgers for those years before the war, there frequently appear a debit item listed "Cash for treat'g Ladies"—which meant taking them to a play. The frequency of this entry attests to his habitual presence in the theatre. The plays were sometimes by Cibber or Vanbrugh, Garrick or Rowe or Steele, but more often by Shakespeare.

When grim business called him away from the pleasures of Tidewater life, his love for "the play" did not diminish. During his early soldiering days, in 1757, his ledger lists a contribution of one pound to the players at Fort Cumberland. And once he had married Martha Custis and returned to serve as a member of the Virginia House of Burgesses, he necessarily spent much of his time at Williamsburg—the very heart of the Colonial theatre. The ledgers reveal that his attendance grew even more frequent.

In Williamsburg, the Raleigh Tavern in the Duke of Gloucester Street was the popular rendezvous after the play and here the much-admired Mrs. Beatrice Hallam held court. Attendance at the theatre usually meant going to a dinner party somewhere beforehand, and to the Tavern afterward for punch. Even when Washington was at home at Mount Vernon, he rode into Alexandria for court days and was likely to stay in the city overnight if a play were being performed. His ledger shows that he frequently played host at a box-party of friends—although Martha seldom appeared as hostess, for she did not share her husband's affection for playhouses and was almost prudishly particular about what "shews" she would attend.

Not so her young son by her first marriage, John Parke Custis. John was sent to study at Annapolis and there he became desperately enamored of lovely Miss Sarah Hallam, then still playing secondary parts. Washington was hastily summoned to Annapolis to remedy this unsuitable situation. And remedy it he did by removing young John from Annapolis, escorting him to New York to be entered at King's College, now Columbia University. While in the city, on the evening of May 28, 1773, Washington wrote in his journal that he "Dined with Mr. James Delaney and went to the play and Hull's Tavern in the evening." The play was *Hamlet*.

Even when there was a war to be fought, the Commander of the American Army was decidedly out of sympathy with the prohibitions the Congress had placed upon theatre attendance. He encouraged regular theatricals as soon as spring had eased the grim rigors of winter at Valley Forge. During 1778, plays were being published (if not performed) "at the desire of some of the officers of the American Army"—and Washington was sufficiently interested to make personal contributions to the ventures. When the French with their fondness for theatre became his allies, he felt impelled to ignore the commands of his own Congress to entertain the foreign officers suitably— especially on the birthday of the Dauphin, when plays were their traditional form of celebration.

When the war was over Washington returned to Mount Vernon, to occupy himself with restoring the prosperity of the plantation, and for a few years apparently went to the theatre seldom if at all. But in Philadelphia performances were being given, although they styled themselves *Spectaculum Vitae* to evade the local law. Washington was summoned to Philadelphia in 1787 for the meeting of the Federal Convention to form a new Constitution, and once again his theatregoing commenced, even more enthusiastically for the period of privation. One diversion he is known to have attended was "an opera called *The Tempest*—Altered from Shakespeare by Dryden."

When he was sworn in as first President of the United States of America at New York City in 1789 the future acceptance of theatre was assured. Only ten days after he took the oath of office, Washington went to a play at the John Street playhouse, and his arrival at another performance shortly thereafter was described in the *Gazette of the United States:* "On the appearance of the President, the audience rose, and received him with the warmest acclamations—the genuine effusions of the hearts of freemen."

The gradual return of the theatre in the few years after 1785, with Hallam the Younger and John Henry as its chief stars, had made certain inroads on prejudice in Baltimore, Philadelphia, and New York. But even in the cities most inclined to be tolerant, there had been dogged opposition. "There is a loud call for industry and economy," protestors against the theatre reminded the public. Supporters replied by declaring that the theatre was "a school for virtue, elegance and politeness." Now, with Washington himself giving approval by his presence, the protests dwindled.

Hallam was starring once again in *Richard III, Hamlet,* and *The Merchant of Venice* before the new Republic was firmly under way. And a Will Shakespeare already known for his histories and tragedies was earning a new American name for himself as a writer of comedies. *As You Like It* made its first appearance on this side of the Atlantic with the popular Mrs. Kenna as Rosalind, and the season of 1787 brought America *Much Ado about Nothing.*

The latter event, however, was somewhat overshadowed at the time by the debut of the first major play by an American. He was Royall Tyler, and his play was *The Contrast.* Nationalistic pride demanded that it be greeted with loyal praise. When the play was printed by public subscription in 1790, Washington's name headed the list of sponsors. When it was played, a feud flared up between the two chief actresses involved, Mrs. Morris and the formerly well-liked Mrs. Kenna, as a result of which Mrs. Kenna was hissed by the audience and driven from the company. It was a sad ordeal for a performer of whom the *Daily Advertiser's* "Criticus" had said, in that very season:

> Mrs. Kenna . . . never fails to do [her characters] justice. To exhibit the tumultuous and turbulent passions of our nature in a masterly manner, appears to be her forte. When she expresses anger, rage, indignation, horror, despair, you think you see a real image— you can scarcely suppose you behold a fictitious character. Nature seems to be actually convulsed.

The roles in which the poor lady had achieved these triumphs, of course, had been those of Shakespeare—not Tyler.

The actors at the time of Washington's early administration were a colorful lot, all rugged individualists. John Henry, whose *Shadows of Shakespeare* had led the theatre back from its wartime exile, was a victim of gout. He therefore maintained a private carriage to tote him between his lodgings and the theatre. This made it possible for Mrs. Henry to dress for her evening's role at home rather than in a drafty backstage area and New Yorkers were frequently treated to a glimpse of Lady Macbeth or Goneril descending from the family vehicle. And there was Beatrice Hallam-Douglass, continuingly pre-eminent, America's original Juliet and Cordelia and Portia, still so well regarded that she was accepted without a murmur playing Juliet to her own mature son's Romeo.

Since there were no traditions of behavior in the young country taking its first independent steps, every eye looked to President Washington for clues as to what was proper. At the theatre he stressed a manner of ceremony and formality. Also, he sought to share his own pleasure in playgoing with others in his fledgling government, although he took great pains not to make his invitations sound like royal commands, which would have been unfitting to a Republic.

Writing to his Chief Justice, John Jay, he especially emphasized his hope that Mr. and Mrs. Jay would not accept one particular invitation unless it would give both of them pleasure. The Chief Justice promptly accepted, writing back with thanks that he much appreciated the President's "delicate attention to my embarrassment . . . which ceased with all question between government and the theatre." A conscientious jurist might indeed have been placed in a delicate position, had not the ill-observed laws against the stage been formally set aside only a few days before the presidential invitation was issued.

In 1790 the seat of government was removed from New York to Philadelphia. The Washingtons moved—and so did the American Company, quitting John Street for this now greener pasture. The Southwark was well established as *the* theatre of Philadelphia, and its east stage box was now decorated with the coat of arms of the United States, festooned with crimson draperies, and proclaimed the Presidential Box. Attendance at "the play"—which meant, above all others, the plays of Shakespeare—became almost an affair of state.

On gala evenings when the President and his guests were to be in attendance, one soldier stood at attention by the stage door and four more paced the gallery. In black satin and wig, Manager Wignell held high a branched brass candelabra as he personally lighted the presidential party to its seats. As Washington appeared and the audience surged to its feet, the theatre orchestra blared out the newly composed *Presidential March*. But when it was over, the audience often shouted its demand for the old *Washington March* they had stepped to in Revolutionary years. There were seldom empty seats when it was known that Washington was expected at the theatre.

Quite frequently, the Vice-President and Mrs. Adams were members of the official party in the Washington box; Martha Washington, almost never. By now, John Adams had served his country as its first ambassador to London. Witty Abigail Adams, who since girlhood had known her Shakespeare as thoroughly (if as academically) as had her husband, had thus had ample opportunity to watch the immortal Mrs. Siddons and the effective Mrs. Farren playing in the master's great roles. Yet she wrote of Shakespeare at the Southwark: "This little playhouse is as good as any to be found outside France, and the acting is adequate." Despite an outwardly cold and reserved demeanor, George Washington evidently rated the acting performances somewhat higher; for it is on the record that he laughed unrestrainedly at what amused him in the plays, and that he was not ashamed to weep when moved.

Nor was the President's Shakespeare altogether confined to the stages of popular playhouses. On at least one occasion, a private performance of *Julius Caesar* was played before a selected audience in the garret of the august Presidential Mansion itself. A member of the immediate family, Washington Custis, was cast as Cassius.

The year of his retirement from the Presidency—1797— was to be the year of Washington's last attendance (in February) at his beloved theatre. He returned then to Mount Vernon, and the playhouses knew him no more. But at his death every stage in the land was draped in deepest mourning. The actors whose art he had done so much to defend and make "respectable" delivered monodies, bewailing the nation's bereavement. They had lost a dedicated friend.

7. Shakespeare in a Raw Republic

Thus quickly, under the leadership of its idolized George Washington, did the victorious infant nation turn to a love for professional theatre. And that theatre was largely dominated by William Shakespeare. The plays of other writers who had enjoyed much public favor during Colonial days—Dryden, Farquhar, Congreve and the rest—fell into neglect as the dawn of the nineteenth century approached. But Shakespeare endured.

It would be pleasant to attribute this durability to some postwar improvement in the taste of our theatregoing ancestors. Unfortunately, the weight of evidence is to the contrary. To an American generation then far in the future, the double-feature motion picture bill was to become an entertainment standard. Its equivalent, in these years following the Revolution, was the "companion piece." This was a second play, staged along with Shakespeare on any theatre night. And the patchwork trash enthusiastically applauded by playgoers does away with any notion that their standards for drama were at all discriminating.

Two factors quite separate from his innate genius were what combined to establish Shakespeare as the *beau idéal* of an emerging American theatre. One was sheer snob appeal. The other was the vigor of the great leading roles, which provided superb showcases for the new stars the public was flocking in increasing numbers to see.

The Revolution had been fought to establish democracy and overthrow privilege. But the citizens of thirteen states so very recently become sovereign were still far from having broken off their lifelong emotional ties with the Mother Country. English concepts of class and privilege still persisted, with one difference. Inherited aristocracy was now replaced in America by an upper class to which any man might aspire— if he could display accomplishments enough, or amass wealth enough, to raise him there. Such a raw new society was naturally diffident about its own tastes. However much it might profess scorn for the dictates of London, it still followed them slavishly in matters of dress, of formal behavior, of literary and artistic and dramatic enthusiasms.

With the 1770s, England had witnessed a great renaissance of homage to Shakespeare. So now her recent colonies followed suit. By doing what England did, they could feel absolutely certain that they were correct and that they would not be looked down upon or made fun of.

Elihu Hubbard Smith, an unsuccessful physician turned equally unsuccessful playwright and critic in the New York City of 1795, wrote in frank appraisal:

How much of the applause which British Plays obtain, among us, arises from our knowing that they have been well received at home? And, beside the prejudice so universal against pieces of our own manufacture, is there not an intellectual cowardice, a fear lest others should despise his judgment, which restrains the spectator from applauding a cis-atlantic drama?

By "British Plays," Dr. Smith meant chiefly those of Will Shakespeare.

In the public journals of his day, Smith was constantly berating his fellow playgoers for their inferior taste. Humanly enough, his displeasure was most vehement when they failed to appreciate one of his own uninspired offerings. Public indifference to his opera *Edwin and Angelina* prompted him to complain in print of Americans who could "crown with applause foreign productions, which, to compare with this, are as a Satyr to Hyperion." The luckless Smith could not even lash out at the popular neglect of his play without falling back upon a line from *Hamlet!*

The reverse of this awe for British taste was of course a wild glee whenever the superior British made fools of them-

selves. It happened at least once during those earliest years of
the Republic.

In England one William Ireland, son of a London booksel-
ler and a young man of no particular education, suddenly
announced that he had discovered a three-hundred-word religious essay written in Shakespeare's own hand. Excited experts examined the document and were quick to pronounce it
genuine. The resourceful Ireland promptly "discovered" original longhand manuscripts of *Hamlet* and *King Lear,* written
in the same distinctive scrawl, and after these a box containing
several locks of the poet's hair. Ireland became the lion of
the literary world. Boswell himself came to kneel in homage
before the scraps of hair and paper, to kiss them devoutly and
declare his "thanks to God that I have lived to see them."

Ireland had thus set the stage for his greatest "discovery"
—an entire Shakespeare play until then unheard of. London
was agog as it was announced that the master's "lost" drama,
Vortigern, was immediately to be produced at the Drury
Lane. Seats sold at fantastic prices. On opening night—April
2, 1796—the streets surrounding the theatre were impassable.
But the excitement, mounting to hysteria, was short-lived.
Vortigern was a dismal failure. Its first performance was also
its last. Shortly thereafter, Ireland admitted that his discoveries were a complete fraud, and that he himself had written
Vortigern. He bitterly, if humanly, blamed the actors for its
disaster.

News that the British had been taken in by the hoax was
greeted by Americans with hearty guffaws. Yet even such
assaults as this one upon the infallibility of British taste could
not to any real degree undermine their reverence for it. The
conviction that they would be considered "correct" in attend-

ing plays by Shakespeare was unshaken. And an equally important fact was that the great acting stars of the day (almost exclusively, English stars) were appearing on American tours chiefly in Shakespeare.

It was an era tailor-made to foster a star system. Spellbinding orators ranked high among the popular heroes. A consuming interest in the potential of the individual was expressing itself everywhere. Shakespeare's subtleties of thought might escape such audiences, but not the opportunities his "big" speeches in his "big" scenes gave their favorite personators to declaim and emotionalize.

Actors who had established their reputations in London (and who, therefore, must be assumed by Americans to be of first quality) had begun "condescending" to cross the Atlantic. Actually, very alluring financial benefits were involved. If a player had been well received "at home," he was assured of capacity audiences in any American city where he chose to appear. One of the first to come was handsome Thomas Cooper, whose *Hamlet* had been a Covent Garden hit of 1795. He was imported to Philadelphia in the following season, and to New York for the season following that. His Hamlet, Macbeth, and Romeo were almost frantically applauded.

Cooper was probably a typical example of the stars of his generation. He was notoriously inaccurate in learning his part, frequently improvising text or "blowing" his lines altogether. But he was good-looking, virile, charming, and could project across the pallid footlights "a sense of superb passion and power." This was what in a later generation would have been called "star quality." And it was quite enough to make him the reigning idol of his day. He married Miss Mary Fairlie, the unquestioned belle of New York City's emerging society, and was firmly ensconced upon his pedestal.

The citizens of our raw young Republic carried a definite chip on their shoulders, however, in any matter of being patronized by their imported celebrities. They were swift to take umbrage at a slight—fancied or real. Woe betide the actor who aroused them to truculent defense of their new nation's dignity.

A decade or more after Cooper's first American triumphs, an equally distinguished English performer—Charles Frederick Cooke—undertook a trans-Atlantic tour. At first, he was cheered at every turn. But Cooke possessed "temperament" which did not fall far short of actual insanity. He was quite capable of pouring vitriol upon those hospitable Americans who had most warmly befriended him. Matters came to a head on an evening when, billed for an appearance in Baltimore, he was informed that President James Madison would be attending the play. Cooke promptly flew into a rage and vowed that if Madison were admitted to the theatre there would be no performance. More than a quarter-century after the Revolution, he would still not set foot upon a stage for the enjoyment of one he called "a king of rebels." Once this story was spread abroad, Cooke became anathema. The incensed American public would have no more of him.

Similarly, when the great Edmund Kean crossed the ocean in the early 1800s with such interpretations of Richard III, Othello, Hamlet, Lear, and Shylock as America had not previously witnessed, he was greeted at first by frenzied adulation. New York and even Boston lay at his feet. But then—a bit heady with success, and ignoring the most earnest advice of his own managers—Kean undertook a summer

season. Warned that during the hot months big-city populations would dwindle, he was still utterly astonished by the
meager audiences assembling to see him. Angered, he refused
to play. Imagining that they were being held in contempt by a
supercilious Englishman, the Americans who had lately
adored him turned on him in fury. National pride had been
outraged. And the man responsible became instantly so
unpopular that for a considerable time Kean was virtually
driven from the American stage and faced financial disaster.

Still, a slavish worship of "fashionable" foreigners—stars
chiefly appearing in Shakespeare's roles—continued to dominate American theatre. Shakespeare himself might have
quoted his own words, that "the play's the thing." But Americans of the early Republic would have disagreed. For them, the
player was the thing—the chief player, the star. Companies
of very indifferent quality were often assembled to support
visiting luminaries from London. But the public wanted a
fashionable Richard to perpetrate his blood-curdling villainies;
or a Covent Garden Macbeth to recoil in horror from Banquo's ghost. The lesser actors could be so poor as to violate
the drama—and still be acceptable.

Accentuation of the star roles to the detriment of the plays
as a whole went to almost absurd lengths. When full production of a Shakespearean play was ruled out—by finances, or
by the size of a potential audience, or by the lack of an
adequate theatre—"readings" from the plays almost equalled
the real thing in popularity. Particularly if the evening's
elocutionist could be advertised as "newly arrived here from
London," a program pieced together from Lear's mad scene,
Macbeth's banquet, Hamlet's soliloquies, and Antony's oration

over the corpse of Caesar—interspersed with music hall numbers for contrast—would assure a packed house.

Certain stars protested this wrenching from context of scenes and speeches. The greatest actress of her day, Fanny Kemble—who would probably have approved John Gielgud's beautifully integrated "The Ages of Man" more than a century later—publically voiced her anger against the rendering of Shakespeare as "patches for declamation." But popular enthusiasm for such performances remained strong. What did it matter that the mood and logic of great plays were lost? One had seen a "name" star tearing passions to tatters, displaying all his skill and versatility, making the rafters ring. One asked no more.

Because Shakespeare provided abundant material for such pyrotechnics, and because unassailable English taste had long since established his genius, Will of Stratford was the undisputed Czar of the Federal stage. Perhaps he himself— who had written to provide vehicles for his own "name" actors at the Globe and the Blackfriars—would have sympathized and understood.

The greatest of playwrights, it might go without saying, has need of a physical theatre. He is frustrated without a stage on which to present his inventions to the public. At the close of the Revolution, American playhouses—such as they were—had fallen into woeful disrepair. Such of them as survived were altogether inadequate to the requirements of a new generation. Even the historic John Street, scene of so much of New York City's earlier theatrical history, was worn out and demoded. Not unnaturally, the 1790s witnessed a considerable remedying of this situation.

The first important new theatre of the postwar era was the

Chestnut Street in Philadelphia, opened in 1791. It was almost instantly nicknamed Old Drury, for its "London" atmosphere. Its innovations of design (all widely publicized as having been patterned after the Theatre Royal at Bath) were aimed at satisfying a new sort of American audience. This was an increasingly wealthy class, riding the upsurge of national prosperity, which could afford to pay generously for its entertainment. The boxes became more numerous and more ornate, stages themselves for the display of jewels and velvets. Pit and gallery shrank correspondingly, to make room for the new aristocracy.

Until now, playhouses generally had been flimsy, barnlike structures, crudely built. In many, the seats had been mere rough, backless benches. The typical source of heat had been one large, round stove somewhere out in the foyer near the street doors, where during intermissions a half-frozen audience could flock to thaw out. The prudent theatregoer brought with him, in winter, his own foot warmer—a square, perforated box with a metal lining in which hot embers could be carried to the play. The capacity of a typical theatre had seldom exceeded three to four hundred seats. No theatre floor had carpeting, and many had been covered with sawdust or sand like circus arenas. But in the early Republic all this was to be changed. In the theatres now coming into being, elegance was the chief concern. A prosperous audience, accustomed—or becoming accustomed—to luxurious possessions, and garbed for their pleasure outings in "Alamodes, Lutestrings, Ducapes, Damasks, Padusoys, Velvets [and] India Taffities," demanded comforts and refinements previously undreamed of.

Boston, the citadel of culture, could boast in 1790 not a

single playhouse—although Virginia by then had patronized the theatre for three-quarters of a century. Following a playhouse riot in 1750, a law against "shews" had been enacted in Massachusetts. In changing times, this ordinance now was assumed to be obsolete. On Board Alley, in 1792, a structure known as the New Exhibition Room was erected. Here *Othello, Hamlet,* and *Romeo and Juliet* were presented as "moral dialogues," Charles Stewart Powell was the leading actor. In November, he took the risk of staging *Catherine and Petruchio,* and the authorities made no protest. Encouraged, he essayed *Richard III* on December 3, and on December 5, the sheriff's men swooped down with writs and padlocks to close what was obviously a theatre.

Public indignation grew rapidly. Repeal of the outmoded law was loudly demanded. Among other prominent citizens, Boston's John Gardiner appeared before the Commonwealth's House of Representatives to plead that, "This unsocial, this illiberal, irrational, unconstitutional, prohibitory . . . this Gothic act is contrary to, and an infringement of, the inalienable rights of man. . . ."

Another stout defender of theatre in Boston was Elbridge Gerry, that member of the first Congress whose name has endured in American politics through a dubious procedure known as gerrymandering—in the modern dictionary definition "manipulating to gain an unfair advantage." Mr. Gerry made public his fears that his home Commonwealth would be left behind the nation because of her narrow-mindedness in matters theatrical. "Love for such amusements," he protested, "which are supposed necessary to polish the manners of citizens, may give to those of other states an advantage in this point over the citizens of Massachusetts."

Many advocates of repeal of the anti-playhouse law—the vast majority of them indeed—had been raised as were the Adams family, in a climate of reverence for Shakespeare. His influence—in the library if not on the stage—was strong upon their thinking. Thus championed, theatre won its battle in Boston. The odious law was rescinded. In 1794 the Federal Street theatre, designed by the famous Charles Bulfinch, opened its doors.

A popular subscription solicited to raise funds for the enterprise had been enthusiastically filled. Unusual adjuncts to the playhouse were tea and card rooms for those of the audience who might weary of the play. Over the stage opening an artist painted lavishly draped crimson hangings. Against these, the masks of tragedy and comedy shared display space with the arms of the new United States and the Commonwealth. Dangling from the arms on gala ribbons was the legend: "All the World's a Stage." Thus was Shakespeare welcomed to Boston.

A regular employee at the Federal Street Theatre was the master of ceremonies, whose chief duty it was to suppress incipient rioting in the audience. In Boston, still easing its way into new ways of thinking, no more than three preformances a week were permitted even now, and none of these might conflict in time with a scheduled church service. But almost at once, humbler elements in the city began protesting that the new Federal Street was catering to the powerful, moneyed Federalists. A second, less elegant house—the Haymarket—was soon erected to satisfy democratic preferences.

New York City, not to be left behind, replaced its crumbling prewar playhouses with the elaborate new Park Street Theatre. The extent to which theatre was becoming a profitable business is indicated by the fact that, only a few seasons after the Park Street's opening, the financially shrewd John Jacob Astor saw fit to buy the house and invest the then astonishing sum of fifteen thousand dollars in refitting it. Prosperous patrons now enjoyed a princely lobby, newfangled gaslights, lounges, coffee rooms, and mirrors so angled as to reflect back upon itself the brilliant pageant of the audience. Interestingly, Astor provided four tiers of boxes instead of the usual three, and the house thus provided more box seats than pit and gallery seats combined. Astor's financial acumen was seldom questioned, so it is reasonable to suppose that he knew what would make his public pay for tickets.

The physical influence of Shakespeare upon all this theatre construction was considerable. Many architectural features of the new playhouses harked back to the stages of his era. Notable among these was the extended stage, which brought a star actor out into close proximity with his audience, so that they might savor to the fullest his bursts of declamation. In Philadelphia, the "Old Drury" apron thrust a good fifteen feet past the proscenium arch, clear past the first section of boxes. It gave actors working space much like the Elizabethan stages upon which Burbage had first created many of Shakespeare's roles. So marked was this similarity, and the source from which it sprang, that the critics' box at the Park Street in New York was popularly known as "the Shakespeare." Here sat the youthful Washington Irving, jotting performance notes for the critiques he was signing as "Jonathan Old Style."

Despite all the new elegance of the theatres, despite the "carriage trade" which filled their boxes, the occupants of gallery and pit in the administrations of Washington, Adams and even Jefferson remained as vociferously independent as ever they had been. The groundlings of Shakespeare's Globe would have recognized kindred spirits. These humbler elements of the audience were accustomed to expressing displeasure or differences of opinion in direct and physical terms. Let something upset or excite them and they would swarm over the footlights to make their feelings known. They would erupt from the pit like lava from a volcano, with actors and scenery no barriers to their brawling.

One heated outburst of the kind occurred in November, 1796, in New York City, when a pair of sea captains attended the play. They entered the theatre with enthusiasm bolstered by a preliminary session in a grogshop. During the overture, they patriotically, if tipsily, shouted demands for *Yankee Doodle*. Unsympathetic neighbors from the pit promptly invaded their box and tossed them from the theatre. But the bruised and ruffled captains lurched down the narrow streets to the waterfront and rounded up their brawny crews for a return in force. Midway of the drama, the theatre's street doors burst open and the wharf army flooded in. A full-scale melee ensued, in which several heads were cracked before the law arrived to restore order.

Even on ordinary occasions, the occupants of the cheap seats were quite accustomed to making their judgments clear. They behaved, in general, like fans at a modern major league baseball game, stamping and yelling catcalls, or cheering and roaring their approval. Rotting vegetables were hurled freely, and one gentleman's private diary records that, "The egg as a vehicle of dramatic criticism came into early use in this Continent." There is no evidence that a work of Shakespeare's ever inspired such a reaction; but more than one actor who misplayed him did.

The prosperous elements of an audience were equally subject with actors and playwrights to the gallery's displeasure. In his *Memorial of the City of New York,* a theatrical historian named Wilson reports:

It often happened that the moment a well-dressed man entered . . . he at once became a mark for the wit and insolence of the men in the gallery. They would begin by calling on him to doff his hat in mark of inferiority, for the custom of wearing hats in the theatres was universal. If he obeyed, he was loudly hissed and troubled no more. If he refused, abuse, oaths and indecent remarks were poured upon him.

Such "audience participation" must have made play-going a lively affair in the lusty late eighteenth-century America!

Alexandria

Fredericksburg

Richmond

Norfolk

Thomas Wade West's

first

American

Theatre Chain

Charleston

8. Southern Exposure–Northern Lights

Those northern cities where
Shakespeare long had flourished were by no means the ex-
clusive beneficiaries of the post-Revolutionary upsurge in
theatrical fortunes. In a sense, the cities of the South bene-
fitted even more. For there the first true American theatre
chain was being created—a modest forerunner of the monster

syndicate destined to dominate America's stages in the late nineteenth and early twentieth centuries. The genius responsible for this pioneer activity was an Englishman, Thomas Wade West.

This early entrepreneur (himself by all accounts an indifferent actor, yet pre-eminent as a manager) arrived in Philadelphia in 1790. He had with him his wife Margaretta and their family—which included a highly talented son-in-law, John Bignall. Respected, although not outstanding, theatre folk "back home," they brought with them a letter of introduction to Lewis Hallam, Jr. Hallam's Old American Company was still the standard for the American theatre.

Hallam was sympathetic, and offered the Wests and the young Bignalls places in his company. But the salaries were modest, a mere two guineas a week. Moreover, the roles available (since the company already possessed its full roster of leading players) were secondary and uninteresting. With considerable courage, West decided to turn down the offer. Instead, he set about forming his own company. His eye was fixed upon the promising regions to the south, where relaxed and pleasure-loving ways of life had long included enthusiasm for the theatre.

West's business ability was evident from the first. He seems never to have encountered difficulty in raising the money his ambitious projects required. And these sums were considerable. He first turned his attention to the flourishing city of Richmond, which had recently replaced Williamsburg as Virginia's capital. Even West's first season there revealed to a delighted public a new conception of how the great plays they enjoyed ought to be mounted.

The hit of that season was a production of *The Tempest*

such as had never been seen in America before. Managers
of less vision had been content to put on the play, as was
customary, against stock forest flats which were standard
equipment in any established theatre. Not so Thomas Wade
West. An advance notice of his offering, appearing in the
Virginia Gazette and General Advertiser for December 16,
1791, described his vision in full:

The opening discovers a troubled Horison and Tempestuous Sea,
where the Usurper's Vessel is tossed a considerable time in sight,
and gives a signal of an approaching storm, amidst repeated claps
of Thunder, Lightning, Hail, Rain &c and being dashed on a Chain
of Rocks (which both sides of the stage strikingly represent) and at
the same instant, a dreadful shower of fire, pouring from the dis-
tempered Elements, the crew gives signals of distress, the Waves
and Winds rise to an affecting degree, and the vessel sinks in full
view of the audience. The Scene altogether forming a most awful,
but perfect picture of

A SHIPWRECK.

The hurricane (which is supposed to be raised by Magic) ceases,
a delightful prospect of the Inchanted Island appears, also of the
Enchanter's dwelling. Here the business of the Play commences;
and through the course of it (which abounds with Poetic Beauties)
is represented the strange being of CALIBAN, a Monster of the Isle,
dressed from Nature, and agreeable to the Author's fancy of that
wonderful and truly original Character. . . .

Small wonder Richmond was at West's feet!

Play after play he presented with similarly elaborate staging
and special effects. The very bulk and weight of his scenery
determined what other cities should be chosen for seasonal
visitation by the company, following the close of their Richmond run. Populations were still too sparse to permit the
players to concentrate the year around on any one city, but,

overland transportation of such sets, machines, elaborate properties, and costume trunks was out of the question. Centers which could be reached by water-borne barge were selected.

Soon, Norfolk, Virginia, became home to the West organization, and there West built his next theatre. Adjoining it, he put up a house for his family and their beloved furniture and silver and paintings. But after a time the chief scene of their professional activities was Charleston, South Carolina, with its fine harbor and a large public already long devoted to "the play."

In Norfolk or Richmond, West billed his actors as The Virginia Company. In Charleston, the same players in the same roles tactfully became The South Carolina Company. By either name, like Shakespeare's rose, they "smelled as sweet." Star of the repertory was the family's son-in-law. John Bignall had developed into an outstanding actor, with a range of parts which embraced tragedy, melodrama, and slapstick farce. Margaretta was more than adequate in the somber roles—Lady Macbeth, Queen Katherine, Goneril. Their daughter, Mrs. Bignall, was considered an effective Ophelia and Juliet. Thomas himself played First Gravedigger to his son-in-law's Hamlet, at least adequately, in every major city from Baltimore to Savannah. But it was as manager and producer that he truly starred.

The company was home at Norfolk in the summer of 1794 when, without warning, an already crowded port was swamped by the arrival of well over one hundred unexpected vessels. These ships were loaded to their waterlines with citizens fleeing an outburst of savage civil war in Santo Domingo. Among the polyglot horde, which included all social and financial classes, were several actors. The refugees at once sought out their prospering English fellow thespian and threw themselves upon his charity.

Sympathetic to their woes, West engaged five of them to play in his company—already an excellent and close-knit unit, boasting recruits even from Hallam's long-established Old American Company. He also hired two French artists to paint new backgrounds for several of his productions.

Although from the first the introduction of so exotic an element promised trouble, the refugees remained grateful—until, in the course of the next season's travels, the company reached Charleston with its considerable French population. Here, the St. Cecilia Society was moved by their dramatic plight, and it offered a benefit performance for them. The actors, sensing additional gain from such public sympathy, soon set themselves up in a rival organization which they called the French Company. They were headed by one Alexander Placide, who billed himself as "rope dancer to the King of France."

The French Company became the fashion of the season. And not even theatre-loving Charleston could support two competitive troupes of actors. But instead of vying for supremacy over his rivals, West exercised his usual business acumen and cajoled Placide into rejoining forces. Combined, the companies could stage Shakespeare's most ambitious dramas, with elaborate processions and mob scenes and battle arrays. In circumstances where such resources were not required, small units of actors could be sent out to the rural towns where perhaps no theatre better than a tavern was available. There they could offer entertainment which, while modest by comparison with the full West "treatment," still outshone anything else the people had had opportunity to enjoy. Because of this exposure to high standards of stagecraft, the rural south early grew accustomed to theatre of a quality unknown to corresponding backwaters farther north.

In the season of 1796 alone, West presented 111 different plays. By 1797, he had built new theatres at Fredericksburg and Alexandria. Those already built and operated by him in Richmond, Charleston, and Norfolk were prospering. Five theatres in almost the same number of years! On the closing night of his Richmond run in January 1798, he suffered a staggering blow when the theatre caught fire and burned to ashes. But even this loss, estimated at three thousand pounds, did not alter his policy of sparing no expense in the production of his theatrical offerings. His company still numbered between forty and fifty actors. His sets and costumes put to shame those of any of his competitors.

One of the few economies Thomas Wade West ever practiced, even after the Richmond fire, led to his sudden death. In order to cut expenses, he had incorporated quarters for himself and his family into the Alexandria playhouse. In the dead of night on July 28, 1799, when the Wests were sleeping there, he awakened with a feeling that something was amiss. He got out of bed and prowled into the unlit gallery of the theatre (which adjoined the sleeping quarters) on a round of inspection. A backstage lantern had been left burning, and when he saw its fitful flickering—doubtless with memories of the Richmond fire to spur him—he broke into a run in the direction of the glow. A taut rope, probably essential to some effect in the play of the evening before, still stretched across the gallery aisle, and in his haste, West tripped over it. He was flung across the gallery railing to the stage below, and within minutes he was dead of his injuries.

Yet the chain of playhouses he had established still carried on with amazing vitality. Under the management of various of his heirs, the circuit flourished as late as 1812, when the outbreak of a new war with England finally put an end to its prosperity. In all the years of the young Republic no man did more to foster America's enthusiasm for the theatre and the works of Will Shakespeare than did Thomas Wade West.

In the North, where West was almost unknown, the long-time mighty Hallam company was at last disintegrating. A less scrupulous management had maneuvered its control away from Lewis Hallam and John Henry. New lights were replacing the old on Philadelphia and New York and Boston stages. Having so recently achieved its legal right to theatre, the Commonwealth of Massachusetts had considerable catching up to do. As a new century came in, it was earnestly making up for lost time.

For two season Boston's dauntless defier of sheriffs, Charles Stewart Powell, had managed the handsome Federal Street Theatre. But his business ability was not so great as his crusading zeal and he retired bankrupt. In the season of 1800 a new actor-manager, Giles L. Barrett, starred with some success as Shylock and as Cardinal Wolsey in *Henry VIII,* and staged *Romeo and Juliet.* Barrett had suffered business reverses in a previous season at the plebeian Haymarket and had gone off to New York, there to open a fencing school. But once he was solvent, back to Boston he hurried; and this time to rich rewards. Shakespeare drama was performed successfully that season in competition with ballad operas, masques, pantomimes and farces, and, during January and February, with the flood of eulogies and dirges mourning the death of George Washington. But the season's outstanding favorite was a new play by Thomas Hood, called *Speed the Plough.* In it was one line of dialogue destined to become immortal—"What will Mrs. Grundy say?" That question has worried Boston through all the generations since it was first spoken!

Actually, for the first time since his plays had come to America, Shakespeare came close at the beginning of the century to being eclipsed by another playwright, August Friedrich Ferdinand von Kotzebue. A tide of adulation had arisen for Kotzebue's nearly two hundred dramatic works, notably for *Pizarro,* which he had written in German, and which had been adapted by Richard Brinsley Sheridan. A German employed by the Russian civil service, Kotzebue was much in vogue. One New York newspaper proclaimed him Shakespeare's "successor." But Shakespeare continued to draw good houses, though the plays were hampered by the extravagance of the "novelties" characteristic of the time. Giles Barrett's *Henry VIII* was advertised with the announcement that a new episode had been inserted after the coronation of Anne Bullen showing "the mode and manner of delivering the usual challenge given by the Champion of England, on horseback on the stage." This craze for novelty went so far that one Shakespearean performance was enriched by an acrobat named Maginnis who danced "the much admired Spanish Fandango, blindfolded over thirteen eggs, playing the castanets."

John Howard Payne—remembered now for having written "Home, Sweet Home" and not for his playing of Hamlet—was a favorite in the North in the early 1800s. Described by the press as "a very Cupid in his beauty," Payne was one of the first important stars born an American. This doubtless added greatly to his popularity in years when a second war with

England was brewing over the impressment of American seamen into the British navy.

Another popular player at the Federal Street theatre was beautiful Elizabeth Arnold Poe, who arrived in Boston with a young Baltimore law student she had met and married while on a recent tour. David Poe had abandoned his law for her stage, although he showed a minimum of acting talent. Elizabeth, however, was admired by audiences. She played Cordelia to Mr. Fennell's Lear, following the fashion for novelties by incorporating a sad ballad "Nobody Coming to Marry Me" into her performance. She was pregnant at the time, and on January 19, 1808, her baby was born—a boy whom the Poes christened Edgar Allan. Within two years, both David and Elizabeth were dead of consumption, leaving a tiny son without parents and a Boston stage without its delightful Miss Arnold.

One early Boston performance of *Romeo and Juliet* was distinguished by a novelty not intended by the management. The Romeo of the evening lay dead in the crypt, and a reviving Juliet was lamenting over him when outside in the night, an insistent bell began pealing. The audience stirred uneasily, suspecting fire. Whispers grew louder as fear swept through the house. Romeo was compelled at last to raise himself up on one elbow and make a speech: "Ladies and gentlemen, do not be alarmed. I assure you that is only the Old South Bell." Whereupon, he collapsed once more into his grieving widow's embrace.

As tension between England and her recently liberated colonies grew more critical, nationalism increased in the theatre as it did in every walk of American life. By 1811, the Federal Street—in announcing its complete redecoration—

featured in big print the fact that it would be "lighted with new constructed lamps of AMERICAN MANUFACTURE." In Washington, young Henry Clay was exhorting Congress to halt the hateful impressment of America's sailors. In Boston, a new play called *The American Captive; or, The Siege of Tripoli* was drawing in patriotic crowds by its promise of a scene depicting Tripoli harbor with "the American fleet drawn up before the town—consisting of the CONSTITUTION, frigate, the HORNET and SPITFIRE, brigs, two Bomb Ketches and four Gun Boats." The public needed balm for its challenged pride.

War fever had its effect even on Shakespeare; for now the characters of established plays were being altered into Americans, and the great Shakespearean roles did not easily lend themselves to such transmutation. In the summer of 1812, Americans were gladdened by news of their country's first great sea victory—the *Constitution* over the British *Guerrière*. A storm of popular enthusiasm compelled the song "Huzza for the Constitution" to be interpolated into even the most obviously non-American of the standard plays. It fitted as poorly into *King Lear* and *Othello* as into other foreign or period pieces; but it was demanded, it was sung, and it was received with cheers.

Further naval triumphs in the summer of 1813 increased those displays of patriotic passion. "Your Vessel Defended; or, The Death of Lawrence" was the ballad of the day, rendered by singers in uniform between acts of the most unlikely dramas. A play about Perry's stirring victory on Lake Erie, *Heroes of the Lake,* was so in demand for that season alone that performances of Shakespeare—and even of Kotzebue—were canceled to make room for its frequent repetition. It was followed into fashion during the 1814–15 season by another thriller of the same kind, *Lafitte and the Pirates of Barrataria,* which told of the proud if unnecessary victory of Andrew Jackson at New Orleans.

A wartime feature in the theatres, against which no mere dramatic classic could compete, was the display on stage of elaborate "transparencies." These were unconnected with the business of most of the plays, but pandered to the flaming nationalism of the day. Hamlet's somber soliloquies might suddenly be interrupted by the lowering of a spectacular painted scene, lauding the current naval or military hero. One favorite presented "a whole length figure of the Genius of America, Treading under foot the DEMON OF WAR." Another showed an eagle rampant above a scroll containing the names of dead war heroes, the streamers in the defiant bird's beak lettered: "Immortality to the Brave Defenders of their Country!" What chance had, say, the erstwhile popular *Richard III* by comparison?

But the war was short-lived. It ended in a second American victory and the city of Washington, burned by the British, was rising phoenix-like from its ashes. And Will Shakespeare came back into his own again.

9. Go West, Young Bard, Go West!

Hardly had two determined wars for liberty been won when the more daring citizens of the vigorous new American nation began to turn their faces westward in increasing numbers toward the rich wilderness beyond the Allegheny Mountains.

Trails had been hacked through the virgin forest, and mule carts and Conestoga wagons lumbered along them carrying more and more settlers toward their great adventure. Territory after territory was staked out, wrested from the Indian owners, tamed by incredible feats of courage and persistence, and formed at last into a new state with its own star in the American flag.

The very nature of such a frontier is a compound of rawness and crudity with its vitality. Therefore, it might seem incongruous that the poetry of Will Shakespeare should march westward virtually at the heels of those backwoodsmen. But it might almost be said that while Daniel Boone was stalking his bears, Shakespeare was stalking him. The affinity of such hearty characters for Shakespearean theatre is really not so difficult to understand. The plays had been written in the first place for their lusty forebears at the Globe. Because the audiences of his own day had demanded plenty of bloodshed and melodrama, Shakespeare packed his works with violent action. Because the public had demanded broad comedy, he gave them broad comedy. These same qualities now spoke out to the American frontiersmen. The hearers might miss beautiful subtleties in the plays' lines; but they responded enthusiastically to the unmatched power of the basic tales.

It was an age of declamation and oratory. The political giants of the day were men gifted in the art of roaring at a crowd, beguiling it, wooing it, until a necessary point was carried. Natural successors to the eloquence of Patrick Henry, these later spellbinders—Henry Clay, Andrew Jackson, Daniel Webster, and their like—sharpened the public ear for oratory.

To the citizens of this lively frontier, Antony's harangue over the body of Caesar or Othello's address to the Senate were true to their own time. Their own public men had to be such speechifiers as the Roman and the Moor. Moreover, an apt quotation from Shakespeare was one of the frontier orator's chief stocks in trade. It was said of Mirabeau B. Lamar, whose persuasiveness in public addresses swept him into the presidency of the Republic of Texas, that he "had Shakespeare at his tongue's end and could quote him directly and at pleasure...."

The actors who followed the Conestoga wagons westward traveled in almost as crude fashion as the settlers who preceded them. Along trails still nothing but wheel ruts in the forests, they forced their awkward wagons—stocked with what scraps of scenery, and odds and ends of costuming they could assemble—from settlement to settlement. They played their pieces at whatever tavern or public room might be available. Staging was, of necessity, sketchy in the extreme. "Wardrobe" was often mere imagination.

In one recorded production of *Julius Caesar,* Cassius was clad in the "nankin pantaloons, boots, spurs, gauntlets" of the everyday pioneer, with only a spangled cloak and a "slouched hat and feathers" to set him apart; Brutus appeared in his own ruffled shirtfront and with his own two pistols strapped to his waist. Their sole makeup kit consisted of a scrap of burnt cork. Yet the audience accepted them, cheered them, and demanded encores.

Sol Smith (of whom more is to be said) wrote that at one frontier community, in 1823, he and two actor companions played scenes from *Richard III* at a wayside inn with Richard garbed in a shabby buff-and-blue coat left over from its owner's service in the Continental Army, and with Richmond togged out in a convenient Highland plaid kilt. Again, there was no complaint from the customers. Shakespeare could speak to those folk of the frontier without any trimmings at all.

The theatres where such productions were staged—although they rapidly improved as settlements grew from hamlet to town to city—were at first often the meanest makeshifts. In 1816, the booming community of Lexington, Kentucky, had a "theatre" in the upper story of a brewery. It was equipped with folding canvas seats, uncomfortable enough to require true devotion to the drama by those who remained sitting in them to the end of the usual fifth act. In Tuzewell, Georgia, a hotel dining room (with a gallery "about six feet long by two and a half feet wide" for its stage) was pressed into theatrical service, even though frequently the din from the directly adjoining public bar drowned out the dialogue. Whatever was available was made to serve. And the public attended, the actors prospered.

Gradually, however, theatres intended as theatres came into being. By 1838, according to Joseph Jefferson, who in that year saw with a small boy's eyes the "new town of Chicago . . . just turned from an Indian village into a thriving little place," a theatre existed in that promising community of two thousand souls. His parents had arrived there to play an engagement in it. He later recalled that above the curtain was a wretchedly painted medallion of Shakespeare, who looked at though he were afflicted with "a severe pain in his stomach." Regardless of artistic flaws, the presence there of the portrait indicates that a sunbonnets-and-deerskins frontier suitably recognized the Bard as the presiding genius of its drama.

A year before this, in 1837, St. Louis could boast a fine theatre, with "parquet," dress circle, family circle, and gallery. Here, in a recitation of poetry composed especially for the opening night, faulty in construction but noble in mood, Shakespeare was urged to bless "thy first temple in the far, far West"; and a procession of his famous characters—all unquestionably familiar to the audience—was woven into the verse.

Other playhouses might not be quite so refined, yet they continued to rise throughout the frontier lands, and to honor Will of Avon. In Columbus, Georgia, in May 1832, one of these—a structure seventy feet by forty—was erected and made ready for actors in only four days. According to the local newspaper, the undertaking was "commenced Monday morning last . . . and finished on Thursday afternoon, in season for the reception of Mr. Sol Smith's company on that evening. A great portion of the timber, on Monday morning, waved in the breeze in its native forest; fourscore hours afterward, its massive piles were shaken by the thunder of applause in the crowded assemblage of men." Accustomed to frontier house-raisings and barn-raisings, Columbus undertook a theatre-raising rather than forego its drama. *Macbeth* was the second play performed in the building.

Sol Smith—Solomon Franklin Smith—was a true devotee of the theatre; no genius at acting, but a vigorous and enterprising manager, he was a definite influence on the frontier theatre prior to the Civil War. His first appearance behind the footlights was an accident. As a stage-struck youth of sixteen, he had crept behind scenes to watch a performance of *Richard III* in the venerable Green Street theatre in Albany, New York. In order to see without being seen, he hid in a wooden box standing handy in the wings. While the evening's Richard was wooing his Lady Anne, four actors in the chain mail of soldiers marched toward the box. Young Smith hastily dropped the lid.

But the box was an important property, the coffin of King Henry. Suddenly, Sol felt himself lifted and borne out into the scene, while behind him trooped the sobbing retinue of mourners. The lad in the coffin was badly bumped about before good Henry was finally carted off. The pallbearers had not quite reached the wings when he had to call out to them to treat him a trifle more gently. Four terrified actors thereupon dropped their burden and bolted from the stage in panic, leaving a talking corpse to escape his predicament as best he might.

By 1823, not a bit soured on the theatre by so unorthodox an introduction to it, Sol Smith was on the frontier and commencing his thirty years of ministering to its dramatic needs. Columbus was not the only Georgia community indebted to him for its Shakespeare and other drama. In 1833–34 he took a company to the then state capital, Milledgeville, to play a full season while the Legislature was in session. He wrote of the only theatre available there that "Thirty barrels of lime were used in the cleaning of this temple of Thespis [built 1817] and even then it always retained a rather unsavory odor." The difficulty here lay in the frontier's addiction to plug tobacco. Years of "chew-and-spit" had left souvenirs too formidable to be eradicated.

But the audiences came to his plays. That season *Macbeth, King Lear,* the inevitable *Richard III, Much Ado about Nothing, The Merchant of Venice,* and *Romeo and Juliet* were all enthusiastically received. Perhaps the special taste of the patrons—to which any wise manager cocked an attentive ear —ran more toward the uproar and bloodshed in the plays than to their philosophy. Actors probably had to adapt a scene to naïve but positive frontier standards, or be hooted off the stage. Yet when the players gave their customers what the customers wanted, they were cheered until the rafters rang.

One special problem of those wooden frontier theatres was their lighting. The gas lamps by then standard in theatres of the eastern cities were unknown. The substitutes were generally sperm oil lamps with floating wicks, and the constant vigilance necessarily maintained against accidents by fire could not have failed to cramp the acting severely. In St. Louis as late as 1845 an important English touring star, Ellen Tree, had to interrupt her balcony scene in *Romeo and Juliet* to beseech the stage hands to put out a spreading blaze which only she could see from her lofty position on stage. In Houston, Texas, an early Richard III made his entrance with plumes aflame after they had brushed a sperm-oil lamp in the wings. More than once, the Venice of Othello and the Forum of Caesar went up in smoke before the startled eyes of an audience.

In all this vigorous but crude frontier theatre world there was one exception of marked elegance that Paris itself might have been proud of. At the mouth of the Mississippi, New Orleans had been a populous shipping center under the flags of France and Spain long before America's westward migrations began. Here were no horny-handed woodsmen in buckskins, no weathered frontier women in calico. New Orleans had style and sophistication.

Well before English drama first reached the city in December 1817, French classics had been meticulously performed at the Theatre D'Orleans. When James H. Caldwell (like Sol Smith, a great name in the Western theatre management of his day) reached New Orleans with his "company from Virginia," he found an audience with an already well-developed theatre taste. His performances opened at the lesser St. Phillips' Street theatre, but he was soon appearing at the more

distinguished Theatre D'Orleans, alternating three performances a week with the French company there. Each cast
acted in its native language.

By 1818, New Orleans audiences were already flocking to
Shakespeare plays which equaled the finish of those to be seen
in the East. The English tragedian Cooper played an engagement there during this season, and was paid $333 a night,
a figure the wilderness upriver would have considered fantastic. By 1827 the senior Junius Brutus Booth, father of
Abraham Lincoln's assassin, was treating New Orleans to his
great King Lear and Richard III.

In 1835, after fifteen highly successful New Orleans seasons, Caldwell built there the first St. Charles theatre. A
visiting foreign star—the Irishman, Tyrone Power, first of
three generations of that name to claim respected places in
America's entertainment world—described the St. Charles as
"decidedly the most elegant looking auditory of this country."
At this majestic playhouse, ladies in jewels and satins first
moved out of their boxes and were seen also in the pit or
"parquet." This innovation, exercising a notable influence
upon masculine playgoers, brought about a great improvement
in audience behavior.

But New Orleans was a special case in western theatre
standards. The rest of the frontier substituted vigor for elegance. For several decades of the nineteenth century, it surprised eastern audiences—even eastern actors—that theatre
existed in the wilderness at all.

Thus, when in 1832 the adored Fanny Kemble first arrived
from London with her renowned father, Charles, they took
New York and Boston and Philadelphia and Baltimore by
storm with their *Hamlet* and their *Romeo and Juliet*. Yet Miss

Kemble expressed astonishment in her journal upon hearing that a peddler had taken a print of her own portrait by Sir Thomas Lawrence across the Alleghenies and into the "wilderness" with him; and that there, in wild forest country, it had been auctioned off—after spirited bidding—to a young engineer "out there upon some railroad construction business." The West itself could have found nothing unusual in such a purchase. It was well aware of who Miss Fanny Kemble was; and of who Juliet and Ophelia were, as well.

Strangely, the theatre's chief opposition in those frontier territories of the 1820s and thirties and forties came from religious leaders. It was strange because the true reason for this enmity was not at all the moralistic reason which in an earlier time had motivated Puritan Massachusetts and Quaker Pennsylvania to frown upon play acting. Here in the West, religion—like every other phase of life—tended to be more highly colored, more violent, more emotional, than elsewhere. It was in large part the religion of the camp meeting, the revival, the "shouting-hell-and-brimstone." Itinerant preachers and revivalists were primarily flaming orators. As has been said, it was an age of oration, as had been Shakespeare's own, when Queen Elizabeth had aroused his groundlings to fight off the Spanish Armada by a fiery speech to them. Bombast could move such crowds, whether it came from a stage or a pulpit. Frontier churchmen rightly recognized the actors of Shakespeare as their rivals for public attention. They used every trick in their carpet bags to ban or badger the competition. They howled: "Immorality!" and swore out injunctions.

While still a boy, in 1839, the great Joseph Jefferson was traveling the western circuit with his actor parents. They came to the log cabins of Springfield, Illinois, and found a legal restraint against performance awaiting them, the result of the self-interest of local preachers. A youthful lawyer of the town, with a passion both for justice and for Shakespeare, was angered by the prohibition and offered the embarrassed company his legal services free of charge. He appeared in their behalf before the town council and so persuasively argued the cultural and moral benefits of the drama that the injunction was lifted and the scheduled performance took place. Jefferson recorded in his memoirs that the name of the tall young attorney was Abraham Lincoln.

Over and over again, such popular opinion—bolstered by the respected name of Shakespeare—worked to remove stumbling blocks from the path of public performances. The frontiersmen were set on having their Shakespeare. Recognizing a kinship between his own exaggerated, colorful speech and that of the characters in the dramas, and responding to the larger-than-life emotions portrayed, the pioneer felt almost as much at home with the Sweet Swan of Avon as had his own contemporaries.

Surviving records of those early western playhouses reveal that Shakespeare's works were more often acted than those of any other single playwright. Not even the crude native melodramas which were gaining an impressive popularity could outstrip him statistically. One researcher has reckoned that once in every eighteen times a frontier theatre curtain rose, between 1800 and 1840, it rose upon one or another of Will Shakespeare's plays.

10. Selling Shakespeare down the River

America's westward expansion increased its pace all through that earlier half of the nineteenth century. It naturally followed the courses of the wide rivers which made easy highways through a wilderness. Inevitably, then, theatre—and Shakespeare—would follow the rivers as well. On the river banks were mushrooming the raw new towns which meant audiences. As the settlers eased somewhat from their first struggles, they were in a high mood for theatrical entertainment.

The problem at hand was how to bring theatre to them. And the man who first solved it was William Chapman, who had once played Shakespeare in London's Covent Garden and who was the patriarch of a respected theatrical family recently arrived in America from England.

At first, dispersed over the eastern theatrical landscape from Philadelphia to Albany, the various members of the Chapman clan plied their acting trade in traditional fashion. But old William, anxious to hold the family together, found his means of doing so while playing an engagement in the booming new western metropolis called Pittsburgh.

At Pittsburgh, where the Monongahela and Allegheny rivers joined to create the great west-flowing Ohio, Chapman noted the bustle of river traffic; the literal armada of all sorts and descriptions of craft which daily came and went across that inviting water. The notion this observation sparked in him was submitted to careful examination, for Will Chapman was an experienced theatrical manager, not a brash adventurer. But having played further engagements in bustling Cincinnati and in Louisville, he became convinced that his idea was a sound one. A boat converted into a playhouse could travel these rivers easily, tying up for a night or two wherever people wanted to see a play. Theatre need not be limited to the few western cities where permanent theatre buildings might profitably be constructed. Moreover, such a boat could serve as a family home. It could house the several generations of his kinfolk who would be parts of such an enterprise.

He took the plunge and placed his order for a big flat raft of oak and white pine. While it was being constructed, with a small theatre shack on its deck, William summoned his relations to Pittsburgh. The company was reunited and its initial repertory ready, by the time their floating theatre could be launched. Down the river they floated; down an Ohio still un-blemished by industry, its water jewel clear, its banks jade green. The raft, original ancestor to all the beloved cake-icing showboats which would come later, had no proper name. It was simply known to its frontier public as *The Theatre*.

Wherever Chapman chose to put in to shore, word spread like magic through the surrounding country that the actors had come. By nightfall, riding mules or farm wagons or trudg-ing afoot, an audience would have assembled. Perhaps Will Shakespeare was never played to listeners who came to him under more difficult physical circumstances. Yet come they did. *The Theatre*'s arrival was, for most of them, the year's great event. Conscientious showman that he was, Chapman sought to reward them with the best performances his limited resources could create.

Sometimes, the river itself seemed ambitious to "get into the act." The Ohio, teeming with fish, was a temptation to the hopeful "Izaak Waltons" of the company. One evening, the bill was *Othello*. Young George Chapman, actually a come-dian by nature, was playing Iago to the old man's Moor. While awaiting his first scene, George could not resist the temptation to drop a line overside. Still hopeful of a catch when his entrance cue was spoken, he hastily tied the line around his ankle and appeared on stage.

The scene played well. The house sat in rapt attention. But suddenly Iago's foot shot out from under him as the line went taut, giving the jerk which means a healthy bite. He fell headlong at Othello's feet.

Realizing what had happened even as he went down, he improved upon Shakespeare by crying out: "My lord, in my great love for you I have gone too far! I will leave you to your thoughts one moment, and return anon!" The last of the speech was delivered as he raced off stage to make sure of his prize. Thus abandoned, Othello paced in supposed reverie while awaiting his coactor's reappearance.

But the fish played George as false as ever Iago played his master. George was pulling on the line, straining every muscle to hold it, when the scaly creature abruptly shot up out of the water and landed on deck. The unexpected action sent Iago hurtling back on stage, arms flailing, dragging an impressive weight of flopping catch in his wake.

Another incident of that pioneering voyage also involved the sometimes unreliable George. He was tending to his fish lines rather than to the lines of the play one evening, and completely missed his entrance cue. On stage, the veteran William improvised every scrap of "business" he could devise to cover the long wait. At last, he faced toward the wings and shouted the name of the character George was playing. No answer. He shouted again. This time, still flushed with struggle and success, the tardy George burst in.

"Did you not hear me call?" interpolated William in thundering tones to match Shakespeare's true lines. "Why didst thou not come?"

"Because," panted George, still lost to the play, "I was just hauling in the biggest damn catfish you ever saw!"

Beloved though they were by their frontier audiences, the Chapmans were a considerable mystery to the people of the river hamlets. A rumor spread that they were gipsies, because no one could understand them when they talked together. Actually, they were only having fun with the frontiersmen by conversing in the Cockney they had picked up in London along with many other useful dialects. On stage, their diction and delivery were impeccable.

Money—hard cash—was scarce along the rivers. So *The Theatre* operated on a barter system. Poultry, cured meat, homespun cloth, vegetables—almost anything was acceptable at the boat's box office in exchange for admission. For the most part, this system worked admirably.

On one occasion, however, the shrewd citizens of a backwoods area attempted to take advantage of it. One of the half-grown Chapman children had been put in charge of the door. A dressed chicken, bartered for a ticket by one customer, was slyly purloined from the box where such contributions were deposited. Passed back to the crowd on the gangplank, it was tendered again. And again. And again.

Old William, having played the evening's first act to a crowded house, checked receipts during intermission. It quickly became obvious that some 80 per cent of his audience were enjoying free Shakespeare. During the second act, while they were being held spellbound, he cast off *The Theatre* from her moorings and let her drift four miles downstream before tying up again. After the performance, his ticket-filchers faced a healthy hike back to where they had left their mules and wagons.

Down the Ohio, then down the Mississippi, *The Theatre* drifted her prosperous way. Wilderness which had never seen drama now thrilled to its magic. William had intended his venture as a seasonal matter, with the family returning overland in time for a proper season in the eastern cities. But his project proved so successful that a full year passed before *The Theatre* floated into New Orleans, last stop on the tour. Here (since there was no profitable way to get her upstream again) the raft was broken up and sold at a profit for scrap lumber.

The company did return overland; but not to resume careers in Philadelphia or New York. By the beginning of another summer, William had a bigger and better floating theatre ready at Pittsburgh. Veterans of the river by this time, the company in 1832 launched upon a second and even more successful descent of the Ohio and Mississippi. A young theatrical apprentice named Noah Ludlow, destined to become one of the new West's chief managers and producers, wrote in his old age of this second floating theatre of the Chapmans that he had seen it pass upon the river—"a large flatboat with a rude kind of house built upon it"—and described its "ridge roof" which was surmounted by a flagpole flying a pennant lettered with the single word THEATRE.

And Irish Tyrone Power, although himself playing only the land-anchored theatres of larger frontier communities, wrote his observation of the company which sometimes tied up nearby to offer him competition. He described it: "Composed of members of his [Will Chapman's] own family, . . . which is numerous and, despite alligators and yellow fever, likely to increase."

The Chapmans did not have the rivers to themselves for long. Another company, and an excellent one, headed by Samuel Drake, had trekked westward from a considerable success at Albany in 1815. It played the overland way stations between the Hudson and Pittsburgh, surviving several encounters with Indians and wolves along the trail, putting up a curtain and borrowing such chairs as might be had, to make a theatre of whatever inn might be found along the way. They played for their lodging and meals, and derived their true payment from the excitement and adventure of their journey. When they arrived at last in coal-blackened Pittsburgh, where a real audience and a theatre of sorts awaited them, Drake, too, was swift to appreciate the possibilities of water-borne drama. Already committed to appearances in Lexington, Kentucky, he invested his capital in a "longhorn"—a raft with a cabin, having one steering pole at its stern—to take them into the wilderness.

"Old Drake," not then so very old in years, yet invariably known by this title to his company, used to rouse his players at daybreak with appropriate stately speeches from Shakespeare. His magnificent "double-basso" voice struck echoes from the green valley walls as he strode the cramped deck and declaimed Friar Lawrence's lines from *Romeo and Juliet:* "The grey-ey'd morn smiles on the frowning night. . . ." No alarm clock or ship's bell could have awakened sleeping actors so fittingly to a new day's labors.

The ladies of the company could sleep aboard; but, except for summer nights mild enough for sleeping on the open deck, the men had to find lodgings wherever the ark made a twilight landing. On at least one occasion, Will of Avon gained accommodations for them.

A farmer near the night's mooring had agreed to put up the actors, but soon after they had settled in, two other would-be guests applied to their host for sleeping space. The new arrivals were quartered in the same room. They were mule skinners chaperoning a flatboat load of the beasts downriver; and they stank of their trade. The actors protested, but the farmer, double profit in his pocket, reminded them piously that in the wilderness lodgings were rare and all comers should be glad to share such as there were with fellow travelers.

It was a case of sleeping in quarters reeking like a stable or getting rid of the unwanted roomates. Sam Drake solved the problem for his fellow troupers in terms of pure Shakespeare. One of them returned to the boat and got himself up in the gear of the ghost of Hamlet's father, a white canvas cover-all painted like armor. His face was blanched with flour and given a corpselike hollowness with charcoal shading.

When bedtime arrived, the odorous mule handlers made ready to retire. Drake and his companions sat talking, projecting their voices just sufficiently to be heard by the strangers. They went into a familiar scene as though it were normal conversation. "What, has this thing appear'd again tonight?" . . . "I have seen nothing." . . . "Horatio says 'tis but our fantasy, And will not let belief take hold of him Touching this dreaded sight. . . ." By the time they reached the cue for the entrance of the ghost they had their unpopular listeners' full attention.

Drake intoned his line: "Peace! break thee off! Look where it comes again!" And the ghost of Denmark's murdered king loomed, silent and awesome in the shadows of the rear doorway. The mule handlers let out fearful yells, grabbed their clothes and departed for their flatboat at a run, not even listening to Drake's ringingly delivered: "Angels and ministers of grace defend us!" The actors aired out their quarters and slept well.

Although prosperity attended those early raft-theatres, their inability to drift upstream as well as down limited operations. But back East, Robert Fulton's adaptation of steam to navigation had caught on with such rapidity that even now the answer to the problem was obvious. A steam-powered floating theatre could ply the rivers in both directions; could facilitate

longer travel between moorings, so that only the more populous river settlements need be visited. Moreover—and this
was no mean advantage—it could eliminate the long and
actually hazardous return trip overland. The frontier trails
were haunted by highwaymen who thought nothing of murder
and butchery.

At the end of their second river season, the Chapmans again
sold their theatre for scrap lumber. Their profits were great
enough to buy a wagon and horses for the eastward trek, and
still leave enough in cash to pay for the steam-equipped theatre
William envisioned for their third water-borne tour. Off from
New Orleans they rolled, along the lonely, rutted trails. Three
weeks into the wilderness, they came upon what all travelers
of the period dreaded—an ambush by brigands.

Blocking the trail ahead as his gang closed in at either side,
the ugly leader bellowed fearsomely: "We are the Skeltons!"

"We are the Chapmans!" boomed back George, in fine
dramatic style.

Somewhat disconcerted, the bandit demanded further information about them and was told they were starving actors
trying to reach home after a disastrous engagement in the
South. Having heard of actors but never encountered them,
Skelton compelled them to tie up their wagon and put on a
show forthwith in a trailside clearing.

It had never been quite so important that the Chapmans
please an audience. Grizzled William led off with two Shakespearean "curse" scenes—from *Julius Caesar* and from *King
Lear*—and with his famous soliloquies from *Richard III* and
The Merchant of Venice. Each of the other members of the
company did what he or she thought might best amuse the

gaping ruffians. There were songs. There were recitations. There was dancing. There was fiddle sawing.

Once again the Chapmans scored a hit. At the end of the performance Skelton and his band, almost friendly by now, went through the wagon. They handled costumes and properties, but found nothing worth stealing. At the bottom of the wagon, the bandit leader came upon a property casket, used in *The Merchant of Venice*. But as he pulled it into view, dainty little Caroline Chapman (destined to become a great stage favorite in California considerably later) flung herself weeping upon it. She sobbed that Skelton must not open it. George quickly caught his cue.

"In that box," he told the bandit mournfully, "is the remains of this poor gal's baby, that died two days after birth. We're taking it north so it can rest with our kinfolk in Pittsburgh."

Sentimental tears in his eyes, Skelton returned the box. He and his comrades spurred off along the wagon tracks. The actors reloaded the wagon and careened at top speed on their interrupted way. What the casket actually contained was not infant remains but the cash intended to buy their steam-operated showboat for the coming season!

So successful were these floating playhouses that, almost in this instance alone, the usual east-to-west trend of theatrical progress was reversed. By 1842, eastern theatre interests had taken notice and converted into a playhouse an outmoded "safety barge"—of a type towed behind many early steam craft as a precaution in case of a boiler explosion—to tour the hamlets of the Hudson River Valley.

Shakespeare was not involved in this venture. The producers chose a play called *The Rent Day,* a Drury Lane hit of past seasons, but easily adapted to current American conditions. Farmers of the Hudson Valley in those days were fighting a virtual war against the big New York State landlords —Livingstons, Van Rensselaers—whose debt-strangled leasehold tenants they were. The play's honest farmer and his virtuous wife were bound to be a highly popular hero and heroine with such audiences; the rent collector a naturally detested villain. *The Rent Day* successfully played the river until the autumn of 1845, when a considerably more elaborate showboat, *The Temple of the Muses,* was afloat on the Hudson to vie for ticket money.

This *Temple* had once been a southern passenger packet, the *Virginia,* but now was resplendently transformed. In her bow was a roomy salon with two bars for the sale of food and drink, where a nine-piece orchestra played for audiences reflected in polished mirrors. The theatre itself, in the stern, was lit by patented gas devices and had a stage 42 by 45 feet and scenery 16 feet high. It so impressed its opening-night audience that one Manhattan newspaper begged its readers to imagine the city's Olympic Theatre afloat.

The *Temple*'s chief attraction was a wild melodrama concerned with a madwoman aboard a storm-tossed lightship, the captive wife of a fiend bent upon luring hapless vessels to their doom by displaying false lantern signals. When one shipwrecked victim turned out to be the long-lost son of the misused maniac, the audience was treated to a finale as superdramatic as it was ridiculous. This absurd melodrama, like many others of its time was actually written in imitation of Shakespeare, and audiences recognized this.

For half a dozen summers the showboats on the Hudson prospered; and then they lost their popularity. Their prototypes on the Ohio, the Mississippi, and the Missouri, however, grew increasingly popular as each season passed. Some of their success was unquestionably due to the fact that productions included genuine, not bogus, Shakespeare. Equally important was the increasing use of steam power upon the western rivers —the power for which the Chapmans had been returning at the time of their adventure with the Skelton gang, and which by the following season they had in fact acquired.

With all its advantages (such as eliminating encounters with audiences of bandits) the addition of steam to those earliest showboats created new problems to replace the old ones it solved.

By the theatre's first season with steam, George Chapman had become a fairly acceptable Hamlet. The company was advertised to appear at a river town considerably farther away from where they were playing one evening than was usual in their schedule of one-night stands. In preparation for casting off as soon as the audience had gone ashore, the boiler was stoked early. The top of the boiler lay directly beneath Ophelia's grave, with only a flimsy floor between. When Hamlet stepped into the grave the audience was astounded to see him break into a wild approximation of a Highland Fling among the skulls, and come catapulting out of the hole as if devils pursued him.

Because steam propulsion made possible the use of bigger boats providing larger acting spaces, more elaborate productions could be undertaken. The Chapmans had long desired to add *The Winter's Tale* to their repertory, and now they did so. But the extra "talent" required by the play's large cast meant signing on eager novices at each new stop.

One stormy night they had begun the scene in which Antigonus abandons the infant Perdita in the forest and is then pursued by a bear. A local worthy, stitched into the bear's skin, had just come lumbering on stage to give chase when a formidable crack of thunder and a streak of lightning rent the night. Up onto his hind legs reared the bear, a devout churchman, to cross himself in panic. Thereafter, Will Chapman kept a close eye on the weather if he billed *The Winter's Tale.*

William Chapman, first on the rivers, never deserted them. He reached the age of ninety, still playing those briefer roles in the repertory for which he retained sufficient vigor. Some, like the Ghost in *Hamlet* and King Duncan in *Macbeth,* he had played at the start of his long career in Covent Garden with the immortal Mrs. Siddons. And it was for the Ghost that he made up as usual, one night in 1839 when the boat was tied up at Manchester, Ohio. Having played his part without a hitch, he returned to his chair between decks to rest. They found him there later, still in full costume, peacefully dead. His widow took charge of the company and ran it for eight years longer before finally selling out to younger impresarios.

Long before this, steam had become usual rather than novel on America's inland streams. The first modest floating theatres had been elaborated into the gingerbread-lace grandeur of these side-wheeler "showboats" which now are chiefly remembered. Many of these ferried their theatrical wares—including a generous share of Shakespeare—up and down the rivers for decades. The sound of their calliopes became the music of the streams they voyaged. And each of them lived out her own romantic saga.

There was the *Lillie Lou,* for one. She was stranded five miles from water when the Mississippi riverbed shifted during a storm; and years later, after she had become a derelict curiosity prowled over by sightseers from miles around, was suddenly swept back into the water by another unpredictable shift of the river. She tore downstream on a last insane, ghostly ride which was terror to those who watched from the flooded levees. There was the glamorous *Golden Rod,* built with an auditorium that seated fourteen hundred. And there was the last of them all, the famous *Cotton Blossom.* As late as 1934, *The New York Times* reported the end of her theatrical career and told how she had been "sold up the river from Memphis, Tennessee, and, stripped of her calliope and flaming banners, has gone into service as an excursion steamer."

They were gallant river theatres, all of them. Yet Shakespeare was never better served by the most elegant of these later comers than he had been by the pioneer Chapmans and their flatboat kind, who first broke the watery trail on the Ohio and the Mississippi.

11. Shakespeare and the Noble Savage

From the days of the first English colonists, native Indians had played a large part, both as friends and as enemies, in new America's daily fortunes. To the folk of Shakespeare's London, those exotic savages had been one of the most speculated-about features of the New World.

Specimens of their race were so frequently kidnaped from Colonial forests that Puck, in *A Midsummer Night's Dream,* comments upon the practice by saying of Titania that "she, as her attendant, hath A lovely boy, stolen from an Indian king," and then by reference to the boy's mother proves him to be an American Indian. Transported to England, these human curiosities were displayed to crowds often outnumbering the audiences at the legitimate playhouses.

Shakespeare himself must on more than one occasion have attended exhibitions which featured, along with "freaks and monsters," the fascinating American savage. The painted curtains typical of such shows "portrayed the serpents, Mermaids, birds, wild beasts and Indians from America," and were gazed upon with avidity. The historian and geographer Richard Hakluyt, in his edition of Peter Martyr, which Shakespeare is certain to have studied, set down a full description of these arresting strangers to the realm of Good Queen Bess. They were, he said, "tawny like unto the West Indians, whiche are altogether in generall either purple or tawny, like unto sodd Quinces, or of the colour of Chesnuttes or Olives, whiche colour is to them naturall."

In the very year of Shakespeare's death, there arrived in London an Indian who came not as a peepshow curiosity but as a recipient of royal honors. The lady was the daughter of Powhatan, powerful king of the Chickahominies in Virginia. Her own people had named her Matoaka. In Jamestown, captured by settlers there as a hostage for the return of goods and captives taken by her tribesmen, she had been christened Rebecca. But it was by the name of Pocahontas, friend to the explorer Captain John Smith, that she was most widely known. While a prisoner in Jamestown, she had fallen in love with a young Englishman named John Rolfe, and had married him with the blessings both of her father and the Colonial Governor. When her husband took her home with him, two years later, Elizabeth's court feted her lavishly—presumably, to insure peace with the Chickahominies, so essential to successful colonization of Virginia.

Amply exposed to the Amerind, both in person and by the literature of his day, Shakespeare not surprisingly made reference to him in play after play. In *Henry VIII,* a porter comments upon the popular curiosity concerning Indians by asking, "Have we some strange Indian . . . come to court, the women so besiege us." In *Love's Labour's Lost,* the passage referring to "a rude and savage man of Inde" could not mean him to be from anciently civilized India but only from raw new America. And in *The Tempest,* itself inspired by exploration of the New World, Trinculo complains of the current rage for American Indians as freaks—"When they will not give a doit to relieve a lame beggar, they will lay out ten to see a dead Indian." The character of Caliban in the same play was certainly modeled upon the American Indian.

Intrigued he obviously was by these alien beings. But Shakespeare died decades too soon to receive any report as to how those same unlettered savages might respond to his works.

The nameless Indian of Quebec who suffered nightmare in 1640 after witnessing the newborn Dauphin's birthday play, with its "hell which vomited forth flames," is the first Indian theatregoer of record on the new continent. But it was probably not until the first season of the Hallams in Virginia (1757) that the red man was exposed to Shakespeare.

In November of that year, certain Indian dignitaries arrived in Williamsburg to renew a treaty of friendship with the colonists. The *Virginia Gazette* did everything possible to give this deputation the status of a royal embassy, and referred deferentially in its columns to "the Emperor of the Cherokee Nation and his Empress" as leaders of the delegation. Their son and a considerable band of warrior attendants completed the party. Eager to impress the visitors, the Governor decreed a theatre party as evidence of "civility and friendship." The Hallams provided their second Colonial Shakespeare production, *Othello,* as the attraction. While the play's great lines were lost upon the distinguished visitors, the sprightly stage action with its skillful swordplay was not. Witnessing the slash and parry of naked steel with "great surprise," the startled Empress quickly commanded her bodyguards to break up the action and prevent the actors from slaughtering one another.

A decade later, it was again a band of Cherokee notables who were treated to Shakespeare—*Richard III,* this time—at the John Street in New York City, by courtesy of His Excellency, Governor Moore. Such "first citizens" of South Carolina as Chief Attakullakulla (Little Carpenter) sat in polite, uncomprehending amazement beholding England's bloodied crown change hands. According to a report of the evening in *Holt's Journal,* they seemed to be more "surprised and diverted by the tricks of Harlequin" in the pantomime ballet which had been added to the bill.

As theatre in America took to the road in the early decades of the nineteenth century, and as traveling players brought Shakespeare and other attractions to still-untamed frontiers, Indians almost inevitably became acquainted with Shakespeare. Some of the acquaintance was of a sort never anticipated by managers or actors!

Sol Smith, whose theatre career had begun with his adventure with King Henry's coffin in Albany, had by now become an active actor-manager in the West and South. On one occasion, his company arrived at Columbus, Georgia, intending to open an engagement there in Kotzebue's popular historical melodrama, *Pizarro*. Requiring a considerable band of supernumeraries to appear as the warriors of Atahualpa's defeated Inca army, Smith struck a bargain with a local chief of the Creeks. The theatre was to be supplied two dozen red-skinned extras with their own bows, arrows, and tomahawks. Pay was agreed upon at "fifty cents each and a glass of whiskey," terms completely acceptable to the Indians.

Presumably *Pizarro* was a success with cast as well as audience, for on the following evening the entire delegation of warriors with their native arms again turned up at the stage door. Unfortunately, the bill for this second performance was *Macbeth*. In dismay, Smith "most positively declined their valuable aid." But the disappointed Creeks, seeing no difference between an army of Incas and an army marching against the battlements of Dunsinane, created such an angry disturbance that the curtain was considerably delayed in rising.

Sol Smith, during his long and colorful theatrical career, was to have considerable experience with Indians. On another occasion, so short a time before the outbreak of bloody hostilities between Creeks and white men that ill-feeling must even then have been bitter, he was transporting his company from stop to stop through the very heart of Creek territory. They were traveling the rough frontier roads in a line of barouches, their luggage and Shakespearean scenery aboard a large Philadelphia road wagon rumbling awkwardly behind. One of the company was a self-important actor named Carter, possessed of two great fears—one of the Indians, the other of having it discovered he wore a wig to conceal total baldness.

The jouncing procession halted one afternoon at an Indian

settlement along the trail. There, some hundred warriors were gathered at the headquarters of their Chief for a tribal revel. The Creeks were hospitable enough and offered refreshments. Taking the Chief aside, Smith arranged with him a practical joke designed to puncture poor Carter's pompousness. A petulant remark by the victim about the prices being charged them for their food and drink was seized upon as a pretext. The Creeks made a threatening show of resentment.

Shouted at to run for his life by fellow troupers in on the joke, Carter vaulted astride the nearest saddled horse and took off like the wind. The Chief had detailed four braves to give chase. Carter's wig flew unnoticed from his head as he fled for his life. It was brought back to camp as a scalp amid general hilarity. Afterward, in a published interview, and never dreaming that he had been made a fool of, Carter announced that he had outridden a pursuing force of no less than fifteen hundred blood-thirsty savages.

Theatrical wigs were often confused with the real thing in those early frontier meetings between Shakespearean actors and Indians. Well before his national reputation as a great Hamlet had been made, young Edwin Booth was one of a company touring California's mining towns with a partly Shakespearean repertory. The caravan reached the town of Diamond Springs, near which the Digger Indians had consecrated ground to burial rites for their dead. Perhaps too near to this sacred plot, the actors set up a night's camp. They promptly set about airing out their travel-dusty costumes and properties to make them ready for the next performance. They had stretched clotheslines between the trees and were hanging out their wardrobe and wigs when a party of mounted Diggers rode up in unfriendly mood. But it took only one glimpse of the impressive array of "scalps" and warrior regalia to turn the raiders back with frightened yelps. The last the actors saw of them, the Indians were spurring for the hills at the fastest speed they could kick from their tough ponies.

Less amusing for the theatre people involved was an incident of the early 1840s in Florida, where the second Seminole War was in progress. A traveling troupe headed by William A. Forbes made bold to penetrate the disputed territory and, foolhardy enough to go from one military station to another without armed protection, the actors were swooped down upon by raiding Seminoles. Two of them were taken by the Indians and ruthlessly butchered. The wagon containing the costume trunks was captured and soon the garrison of the nearest fort was challenged by a party of savage riders who circled their position whooping and yelling—but safely out of shotgun range—clad in the Roman togas of *Julius Caesar,* the Highland plaids of *Macbeth* and the Italian velvets of *Romeo and Juliet.* The popular star Joseph Jefferson, who often recounted this story, described the Seminoles as being "decked in the habiliments of Othello, Hamlet and a host of other Shakespearean characters, for [and here he made the vital theatrical point] *Forbes was eminently legitimate.*"

Sometimes it was not contact with unfriendly Indians, but steps taken to avoid such a contact, which added a fresh detail to that era's growing stage legend. By the middle 1840s, Jefferson had won his own special place on the dramatic heights and, with his company, he was playing an engagement at Houston, Texas. Three hundred miles of Indian country away, at San Antonio, a former actor-manager named Stanley—now reduced to operating a bar with faro and keno games on the side—learned with excitement of the star's arrival. Ignoring all danger, Stanley rode the long distance to beg Jefferson to extend his tour to San Antonio. But Jefferson was more prudent than his visitor. He remembered the fate of the Forbes troupe and refused to risk the uncertain journey. In recognition of Stanley's former status in the theatre, however, he did urge the older man to remain in Houston long enough to play a special performance of *Richard III*.

For several days, Stanley rehearsed with the company; boomed out the role's soliloquies in his outmoded, fervent style; practiced the villain's gestures; built up an impressive humpback for himself out of raw cotton, to lend his coming performance verisimilitude.

But he had failed—as had Jefferson—to take into account one special circumstance of the Houston audience. These men all knew Stanley. They had drunk at his bar and lost money at his gaming tables, and now they were not going to let themselves be seduced into a belief that he was England's King, the last of the Plantagenets. The play had scarcely begun when its action called for Stanley to woo the aloof Lady Anne. A booming voice from the audience warned her of the true circumstance of her suitor.

"Don't you believe that polecat, ma'am!" the well-informed spectator shouted. "The no-good so-and-so's already got him two Mexican wives back in San Antonio!"

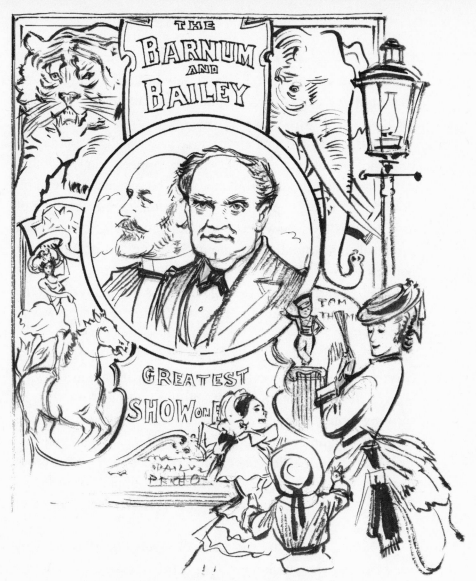

12. Circus Boy William

Of all forms of public entertainment, the one perhaps most generally thought of by Americans as peculiarly their own is the circus. Whole generations in this country have grown old warmed by memories of calliope music and spangles and sawdust, of daring young men on flying trapezes, of elephants and acrobats and equestriennes and clowns.

Actually, the modern circus first saw the light of day in England. A former English cavalry officer named Philip Astley was its pioneering genius, and he opened his "exhibition" to the London public in 1770. Almost from the time of its debut, Astley's show was a traveling affair that crisscrossed the rural shires month after month in a caravan of lumbering painted wagons. Its success quickly bred imitation. Within a few years, various similar organizations were invading the provinces. And from provinces to former colonies was a logical step.

As early as 1792 in Philadelphia and 1795 in New York City, an English outfit known as Rickett's Circus was drawing crowds. It was followed in 1797 by the Lailson Show with its thrilling female rider, Miss Venice. Within a very short time, Rufus Welch and other American exhibitors were edging into the circus field. During the earliest decades of the nineteenth century the rolling, hilly farmland of upper Westchester County, not far north of Manhattan, had become a cradle of American circus activity.

In 1808 a farmer by the name of Hachaliah Bailey, living near the tiny town of Somers, New York, received as a present the second elephant to appear in America since times before the Ice Age. Bailey's brother, a sea captain, had purchased the huge beast in London. For reasons lost to history, he considered Old Bet an appropriate gift.

Old Bet was brought by sloop to the Hudson River town of Sing Sing (now Ossining) and herded overland to the Bailey farm. Here, the curiosity she roused among the local gentry

quickly convinced the canny Hachaliah that he had acquired
a money-maker. He put a crude canvas wall around the field
where Old Bet grazed and started charging admission for a
look at her. The "monster" was moved from field to field by
night, as grazing required, to prevent people from seeing her
free of charge. The customers flocked in. Bailey found himself
with a new career, as exhibitor of wild animals.

In the first months of her life in America, Old Bet earned
enough for her owner to entice two businessmen into investing
the then considerable sum of twelve hundred dollars in a two-
thirds interest in her for a single year. As a traveling exhibit
she proved a steady money-maker right up to the black day
when a resident of the Maine backwoods, terrified by his first
look at what he took to be the behemoth he had read of in
the Bible, grabbed a gun and shot her dead. But by then
Bailey's road-show ventures had made him a comfortably
wealthy man. He built a hotel in Somers which he named the
Elephant; and on a granite plinth in front of it, he placed a
statue of his original attraction. Old Bet's likeness was carved
from solid blocks of wood, meticulously fitted together and
painted with gold. The hotel is now a circus museum; and the
statue still stands before it, weathered from its original bright
gilt to a suitable elephant gray.

Inspired by Bailey's success, a veritable circus fever spread
through the region from the Hudson River eastward into
Connecticut. Many a fortune was made in the region from
traveling shows created in imitation of the original venture.
The menagerie as a feature of the modern circus stems directly
from those early caravans. Performers and animals set out
from the farm barns where they had wintered as soon as the
rutted country roads were free of snow in the spring. Pulled

by strong dray horses, often mired to their hubs, the gaudy wagons forged as far westward as the Mississippi and as far southward as Georgia. Kentucky knew them, and Michigan, and Indiana, and Ohio, and every place between where paying audiences could be found. The circus was firmly woven into a young America's pattern of life.

Had he been born in a different century and in a different place, the lad who once ran off from Stratford-on-Avon with a company of strolling players might well have fallen victim to the glamour of the those rolling wagon shows. He might, like many another youth, have cast his fortunes with one of them. As things were, Will Shakespeare's works had to do Will Shakespeare's circus-chasing for him—or perhaps it was the circus that chased Will.

At any rate, the first record of their joint activity bears the date 1829. In that year, in Louisville, Kentucky, the Noah Ludlow who had ventured westward with "Old Drake" united his assets with those of a circus manager. A "combination of dramatic and equestrian performances" was what the partnership proposed to offer their river-towns public, by setting up both a stage and a riding ring wherever they stopped to entertain.

Ludlow selected for his half of the bill Shakespeare's *Taming of the Shrew,* in its watered-down version of *Catherine and Petruchio.* The first stop on the tour was Cincinnati. Here the partners discovered and rented a flimsy old bathhouse which included a stable of sorts for the animals. For two weeks, the Shrew was tamed nightly, either before or after, or in counterpoint to, the galloping hoofbeats of trained horses.

At the end of this brief period, the circus man for some reason pulled up stakes and departed. To recover from the blow, Ludlow at once put on *Julius Caesar* in the bathhouse, Shakespeare being what he knew best. The building was wretched, the production woefully pinched, the acting shoddy; and even so provenly popular a drama failed to attract an audience. So Ludlow fell back on circus embellishment once more and combined the performance of two-legged Romans with the act of a trained dog appropriately named Nero.

How many such combinations of *The Tempest* with trapezes, of *Macbeth* with menageries, of *Lear* with lions and leopards, may have been performed throughout rural America during the first half of the nineteenth century, nobody knows. But judging by surviving records they were far from infrequent. As Ludlow himself prospered, he employed many a circus act to bring in the customers who were not impressed by the name of William Shakespeare. Many of the newer, more elaborate showboats (by then numerous on American rivers) were planned for circus rings rather than for stages. The horses pranced, the jugglers juggled, and when Shakespeare's turn came he could be presented in the round.

The entertainment world of the early-to-middle 1800s in America was not large, and all but inevitably its two chief giants eventually locked horns; Stratford's Will Shakespeare came to grips with Bridgeport, Connecticut's, Mr. Phineas T. Barnum. Barnum's name, a hundred and more years later, still means "circus" to millions of Americans. At the time, however, he had not yet formed his famous partnership with James Bailey; and the day still lay far in the future when their circus would combine with its Ringling rival into the undisputed "Greatest Show on Earth." Each man—Bard and Barnum—in his very different way was unquestionably the dominant showman of his particular generation. And since

Shakespeare's way had proved sufficiently durable to carry him over the centuries into Barnum's age, the eventual meeting of their spheres was only a matter of time.

In New York City, in the early 1840s, Barnum opened a theatre in his famous Museum. In order to woo the puritans of a Victorian age, however, he had styled it Barnum's Lecture Room. All public references to it avoided the word "theatre." Of the three thousand who were an average day's audience for Barnum's moral offerings, most would have been profoundly shocked by the idea that they ever had entered a playhouse.

Contrary to the custom of the day, there was no bar at the Museum where liquor was served. Patrons who left the premises between acts for "refreshment" in nearby taverns were refused readmittance. Advertisements which solicited the patronage of women and children piously announced that the entertainment to be enjoyed was "for all those who disapprove of the dissipations, debaucheries, profanity, vulgarity and other abominations which characterize our modern theatre." What appeared upon the stage was of the highest moral—if not artistic—quality. *The Drunkard,* a play with dire warnings against the evils of the Demon Rum, was a perennial favorite. *Uncle Tom's Cabin* was given some of its earliest performances there.

Despite the moral tone of his entertainment, Barnum never made the mistake of boring his audiences. Many prominent performers in the amusement field made their debuts at the Lecture Room. One of the favorites there was the greatest of all American clowns, Dan Rice. Rice was first successful as a jockey, but began his successful theatre career as "straight man" to an educated pig named Lord Byron. His "character" was Uncle Sam, bewhiskered and coattailed, and it was Rice who made this personification of the nation truly famous. With (and later without) Lord Byron, he was a sensational success until the years just before the Civil War. At that time his undisguised sympathy with the southern cause cost him much of his popularity. After the war he published a newspaper, ran for Congress in Pennsylvania and was defeated, and even actively campaigned for nomination for the presidency of the United States.

Rice was in his heyday at the time of Barnum's Lecture Room, however, and it is understandable that with such attractions to offer Barnum came to Will Shakespeare slowly. Doubtless the prestige of the Bard fitted neatly with the dignified atmosphere of the Lecture Room, and at length Barnum decided to produce the lusty comedies and the passionate dramas. But he was wary. He announced to his public that the plays would be "shorn of their objectionable features when placed upon my stage." Bowdlerized to suit the most finicky of his lady customers, Shakespeare thereupon shared that stage with Dan Rice and his educated pig, and with Mme. Clofullia, the Museum's celebrated Bearded Lady.

Barnum's greatest artistic venture was his importation of the famous Swedish Nightingale, Jenny Lind, for her American tour. But the greatest money-maker of his career was, in all probability, General Tom Thumb. This popular midget performer was one of the outstanding attractions of the nineteenth century, not only in America but also abroad. And it was while in England in 1844, on tour with his vest-pocket star, that Barnum was stirred by his great Shakespeare inspiration.

The General was playing in Birmingham and drawing crowded houses. Barnum's friend, Albert Smith, "a jolly companion as well as a witty and sensible author," had come up from London to do a bit of sight-seeing with the visiting America impresario. Early one morning, the two men mounted the box seat of an English mail coach to begin the thirty-mile ride to Stratford-on-Avon. At a brisk twelve miles an hour, they sped across the delightful countryside. Barnum was academically interested in their destination, but his interest was sharply increased when, still four miles short of the birthplace of the Bard, he spied over a wretched hole-in-the-wall barber-shop the legend: SHAKESPEARE HAIRDRESSING, A GOOD SHAVE FOR A PENNY. Recalling the maxim about prophets unhonored in their own lands, he was impressed by the realization that even here, in his home town, Master Will had commercial drawing power.

The two friends breakfasted at the Red Horse in Stratford and Barnum asked for the best available guidebook describing the poet's birthplace and grave. His American pride was stirred when this proved to be *The Sketch Book* of his fellow countryman, Washington Irving. Perhaps, at the time, he also recalled that in the youngest days of the Republic the two illustrious founding fathers, John Adams and Thomas Jefferson, had made a pilgrimage to Stratford together. Their known esteem for the poet bespoke the reverence of their journey, although Jefferson's account of it in his diaries for that year of 1786 recorded only the blunt fact; and then, "for seeing house where Shakespeare was born, 1s; seeing his tomb, 1s; entertainment, 4s 2d; servants, 2s."

The morning was devoted to visits. The two men went to the parish church where Will sleeps near the northern wall of the chancel, under a slab bearing the epitaph he was supposed to have composed himself:

Good Friend for Iesus sake forbeare
To digg the dust enclosed heare;
Bleste be the man that spares thes stones,
And curst be he that moves my bones.

But it was the poet's birthplace which most intrigued the show-man from America. From the moment he entered the simple cottage, which had been so utterly neglected with time that its living room had deteriorated into a butcher's shop, Barnum's active imagination responded.

The old plaster of the kitchen walls was crisscrossed with the signatures of generations of visitors who had hoped to leave at least this much of themselves in what they obviously regarded as a sacred place. Scribbled so close together that they seemed like clinging cobwebs, those autographs engaged Barnum's show-wise mind. He was still thinking about them when the post chaise, hired to carry the sight-seers to more aristocratic marvels at Warwick Castle, got under way.

As a result of this musing, and acting with his customary promptness, Barnum a few days later made an offer to purchase the cottage at Stratford. He was, indeed, given a first refusal of it through the intermediary in whose name the transaction was being carried on. His intention was simple. He would have this shrine which thousands visited carefully dismantled, timber by timber, brick by brick, and transported to America. There, eventually, it would be set up as the chief attraction of his Museum. But first, reassembled for touring purposes on a railroad flatcar, it would be taken all over America, as background for an all-midget production based on the life of Shakespeare, to star the ever-popular General Tom Thumb as a watch-fob Bard.

Despite the careful use of an intermediary, word of the project leaked out and was reported by the British press. The public was horrified. Comfortably forgetting their long neglect of the site, they now thought of it as the Kingdom's proudest jewel. Wails of protest arose from every corner. A group of well-to-do Londoners quickly banded together to make a counteroffer on the property, and purchased it from a properly intimidated owner for three thousand pounds. They then transferred title to an organization formed to receive it, the Trustees of Shakespeare's Birthplace, who in 1857 set about restoring the property and eventually established it as a national monument.

Barnum was philosophical about the prize that had been snatched from his hands. He wrote later: "Had they slept a few days longer, I should have made a rare speculation. For I was subsequently assured that the British people, rather than suffer that house to be moved to America, would have bought me off with twenty thousand pounds." General Tom Thumb was destined to conclude his illustrious career before the publics of two continents without ever appearing in what might have been the oddest Shakespearean production known to history.

The circus man and the poet would seem, at first glance, to have had little in common—beyond a flawless instinct for what would please their audiences. Yet as recently as 1940, writing of Barnum, William Lyon Phelps (while conceding that Barnum's literary style had been dominated by the exclamation mark) noted a further similarity. Pointing out that Barnum was "the greatest psychologist who ever lived," he claimed for him the title of "the Shakespeare of advertising."

13. The Gold in Them Thar Hills

In 1848, America was turned upside down by the most explosive event—to date—of the century. Gold was discovered at Sutter's Mill on the American River in California! The news burst upon the settled country to the east with what a later generation would describe as atomic force. Previously anchored lives were ripped free of their moorings. The rooted became rootless. Lifelong plans and patterns were abandoned. By 1849, the "Argonauts" were stampeding westward.

Until the glow of gold thus illuminated it, California had been for most Americans terra incognita. Mexican dominion over the Territory had ended as recently as 1847, with the "Bear Flag War" and final defeat for General Mariano Vallejo. As for California theatre, it had consisted chiefly of Spanish religious plays. Few if any easterners knew it even existed.

Actually, the first English-language play to be acted in the Territory was put on with the suave blessing of General Vallejo. Confined under guard to his gracious hacienda at Sonoma, he had with true Latin courtesy built a crude theatre there in order that the troops who held him prisoner might entertain themselves. Here, the soldiers rehearsed and presented a production of Webster's then-popular comedy *The Golden Farmer*. This effort proved such a success that later the amateur actors appeared at Monterey and Santa Barbara.

Gold fever swiftly thrust such modest excitement aside. By each of the three routes then available, thousands upon thousands of avid seekers after precious metal poured into the new El Dorado. Some took the long, wearisome voyage around South America and Cape Horn. Some sailed to the isthmus of Panama, crossed its fever- and bandit-infested jungles by pack mule, and continued by sea along the Pacific coast. Some took the overland wagon trails, braving floods and famine and hostile Indians and the perils of wild mountain passes, in their eagerness to reach California. Those of them who lived to see the journey's end by whatever route rushed to the gold fields where fortune beckoned.

The camps in which the new arrivals lived were wild and wooly. Crime and violence were rampant, emotions were unbridled, sentimentality and ribaldry ran strong. In most localities the law was only a "sometime thing." Convicts from Australia and escaped murderers from Europe, adventurers from several continents, brawling bullies from eastern slums joined the gold rush. The miners were indeed a motley crew.

The gold was there and they tore it out of the earth, or panned it out of the streams, in fabulous quantities. And after they had worked hard, they wanted to play hard. They were willing to pay for amusement. Hardy bands of actors were not long in following after them, ready to serve this new audience and to reap the obvious rewards.

For the first year or two, playhouses were casual. Young Edwin Booth, who arrived in California among the first of his profession, is known to have acted one of his early Hamlets with the stump of a giant redwood tree for his stage; and to have ridden from camp to camp, from performance to performance, astride a pinto pony. Ben Mouton's troupe junketed from mine to mine in a huge covered wagon, decorated with scenes from *Catherine and Petruchio,* their chief attraction. Rowe's amphitheatre, in use by the end of 1849, was a glorified circus tent—yet it served to house *Othello.*

Two of the showboat Chapmans, mature "Young Will" and no-longer-quite-so-young Caroline, were also among the first theatrical arrivals. They played Shakespeare in the shadow of the Sierra Nevada Mountains at Hangtown (later Placerville), in a mountain hall which had a fixed post running up at dead center of its so-called stage to interfere with the action. For this reason it was always referred to in family annals as the "Hide-and-Seek Theatre." Often the Chapman troupe were affectionately escorted from one stand to the next by posses of admiring miners, to protect them from the uglier element infesting the foothills.

California Territory's first real theatre—and it was none too good—was the New Eagle, which opened in Sacramento in the autumn of 1849. Its walls were of canvas, which when wet by a rain turned the interior into a steambath; its roof was of sheet iron; and its ground floor was entirely given over to gambling wheels and bar service. But it could boast a dress circle and even a "parquette"; and it had a real drop curtain, painted with a bilious landscape scene, brown trees in the foreground with yellow skies and lilac mountains in perspective.

For some reason, the stock forest scenery used for many of the roaring melodramas at the New Eagle—and for Shakespeare, as well—was painted in a glaring red rather than in nature's green. It thus prepared the audience for the bloody deeds sure to be afoot. The leading lady was a Cockney with a horrendous accent. But the booted, flannel-shirted miners "out front" applauded her every entrance enthusiastically. Women were few and far between in the mining camps.

During the first feverish months of the gold rush, San Francisco was left a ghost town. Fleets of deserted ships rode at anchor in her harbor. Her streets had emptied of a population now stampeding toward "the diggings." But the city quickly became a mecca for all the newly rich miners with nuggets to spend. By 1851 an ex-cabman and bartender named Tom Maguire, who could neither read nor write, had opened his first Jenny Lind Theatre above a saloon on Kearney Street. San Francisco's fantastic surge to theatrical glory was under way. There has probably never been anything to equal it anywhere in the history of the world's stage.

The Jenny Lind burned twice in the course of its first year. When it was rebuilt after the second fire, Maguire used brick and stone to create a truly handsome edifice enclosing a balcony, three galleries, a parterre, orchestra stalls, and dress circle. He presented the younger Junius Brutus Booth in *Hamlet* to open it. During that season, it is recorded, "miners . . . swarmed from the gambling saloons and cheap fandango houses to see Hamlet and Lear."

Meanwhile, the American Theatre and the Adelphi had arisen to compete with the Jenny Lind. Writing of the American, a French newsman detailed to cover the gold-rush story for his Paris paper declared that, "in many ways the luxury and good taste of this little theatre remind one of the Opéra Comique." In a mere two years since the opening of the New Eagle in Sacramento, playhouse standards had soared.

So had standards for the productions the theatres were to house. A town with almost limitless money to spend on its amusements could afford the best; and to San Francisco, the "best" meant the top stars of the eastern stage, in the Shakespearean roles which had made them famous. The financial inducements offered by the city's growing corps of managers were so impressive that engagements were accepted despite the long, often dangerous journey to the Pacific coast.

Early arrivals were the H. L. Bateman family, with seven-year-old daughter Kate and nine-year-old daughter Ellen as precocious stars. Ellen actually acted in *Hamlet, Richard III,* and *The Merchant of Venice,* playing the Dane, the Usurper, and Shylock to her smaller sister's Ophelia, Lady Anne, and Portia. The city's critics were kind: "They are rather to be compared with children of ordinary capacity than with . . . Macready or Charlotte Cushman. Viewed in this light, how wonderful they are!"

More mature wonders arrived in San Francisco on the

Bateman girls' heels. As the city's population soared (mounting to eight times its former twenty thousand in the ten years following the great discovery at Sutter's Mill), the audience for "the best" mushroomed with it. And they were lavish with rewards for those actors who pleased them. Gold coins, watches, tiaras, jewelry were flung upon the stages with abandon.

When the redoubtable Edwin Forrest appeared to put on a season of Shakespeare, tickets for his opening night sold at five hundred dollars. In that same decade, almost a dozen elaborate playhouses opened their gilded doors to a theatre-hungry city. Huge, draped in red plush, jeweled with immense crystal chandeliers—they could house the most magnificent productions booked into them.

The demand for variety was great. It often resulted in performances too sketchily assembled and too hastily rehearsed. Thus it was reported that Mr. James Stark (starring at the Jenny Lind and a "quick study") put only eight days of preparation into *King Lear,* a play hitherto unfamiliar to him, whereas Forrest had studied the part for five years before considering himself ready to go before an audience. Only the suicide of his leading lady prevented Stark from offering his *Lear* at the end of those eight days; and even so, it was on the boards two weeks later.

Other early San Francisco favorites were the durable Chapmans. Because of the generations of theatre behind them, they were far better prepared than most in their demanding art. Caroline Chapman became the finest actress in Shakespeare, as well as modern comedy, that the city was to see at all frequently during that gold-rush era. A season of Shakespeare in which the Chapmans costarred with the Booths—

Edwin (still a youth), the younger Junius Brutus, and their now aging but still commanding father—would have elicited cheers even in New York. *Othello,* with the elder Junius Brutus as the Moor and the younger one as Iago, created a genuine sensation.

And there was Lola Montez, the notorious former darling of the King of Bavaria, who appeared on the streets with a huge parrot perched on her shoulder and who kept two dangerous bears chained at her doorstep. Montez made up in colorful eccentricities what she lacked in talent as an actress and a dancer. Full houses attended her performances. Homage also was paid to Forrest's recently cast-off wife, Catherine Sinclair, who had never acquired high professional stature in the East but whom San Francisco was ready to hail as a genius.

Laura Keene (who would many years later perform in *Our American Cousin* on an evening when President Lincoln would attend it at Ford's Theatre in Washington) enjoyed wide success in a variety of Shakespearean plays, including the infrequently acted *Coriolanus.* Her productions were so magnificently mounted that San Francisco politely failed to notice that she was actually rather a second-rate actress.

The city also welcomed Adah Isaacs Menken, a sensational though mediocre performer, who electrified San Franciscans with her tawdry melodrama, *Mazeppa.* In its great scene, playing a man, she wore a suit of flesh-colored cotton tights and was bound to the back of a live horse—which then circled the theatre on a special ramp, causing ladies to faint and strong men to cheer as it galloped past. Miss Menken evidently believed that having conquered the horse she was ready to take on Shakespeare. She subsequently attempted another

male role, that of Richmond in *Richard III,* and was cour-
teously received even in this because of her former reputation.

The first wild California boom did subside, of course. But
it left behind it a theatre thoroughly established. As one after
another of the roistering mine towns settled down and began
to don the robes of civic virtue, the building of its own
presentable theatre seemed to be the crowning ambition of
each community. The chain of these houses which quickly
came into being formed a California "road" which promised
real profits for touring stars, and attracted them to the West.

What the actors brought to California was in a sense as
precious as the nuggets flung on their stages, or the swollen
receipts poured in at their box-office windows. When one reads
that the unlettered miners in their audiences soon "could
finish lines from Shakespeare before they were spoken," it
becomes obvious that the flow of true treasure across those
gold-rush footlights was not all in one direction.

14. The Shakespeare War

In the very year when Will Shakespeare was taking to the mines of California, and opening up a vast new audience for himself along the Pacific coast, back in New York an open war had developed between the camps of rival Shakespearean actors. Small in scope and brief in duration though it was, it employed real troops who shed real blood. And to the shame of all those connected with it, real graves were filled with real corpses before the shocking violence ended.

147

With its Revolution now six decades behind it, mid-century America was still highly touchy wherever it suspected British condescension. National pride wore a definite chip on its shoulder. This pride was one of the basic reasons for the fantastic popularity of Edwin Forrest. As the first great American-born actor to be hailed abroad, Forrest was the idol of the crowd. They jammed every theatre where he played. Although the aristocracy might still adhere to the cultural standards of England and Europe, New York City's man in the street (whose belligerence and mistrust toward foreigners extended to include the local "upper crust" as well) was violently chauvinistic in his attitudes.

In 1845, the adored Forrest had attempted an English tour. Various London critics had given his fiery, bombastic style of acting cold treatment in their notices. The reigning Shakespearean star of England at the time was William Charles Macready, whose elegant and gentlemanly interpretations of the great roles were definitely preferred. Perhaps with reason, Forrest developed a conviction that Macready himself was personally responsible for the unfriendliness of the critics. At any rate, when Macready was playing *Hamlet* in Edinburgh, Forrest made it a point to attend and to rise in his conspicuous box and loudly hiss the English star. It was a shocking bit of unprofessional conduct, and the newspapers made a sensation of it which further dampened Forrest's foreign reception.

Four years later, Macready accepted an invitation from managers Niblo and Hackett to climax an American tour at their proud new Astor Place Opera House in New York. Twice before this—in 1826 and 1843—he had toured in America, both times with considerable success. But in 1849, with the memory of Forrest's accusations against him still green in partisan hearts, the climate for his reception was vastly different. Forrest had started his career at the Bowery Theatre in New York, and had a fiercely devoted following among the two great Bowery gangs, the "Dead Rabbits" and the "Bowery Boys." These, later described by the city's own press as "rowdies, ruffians, blackguards, rabble," were determined to make a retaliatory show against the Englishmen.

Macready was advertised to open his Manhattan engagement in *Macbeth,* early in May. Manager E. A. Marshall of the Broadway Theatre had already announced that he would present Edwin Forrest in the same role on the same night. The supporters of each of the rival stars drew up their battle lines. A third *Macbeth* of the same evening—that of Thomas Hamblin at the Bowery Theatre—passed all but unnoticed.

A general feeling of trouble in the air spread as far as Philadelphia. In that city the two professional enemies had offered their rival *Macbeth*s at the start of Macready's American visit. There had been at the time an exchange of insults between them in the *Public Ledger*. As a result, Macready's subsequent tour had not been without incident. In Cincinnati, for example, a "Forrest ruffian" in the gallery had heaved a rotting sheep's carcass onto the stage. Macready, to be sure, had not helped matters by his displays of arrogance. He had written of one American leading lady in Boston that she was a Katherine "to make a dog vomit"; and of another that her Desdemona was "fifty, patched up to forty-five." His contempt for his tormentors had been thinly veiled. He had not been tactful. And now the *Public Ledger* was foreseeing fireworks: "The great theatrical warfare which begins tonight is expected to be productive of curious incidents during the evening—and not of the most felicitous character, either."

New Yorkers required no outside predictions to fan the flames. One Forrest supporter later admitted to having purchased fifty tickets to the Macready performance, and to have distributed them among friends pledged to hiss the English actor off the stage. By estimate of the city's Chief of Police, some five hundred Forrest partisans sat among the audience when the curtain went up. And every one of them was biding his time until the star's entrance. Over at the Broadway, thanks to several days of publicity about the feud between the actors, another full house had assembled.

The Astor Place audience greeted each of the players in the opening scenes with an excess of friendly enthusiasm which in itself should have roused suspicion. But the moment Macready set foot on stage, the floodgates burst. Yells, catcalls, hisses drowned out his first speech, and from that moment on the actors might as well have been playing a pantomime. No line of Shakespeare could be shouted loudly enough to be heard above the tumult. Macready was no coward. He stood his ground, refusing to be driven from the stage. But the Forrest crowd were equally determined that the hated detractor of their idol should not be allowed to continue.

When Macready refused to withdraw before a barrage of mere noise, rotten eggs and dubious vegetables began to pelt the stage. When even these failed of their purpose, chairs were ripped loose from their places in the gallery and thrown at the stage—to the very real peril of the audience below. Although a fair force of policemen was in attendance, they were vastly outnumbered and dared not act for fear of enraging the mob further and endangering lives. It was discovered that some of the "ruffians" possessed twists of paper filled with gunpowder, which they intended to hurl into the heavy chandeliers to bring them crashing down if their demonstration for an American hero were interrupted.

At last, to save house and patrons from total destruction, the management rang down the curtain. Having achieved their objective, the "boys from the Bowery" loudly cheered their beloved Forrest and contemptuously hissed Macready and all things English, and took themselves off. Naturally, Macready considered his New York engagement at an end. He packed his trunks and prepared to leave the city.

But the "better element" among the population were shocked and outraged by the violence shown a respected visitor. One city official wrote indignantly of the two actors involved that, "One is a gentleman and the other is a vulgar, arrogant loafer with a pack of kindred rowdies at his heels." A committee of forty-eight of New York's most prominent citizens, including no less a literary pair than Washington Irving and Herman Melville, published a plea to Macready that he reconsider his departure:

> The undersigned, having heard that the outrage at The Astor Place Opera House, on Monday evening, is likely to have the effect of preventing you from continuing your performances, and from concluding your intended farewell engagement upon the American stage, take this public method of requesting you to reconsider your decision, and of assuring you that the good sense and respect for order in this community will sustain you in the subsequent performances.

Urged by a management hostile to Forrest, assured of his welcome by such distinguished gentlemen, believing in their pledges that the public would not permit a second shameful disturbance, and too vain to appear intimidated by ruffians, Macready did reconsider. Niblo and Hackett announced that he would again enact *Macbeth* on the evening of Thursday, May 10. At the Broadway on that same evening, Forrest was to appear in his popular role as Spartacus in *The Gladiator*.

This time, every possible precaution was taken to avoid trouble. Mayor Caleb S. Woodhull—who had taken office only the day before—detailed three hundred special policemen to the Opera House. He also ordered units of the National Guard to stand ready for action at the nearby Armory. As Forrest's supporters had done previously, Macready's now purchased large blocks of tickets for the performance—but with the opposite intention, of insuring that it would be an unquestioned personal triumph for the Englishman.

The opposition, however, was not cowed. On the morning of May 10, people talked heatedly in the streets of "Codfish Aristocracy" and "the English Clique versus the Lower Classes." Posters inimical to Macready appeared:

WORKING MEN
shall
AMERICANS OR ENGLISH RULE
in this city.
The crew of an English steamer have
threatened all Americans who shall dare
to express their opinion this night at the
English Aristocratic Opera House!
We advocate no violence, but a free expression
of opinion to all Public Men.
WORKING MEN! FREEMEN!
stand by
YOUR LAWFUL RIGHTS
American Committee

At theatre time that evening, the Opera House more resembled a citadel than a place of amusement. The management, belatedly realizing that all might not go well, had barricaded its windows. Double guards were set at every entrance. As patrons arrived, only those already holding tickets were admitted—and the doors instantly closed again behind them. Outside, a sullen crowd of Forrest's Bowery Boys had been gathering for hours, hundreds upon hundreds of them, crowding the streets converging upon Astor Place—Lafayette, Broadway, East Eighth. They muttered that only those with tickets bearing a secret mark to identify Macready supporters were being let in. They grumbled that the evening had been rigged to discredit Forrest.

The curtain rose. The play was on. This time, as Macready made his first entrance, a clamor to rival that of the previous occasion greeted him. But tonight it consisted of enthusiastic cheers, with only a small intermingling of hisses. The lines spoken on stage were drowned out this time, not by the audience, but by the crash of windows as rocks were hurled outside. Police had ejected trouble-makers inside, who had paid for their tickets, and these now added their resentment to the brewing fury in the streets. A mounting howl doubled and redoubled like the cry of an outraged beast.

When the temper of the mob attempting to batter down the doors had unmistakably proven itself, a summons was dispatched to the troops waiting at the Armory. By the start of the second act, the clatter of approaching hooves and the tramp of marching feet could be heard above the din.

Down Broadway came the Seventh Regiment, led by a detachment of uniformed cavalry. Word flashed through the crowd like wildfire—"The Military are coming!" The hundreds who had been battering for admission at the Opera House promptly about-faced to close ranks and advance upon the approaching soldiers. The troops certainly had no stomach for the job assigned them, though as yet there was no thought of bloodshed. But they kept on coming.

Those in the front ranks of the crowd pulled up paving stones from the street and pelted them at the van of the military force, howling their wrath. The horses of the mounted troop, trained only for parade duty, were terrified by the onslaught. They reared and bolted, and the riders, struggling to force them under control once more, had no choice but to depart. But the block of infantry kept on advancing, rifles now at the ready.

Grimly, they took up their assigned positions around the Opera House. The seething mob hurled more paving stones at them, and several of the soldiers were injured. Their officers stepped out to instruct the crowd to disperse and were similarly bombarded. Then men in uniform attempted to fix bayonets and herd the rioters back, but their muskets were grabbed and struggled for. Warned that an order to fire would be given unless they departed, the rioters jeered in defiance—"Shoot away!" and "Fire and be damned!"

The threatened command could no longer be postponed. A sharp crack of rifles rang out above the tumult. The first volley was a warning, fired over the heads of the crowd. It only served to enrage them further. One burly Bowery Boy stepped out as theatrically as Forrest in his most melodramatic scene, baring a hairy chest as he bellowed: "Take the life of this freeborn American for a bloody British actor!"

The masses behind him cheered and advanced in a wave.

The second time the muskets spoke, they meant business.

As the shots spurted from their muzzles, several men in the front ranks of the mob went down. Most of them were only wounded, but at such point-blank range it was inevitable that a few were killed. Infuriated beyond all reason at the sight of their fallen comrades, the hundreds behind them flung upon the thin line of soldiers—mad for revenge.

At this point, an emissary from the Broadway Theatre (where, between acts, Forrest was eager for news of how his enemy was faring) reached Astor Place. One incredulous look around was enough to send the messenger back again at a run, the shouts of the defiant crowd loud enough to be heard ten blocks off as they followed him. He burst into Forrest's dressing room panting that the Opera House was aflame, a vast pyre of trapped corpses, and that the streets were too choked with dead bodies to be passable. Only so wild an exaggeration could have outdone the actual scene in Astor Place, where the surging demonstrators were threatening to tear down the building and dismember the soldiery.

"Fire!" a hard-pressed commanding officer shouted again.

The third round of shot was deadly. Many more of the advancing rioters pitched forward on their faces or sank slowly to their knees with red stains spreading over their shirts. Then panic struck. Suddenly, the mob scattered and ran, shrilling curses back at the determined militia. Furious, baffled, terrified, the thousands in the sidestreets gave way with them and ran also.

Like ghosts in the dank mist which had drifted in off the East River, figures began to emerge from the shadows to pick up the wounded and carry them to safety. Even such few lights on the Opera House as had not been shattered were sufficient to illuminate the ghastly trickles of red across the uneven paving. The sudden stillness was filled with groaning.

Nearby apothecary shops and police stations were soon crowded to capacity with casualties. The dead in the streets were being loaded onto canvas litters and carted away. Women who had seen husbands and fathers shot down were wailing inconsolably. And the soldiers who had been forced against their will to do their duty still stood in unbroken line guarding the theatre where, long since, the curtain had been rung down on *Macbeth*.

At the height of the rioting, Macready had been disguised by the police and spirited to safety out a rear exit. After being concealed overnight in the home of a friend, he was put on a train for Boston; and at the end of twelve days in seclusion there, sailed back to England determined never again to perform in America.

As the list of the tragedy's victims was made public— thirty-two dead, over a hundred wounded, many of them maimed for life—New York City was wrapped in a pall of shocked mourning. The incredible truth of what had happened was borne in upon the people. For no grander a cause than a dispute as to which of two Macbeths deserved top honors, a pitched battle had been fought in New York streets.

To the dead, no answer to their argument could matter now.

15. The Henchmen and the Handmaidens

Despite fluctuations, the whole of America's nineteenth century was a Golden Age for Shakespeare. Audiences and actors alike lived in close and exciting relationship to his great plays. The same century's theatre also saw the "star system" develop and flourish. Outstanding actors and actresses served Master Will with the full,

if varying, brilliance of their talents. They deserve acknowledgment of their contributions to his enduring eminence in
America.

Earlier American theatre had regarded a full company as
its basic unit. Beginning with the Hallams, and even with their
haphazard predecessors, the company had acted together;
traveled together. Hallam's troupe, West's, all of them, had
been organizations; those who appeared in the chief roles
had been leaders, yet not the whole show. Now, as the 1800s
advanced, this situation began to change. Touring stars
visited the growing cities where stock companies were ensconced. Each played his own most famous roles, with the
companies for support, and then moved on. The first effect
of the change was largely a disruptive one. William B. Wood,
an actor-manager whose career spanned half the nineteenth
century, described the problem clearly:

When a season is made up of a rapid succession of numerous stars,
the first effect is that nothing can be arranged ahead. The star
is the light of everything, the center about which all must move. He
has . . . his own pieces, his own plan of business, and his own
preferences of every sort. One star is very tall and will play with
no person of diminutive stature. The company must be changed
to suit him. The next is very short and will play with no one of
ordinary height. Everything has to again be unsettled. One star
brings half a company with him, and the stock actors thus displaced,
retire in disappointment. The next looks to us for all his support,
and the manager must get them all back in the best way he can. . . .
What the effect of this is in many departments, let the reader a
little while consider.

The effect was indeed troublesome. If the star had his own
play, unfamiliar to the stock company, they must memorize
long new roles without proper time to do so. The star, arriving

generally on the eve of performance, gave them little time to rehearse with him. So supporting players (who had been trained to take pride in their art) were forced to wander on stage, lines half-learned, and stumble as best they might through action only vaguely sketched out for them. Wrote William Wood: "It was by no means an uncommon thing, when I left the theatre, to hear an actor inquire of another during the performance, 'What is this play about?'."

Casting unfamiliar pieces naturally presented a tremendous problem. Actors who had no physical or temperamental affinity for many longer parts had to be flung into them, if only because they happened to be "quick studies" who could learn the lines in twenty-four hours. Shading and interpretation were impossible. The star, of course, had played his own part until its polish gleamed. His chief purpose was to exhibit *himself,* and audiences were lured to the theatres mainly to watch the Great Name perform. But the plays they attended under such circumstances tended to be sadly deficient, except in the one particular of the star's appearance. Only a monologue could have truly succeeded in the face of so unbalanced a situation.

The great classic stars of the period, Shakespeare's Elite Guard, were the mildest offenders in these matters. Because they toured in the same roles for years, their individual requirements came to be well known. It was almost as though such a star were a fellow stock actor; but one connected with several companies, rather than a single unit. This sort of starring was beneficial, rather than detrimental. It brought welcome variety to a local season. But as transportation throughout the country became simpler—as riverboats replaced wagon trails and the rapidly spreading railroads replaced riverboats—almost any who could foist himself off as a New York actor seemed to try his luck at becoming a road star. Outlying theatres were victimized by insufficiently experienced players, calling themselves stars, who were convinced "that an imitation of some eminent actor would not fail to charm an audience." These performers took over leading roles while they should still have been learning their craft in the lesser ones. Naturally, the theatre suffered.

One star worthy the name, Joseph Jefferson, laid considerable blame for the increasing hold of the star system directly at the door of one Will Shakespeare. He wrote:

If the starring system, as it is called, be an evil, then Shakespeare is undoubtedly responsible for its existence, as his tragedies almost without exception contain one great character on whom the interest of the play turns, and upon whom the attention of the audience is centered. When he introduces two figures for this purpose, as shown in the attitudes of Othello and Iago, Macbeth and Lady Macbeth, they are so closely knit together that the double light shines only with a single ray. . . . There are undoubtedly other splendid characters in the tragedies of Shakespeare, but when brought in contrast with the magnitude of his heroes they are comparatively subordinate.

Jefferson himself, while no stranger to Shakespeare throughout his long career, was primarily an actor of a different sort. But in the greatest of all his hits, *Rip Van Winkle,* he fell back upon the Bard. Various earlier stage versions of the Washington Irving masterpiece had been attempted, none with any great success. Jefferson's version, strengthened for him by the popular playwright Dion Boucicault, deliberately patterned Rip's pathetic reunion with his daughter after the similar situation between King Lear and Cordelia. Even Jefferson's makeup for that final act, with wild white hair and beard floating about his head, was directly copied from the conventional King Lear's appearance.

At first for good, and then increasingly for ill, the star system fastened itself upon the American theatre of the 1800s. For reasons already suggested, those stars whose forte was Shakespeare were among the lesser disruptors of old theatrical disciplines. The plays in which they appeared were more familiar to the supporting companies in the road cities they visited. Their careers tended to be more durable, so that their particular requirements of cast, script, and business were more generally familiar. And as a group, their standards of production were higher, long exposure to poetry of first quality perhaps making it less possible for them to be satisfied with shoddy performances.

The star who set the pattern for what was to come after him in America was the English Edmund Kean. Kean's American tours at the start of the century actually gave Americans their first knowledge of what superb performances of Shakespeare could be. Of Kean's acting, the poet Coleridge said that it was like watching Shakespeare performed by flashes of lightning. Beginning his career as a child prodigy, Kean was still a young man when he achieved stardom at the Drury Lane in 1814. His first interpretation there of Shylock took London by storm. His American tours made theatrical history. His premature death cut short a Shakespearean career in many respects never equaled before or since.

America's first native-born Shakespearean star of first magnitude was the durable Edwin Forrest. Born in Philadelphia in 1806, Forrest, at the age of fourteen, was already embarked upon his stage career. Having played his earliest professional leading role from Shakespeare, Iago, to frontier applause in

Lexington, Kentucky, he established himself as a true star by scoring an enormous success in *Othello* at New York's Bowery Theatre in 1826. His long career included many Shakespearean parts, notably that Macbeth which helped provoke the bloody Astor Place Riot; but his finest was generally conceded to have been King Lear. He was also cheered as Spartacus in *The Gladiator;* and in *Metamora,* a "Noble Savage" drama expressly written for him, which remained in his repertory for decades.

These vigorous, virile parts were what made Forrest the idol of humble, nonaristocratic audiences. Others esteemed him less. An English traveler, Mrs. Frances Trollope, mother of Anthony Trollope (whose scathing account of her American visit from 1827 to 1841 was published as *Domestic Manners of the Americans*), wrote: "When I saw him [Forrest] play Hamlet, not even Mrs. Drake's sweet Ophelia could keep me beyond the third act." In the opinion of New York's intellectuals he was "vulgar" and "a coarse ranter." Yet it was stage-wise Joseph Jefferson's judgment that, "As a melodramatic actor he stood ahead of all his competitors . . . his readings being faultless and full of feeling." Published criticism of his acting enraged the vain Forrest. When attacked, he frequently during performance strode to the footlights to praise his own work and rail at "the irresponsible assassins of the pen" who had ridiculed him. It was said of him that his acting appealed to no one accustomed to sounds softer than thunder. Still, it possessed an emotional power and a physical vitality which swept most audiences before it.

Forrest's reign was long on the American stage. Perhaps the most poignant tragedy he ever played was himself in his later years. As he aged, the rugged health which had sustained him broke down. He became weak and uncertain. Vanity would not allow him to retire; but with the years his old admirers fell away, saddened by the obvious loss of his powers, and he was reduced to touring the outpost areas where audiences still assembled "from a curious desire to see a ruined tower just before it falls." When the tower fell at last, in 1872, Forrest's will left most of the considerable fortune amassed during his decades of stardom to found a home for old actors in his native city of Philadelphia. The home still endures and has offered a haven to many a worn-out servant of an unreliable profession.

Forrest's chief rival in the younger days of his glory was an Englishman, one who came to America not merely on tour but with the firm intention of becoming American. Junius Brutus Booth (later, the words "the elder" were added, to distinguish him from his eldest son and namesake, who also had a long America theatrical career), had scored a great London success in Shakespeare. But his personal life was wildly undisciplined. He culminated a series of scandals by abandoning a wife and two sons to run away with a flower girl from a stall near the theatre.

The lovers eloped to America, where Booth hoped to secure a job as a lighthouse keeper. This, he believed, would keep him and his Mary Ann beyond the reach of his wife's pursuing fury. But he had not reckoned with the strength of the theatre in his blood. Within a very few years, he established a family base in Maryland, took up his career once more, began negotiations for a divorce so that he might marry his sweetheart, and then became father of a succession of children who were to form America's closest approach to a theatrical Royal Family. Three of Booth's sons by his second wife were destined for stage fame—the younger Junius, Edwin, and the doomed John Wilkes.

The father of the family was unquestionably a genius. He also hovered, or seemed to hover, on the brink of madness. He was a heavy drinker. His young son Edwin's career in the theatre first began when the family assigned the lad the chore of accompanying his father on tour to keep him out of saloons until he had completed the evening's stint on stage. The mental instability so often remarked on in the elder Booth, however, seemed rather consistently to manifest itself at times when it might secure sensational publicity for the star. As Shakespeare wrote, "Though this be madness, yet there is method in't."

Once, arriving by steamboat to play an engagement in Cincinnati, Booth—an expert swimmer—jumped overboard within view of the city with a dramatic pretense of committing suicide. He stayed afloat without difficulty until help arrived; and all the way ashore urged his rescuers to handle their oars more carefully, lest they capsize and "have us all drowned."

One of his frequent tricks was to lay on so ferociously during a stage duel (such as the one at the climax of *Richard III*) that his luckless adversary lost nerve and fled; brandishing his blade, Booth then would pursue the poor actor up the stage alley and into the public street, seldom failing to achieve headlines thereby. He finally met his match when one Richmond—more stalwart than the rest—dropped his sword in the duel scene, caught the star by the throat and literally choked him insensible, leaving him limp on the battlefield just as the play's written climax required. After this experience, Booth sought his publicity by other means.

In the days when Booth was Forrest's chief rival as a touring star, the beautiful passenger pigeon was a familiar sight in the American West. Flocks so huge that they screened out the sun for a full hour as they passed, were not infrequent. The pigeons roosted so densely that they could be slaughtered by the hundreds with such simple weapons as a rock or a slingshot. Sold for fertilizer at a nickel a dozen, the once plentiful birds rapidly became extinct. A man who loved animals, and who would not even permit a snake to be killed on his home acres in Maryland, Booth was outraged by this senseless massacre. Arriving to act in one western city, he sent an underling to summon the minister of the leading church to officiate at an emergency funeral service in his hotel suite. The corpse of Booth's demised "friend" lay on the bed, covered by a sheet, and over it the clergyman performed the last rites. Then, with a dramatic gesture, the actor swept the sheet aside. What lay beneath it was a hundred dead passenger pigeons, the butchery of which had sparked his indignation. Next day, the affronted preacher protested from the pulpit this insult to his calling. The town buzzed. And business at the box office was brisk for every performance during Booth's run.

The star was no mere publicity-seeking freak, however. His artistry was of a caliber comparable with Kean's. When he played New Orleans, with the French company there and in their own language, it was said of him that his accent was more Parisian than theirs. He tolerated no shoddiness in the work of his supporting players. His own son Edwin first attempted a speaking role as Tressel in Booth's production of *Richard III*. Ready for the stage, Edwin reported at his father's dressing room for inspection. Booth stared moodily at the lad, who in the play was supposed to gallop up with a message, then asked in icy disapproval: "Where are your spurs, boy?"

Although he was far from being a young man in 1852, the

close of Booth's career was no such anticlimax as Forrest's. In November of that year, returning eastward after solid successes in the gold-rush theatres of San Francisco, he stopped in New Orleans for an engagement of six nights at the St. Charles Theatre. His final performance was as Sir Edward Mortimer in *The Iron Box,* although previously in the week he had played Shylock triumphantly. "To say that he enacted it in a style that delighted everyone," reported the city's leading newspaper, "would be speaking without exaggeration. . . . Talent like that he possesses is so rare now-a-days, when respectable mediocrity is the chief qualification of the American stage, that we cannot make up our minds to part with Mr. Booth."

Yet part from Booth they must, for he had an engagement to fulfill up north in Cincinnati. On his closing night in New Orleans, he caught a severe cold, and aboard the riverboat, already feverish, he made the mistake of drinking river water on the first day out. Strangers found him ill in his cabin and nursed him as best they could. But before the boat docked at Louisville, he was dead.

In Junius Brutus Booth, England had sent America the founder of a great stage dynasty. Ireland's contribution was John McCullough. Born of simple farming folk in County Londonderry, with no trace of theatre in his heritage, McCullough arrived alone in America in 1847 while still short of his fifteenth birthday. He landed at New York City, a husky and attractive young immigrant scarcely able to spell out a few simple words, and managed to make his way to Philadelphia where he had heard that another branch of his family was settled.

Sure enough, walking the streets, he suddenly found himself

face to face with a large sign lettered with his own name: JOHN MCCULLOUGH. He entered the chair-making shop so marked, and soon learned that its prosperous proprietor was indeed the only surviving heir of an uncle who had come to America much earlier. The Philadelphia John McCullough received his kinsman with kindness, and gave him a job as apprentice at the trade of chair-making. Young John had perseverence and a natural aptitude for tools, and earnestly set about learning his trade.

An elderly mechanic named Burke, also employed in the shop, was what nowadays would be described as a Shakespeare buff. As the pair toiled together, Burke habitually recited long passages from Shakespeare's plays, and these delighted John's music-loving Irish ear. Burke frequently "murdered" McCullough with a paint brush, laid him out upon a handy bench, and dramatically declaimed above him Antony's oration for a slain Caesar. McCullough made such a raptly interested corpse that Burke finally presented him with a copy of Shakespeare's plays. The actor himself later said, "From that day the doom of the chair-making business, so far as I was concerned, was sealed forever. To me, the book was a revelation. I had never heard of Shakespeare before."

At first, his reading ability was so faulty that he would sit on the shop steps at the hour when school children would be going home and bribe young passers-by with candy and apples to read aloud from his precious book. His memory, even then, was remarkable and he could retain most of what they read to him. Soon, he was Antony and Burke was noble Caesar's remains. Meanwhile, Burke had introduced him to the delights of amateur theatricals, and to professional theatre at the venerable Arch Street playhouse. Most of McCullough's spare time now was devoted to studying theatre. Before long, he was playing *Othello* with an amateur company in an old sugar refinery where they had set up a crude theatre.

The manager of the Arch Street, attending a performance by chance, was impressed by the young Irishman's strong, melodious voice, excellent bearing, handsome features, and scrupulous command of Othello's lines. A place in the Arch Street company, playing minor roles for a salary of four dollars a week, was offered to McCullough and promptly accepted. Thus, in 1857, one of his generation's outstanding theatrical careers was launched.

McCullough's rise in professional stature from that point on was steady although not sensational. His knowledge of Shakespeare was sufficient to impress the star E. L. Davenport, in whose support he acted in Boston in 1859. By the autumn of 1861, he had caught the eye of the great Forrest, who hired him and took him on tour. He became Forrest's protégé, coached by the now aging tragedian in the supporting roles he played in the company—Richmond to Forrest's Richard III, Iago to his Othello, Macduff to his Macbeth, Edgar to his King Lear. By 1870, John McCullough was an experienced and acknowledged young star in his own right. The only continuing criticism of his acting during his starring career was a probably justified claim that he was too close a copy of Forrest.

McCullough accompanied Forrest to California in 1866. When ill health compelled the older star to return to the East, the younger one remained in San Francisco. He quickly became an idol of the California public. A wealthy banker named Ralston offered to back him, and built for him the California Theatre. In the management of his handsome new playhouse, McCullough took into partnership another rising young star of the day, Lawrence Barrett. Their celebrated joint venture at the California, extending over ten brilliant years, was generally acknowledged to have brought California theatre to its finest flowering. The backbone of their repertory was Shakespeare, with such standard successes as *The Gladiator* and *Richelieu* (both old Forrest triumphs) to give it variety. Macready's greatest part, *Virginius,* also became McCullough's most-applauded role. But Shakespeare dominated. One typical six-night engagement—in St. Louis in 1873 —included *Coriolanus, Othello, Julius Caesar, Richelieu, Hamlet,* and *Richard III.*

Whether in San Francisco or on tour, McCullough continued as a huge favorite with audiences both as an actor and as a man. "There is no other living tragedian in the country, since the death of Forrest," declared the Washington *Chronicle,* "who has taken the hold upon the public and secured their esteem and affection, as has this young and careful student of dramatic art." An on-stage accident suffered while playing *Virginius* in Philadelphia in 1877 is thought to have brought on the mental collapse in which this bright career was ended. McCullough had misjudged his position on stage and was struck on the head by a descending drop curtain "with such force as to temporarily stun him."

His increasingly faulty memory was afterward attributed to this mishap—although he continued playing for several years. Finally, during a rehearsal for *Richelieu* in Chicago in 1884, he broke down altogether and had to be led from the stage by his openly weeping fellow workers. Only the night before, struggling through a public performance of *The Gladiator,* he had stood almost dazed in view of the audience while the play's saddest line was spoken: "General, you are unfit for battle. Come to your tent."

America's first great native-born actress, known nation-wide during her distinguished career as "The Tragic Muse" and "The American Siddons," was Mrs. Alexander Drake. Pretty Frances Ann Denny, born in Albany, New York, where her father ran the inn where Samuel Drake's acting company lived during its 1814 season there, the young lady became both stage-struck and enamored of young Mr. Alexander Drake. She was allowed to attend rehearsals, and was fascinated to see the plays take shape. Old Sam Drake let her read for him, sensed her promise, and cast her as one of Olivia's women in *Twelfth Night*.

During that year news of the fabulous new territory of Kentucky, opening up beyond the western mountains, filtered into Albany. It inspired the elder Drake to head toward the frontier in 1815. By now, the die was cast—so far as Frances Ann was concerned. But her disapproving mother three times refused permission to let her daughter accompany the players. There came a day when the wagons were loaded and ready to roll. They carried west with them "a contractable drop for use as a proscenium, a drop curtain, a set of three-flap wings (one flap painted for exteriors, one for fancy interiors, one for plain interiors), six roll drops (woods, street, parlor, kitchen, palace, garden), and a green baize carpet." Only at the last instant did Mother Denny grant her daughter grudging consent. Joyously, Miss Frances embarked upon her life's career.

The company consisted of the Drake family proper, four actors who were not relations, the youth Noah Ludlow, and the fetching Miss Denny. For the youthful contingent that westward trek, despite its hardships, was a lark. They played at makeshift theatres along the way, mostly comedies and pieces for which small scenery was required; and despite danger from Indians and wolves, arrived safely in Pittsburgh, where their "longhorn" flatboat was constructed and their adventures on the river began. The raw new West welcomed them, and they prospered. Sam Drake built theatres in the booming Kentucky communities of Lexington, Frankfort, and Louisville, and a handsome river-bank home for his brood at what they named Harmony Landing. And Frances Ann married that brilliant young comedian, Old Sam's son, Alexander Drake. With her dramatic flair and regal presence, she was soon establishing herself as the fine actress that Mrs. Trollope lauded while damning Edwin Forrest's Hamlet.

The star of "Mrs. Drake" (as she now was billed in accordance with usual theatrical custom of the day) rose rapidly. Soon New York critics were expressing preference for her in the heavy tragic roles even over the much-admired Fanny Kemble. When she proposed to test her fortunes in London, letters of introduction from such prominent Americans as Washington Irving and John Howard Payne went out to pave her way. But despite acknowledged triumphs east of the Alleghenies, the West remained her particular private empire. She ruled its stages like the queen she was, with the equally, though differently, talented Alexander as her Prince Consort. The seldom-admiring Mrs. Trollope wrote:

Nothing could contrast more than their lines of acting, but the great versatility of their powers enabled them to appear often together. Her cast was of the highest walk of tragedy, and his the broadest comedy, but yet I have known them to change character for a whole evening and have wept with him and laughed with her as it was their will and pleasure to ordain.

And of Mrs. Drake in particular she wrote:

> Her talent is decidedly first-rate. Rich and genuine feeling, correct judgment and the most perfect good taste distinguish her play in every character. Her [acting] is superior in tragic effect to anything I have seen on the stage . . . Mrs. Siddons being set aside.

Frances Ann Drake was a magnificent Lady Macbeth, Ophelia, Queen Katharine, Desdemona. Throughout her career she was also strongly civic-minded. Once when her company was playing a benefit performance for widows and orphans in Cincinnati, she personally appealed to the city's wealthiest citizen, Nicholas Longworth, to buy tickets. Longworth refused her request with the reply that such destitute worthies always could find assistance, and that his own aid would be reserved for the idle, worthless vagabonds whom no one else would help. Mrs. Drake bided her time. Much later she turned up at the Longworth door accompanied by the seediest, most tattered, and repulsive tramp imaginable. Reminding Longworth of his former promise, she made him buy a box for this sorry derelict's benefit, then revealed that the "tramp" was Alexander Drake, made up for his role in that evening's play, *The Ragamuffin of Paris*.

The same queenliness which marked Mrs. Drake's work in Shakespeare also made her an arbiter of Kentucky society. When the Marquis de Lafayette made his farewell tour of America in 1824, the city of Lexington turned out in force to do him honor. There were fireworks, parades, orations, and a gala ball. The opening march was led by the General with Mrs. Drake on his arm. Never a tall man, Lafayette had shrunk with age to a height of five feet, five inches. The actress was toweringly tall. One amused spectator wrote that the old Revolutionary hero seemed like "a plucked wren, while Mrs.

Drake, six feet and over, was a handsome woman and plenty of her."

Tragedy struck time after time at this talented lady. Her beloved Alexander died suddenly at the age of thirty-two. During the Mexican War, their son Richard was killed in the storming of Monterey. When the Civil War came and her younger sons donned uniforms, she retired to Harmony Landing. Her great career was over, but never her affection for the stage. She lived to become an old woman. On the morning of the very day she died, in 1874, she had been rehearsing a group of amateur actors in Louisville.

Partially Mrs. Drake's stage contemporary, and the heiress to her tragic mantle, was Charlotte Cushman. Certainly one of America's greatest tragic actresses, and the first member of the acting profession to be enshrined in America's Hall of Fame, Miss Cushman was born in Boston in 1816. The possessor of a fine contralto voice, she was trained almost from childhood to become an opera singer. She actually made an operatic debut as the Countess in *The Marriage of Figaro* in 1834, but she strained her voice by attempting roles of too high pitch and a year later decided to change careers. She made her first dramatic appearance in 1835, as Lady Macbeth, when she was only nineteen years old.

Joseph Jefferson, who acted with her later, described Miss Cushman as "tall and commanding in person, with an expressive face, whose features might have been called plain but for the strength and character in them." He added: "In the legitimate drama she was more prominent than any other actress of her time." Her first acting years, however, were not quite so distinguished. One Hamlet who worked with her then —she was cast as Queen Gertrude—remarked that "she was

frequently careless in the text and negligent of rehearsals."
She played in New York at the Bowery until that venerable
playhouse burned down, then elsewhere, and by 1839 she was
leading lady at Boston's Park. There she scored her first real
triumph—as Nancy Sykes in *Oliver Twist*. In this role of an
abused, abandoned tigress of the streets, she was hailed as
"fearfully natural, dreadfully intense, horribly real," and
recognized as a potential star of the very first rank.

The great breakthrough in her career came when she was
cast opposite the English star Macready on his second American tour in 1843. Until then her acting had been powerful (she
was called a female Forrest), but rude and uncultivated.
Macready, aware of her genius, remedied that. He worked
with her painstakingly and persuaded her to return to England
with him. In 1844 she triumphed in London. Many thought
her Lady Macbeth the equal of Mrs. Siddons'. When she returned to New York it was as a reigning queen, and she never
lost this eminence.

Of the first three evenings of her triumphant homecoming
engagement, two were devoted to Shakespeare—*As You Like
It,* and *Macbeth*. Undoubtedly Lady Macbeth was Miss
Cushman's greatest Shakespearean role—"one of the most
wonderful exhibitions of histrionics that the modern stage has
witnessed," one critic wrote of it. A part in which she was to
be equally remembered was Meg Merrilies, the "half-woman.
half-demon" of *Guy Mannering*. She was at her best when
portraying a character who was "darkly shadowed, lurid-
tinged . . . with the savage, animal reality of passion, and the
weird fascinations of crime, redeemed by fitful flashes of
womanly feeling."

One conceit of Miss Cushman's, as a handmaiden of

Shakespeare, was the frequency with which she elected to become a henchman instead. She deeply impressed her public with her power in the masculine roles. She appeared as Hamlet less successfully than in most of her other such efforts. She acted Shylock in *The Merchant of Venice,* beard and all, and was triumphant as Cardinal Wolsey in *Henry VIII,* a play in which on other occasions she made a compelling Queen Katharine. She played Romeo to the Juliet of her less illustrious sister, Susan Cushman. Her reason for undertaking these male roles was simply stated. Shakespeare had written many more great parts for men than for women. In the theatre as elsewhere, it was an age of mounting feminism. Strong-minded Charlotte Cushman was unwilling to be cheated because of her sex.

The peak of her career saw her as idolized in England and Europe as she was at home. When she retired from the stage at last, in 1874, her final New York performance was made the occasion for a great tribute to her genius. She was crowned on stage with a wreath of laurels such as adorned the classic Roman heroes. The eminent poet, William Cullen Bryant, acted as spokesman for the presentation.

By mid-century, the sons of Junius Brutus Booth had begun to carry the glory of the family into its second generation. The second Junius Brutus, his father's eldest son, was a much-respected star in California and in the road cities eastward to the Atlantic. He played Shakespeare with honor in New York, Philadelphia, Boston, and elsewhere. The youngest of the three brothers who formed an outstanding trio was John Wilkes Booth—who might have been the greatest of them all had his undisciplined nature not driven him to misuse of his natural talents, and finally to madness and murder. Especially in the Southern states, he was perhaps the most applauded Romeo, Richard III, and Othello of his day. But that day ended suddenly in an act of shocking violence.

The middle brother, Edwin, was the one the elder Booth had marked as his successor. As a lad, in 1842, Edwin made his debut in Shakespeare in his father's company. When the father followed the westward stampede to the gold fields, Edwin traveled to California in his support. And there he really earned his spurs—those spurs the elder actor had noted as missing, on the evening of Edwin's debut! From California he sailed to Australia for a considerable tour; and on the return voyage stopped off to initiate the little capital of the Hawaiian Kingdom, Honolulu, in the majesties of Shakespeare. He then acted in London, arriving as a star on the New York stage only after this virtually world-wide experience.

Forrest had long been King of Theatre during Edwin Booth's early years. No two actors could have been more different, either in physique or in acting. The burly muscular Forrest was still ranting the roof down for his adoring ruffians. Booth played the subtler roles, such as Iago. A portrait of him by Thomas Hicks shows him in that early characterization —"pale, thin, intellectual, with long black hair and dark eyes." Booth's audience did not whoop and cheer. They listened attentively, appreciatively, seldom stirred to strong emotion but fascinated by intellectual brilliance. When Booth's immortal *Hamlet* opened at the Winter Garden in 1864, it played for one hundred consecutive performances—an unheard-of run for its day, when repertory's changing bills were still the theatrical custom. Hamlet is the role to this day most usually associated with Edwin Booth's name. Other Shakespearean parts in which he frequently appeared were Romeo, King Lear, Brutus, Othello, and Benedick.

His life was darkened by the death of his adored first wife in 1861; then shattered by his deranged brother's assassination of Abraham Lincoln in 1865. At this time he retired from the stage and vowed he never would act again. Friends feared for his sanity. But once the public came to realize that no other Booth had been in any way connected with Lincoln's death, popular demand brought Edwin out of retirement to play, once more, in *Hamlet* and *Romeo and Juliet* and *The Merchant of Venice*. After the assassination, however, Booth never again consented to act in the city of Washington, or ever to enter the District of Columbia. If a tour brought him near, he spared no effort or inconvenience to see that he was routed around the capital where John Wilkes had disgraced the family name.

His long-time New York theatre, the Winter Garden, was destroyed by fire shortly after Edwin resumed his career. He then built the famous Booth's Theatre on Sixth Avenue, and opened in 1868 with a spectacular production of *Romeo and Juliet*.

"The stateliest, the handsomest, and the best appointed structure of its class that can now be found on the American continent," his contemporaries styled the new Booth's Theatre. Its frescos and marbles were true works of art. Its influence upon future American playhouses was enormous. For the first time, the stage apron was altogether eliminated and the scene framed by a proscenium. The then-novel box-setting, pretending that the footlights marked a fourth wall of an actual room, had early use here—eliminating the old-style wings. Drop sets could be "flown" up out of sight of the audience to a gridiron seventy-six feet above the stage floor.

The new theatre was indeed the marvel of its era. But it ruined Booth financially. A business panic in 1873 wiped out his heavy investment in the building. He had to tour the country for six years to make good his losses. In 1887 he formed a powerful stage alliance with John McCullough's erstwhile partner, Lawrence Barrett, and together the two stars produced Shakespeare superlatively in New York until Barrett's death in 1891. At this time, Booth himself retired from the stage. His brilliant career, which had ushered in a whole new school of American acting, was much later formally immortalized when his bronze bust was placed among the illustrious few at the Hall of Fame.

A less formal but still active reminder of his greatness is the famous Player's Club in New York, which he founded in 1888. He lived in the handsome club building designed by Stanford White until his death there in 1893.

Booth's last co-star, Lawrence Barrett, born in New Jersey, had begun his stage career in the West, at Detroit, Michigan. Eight years later, when the Civil War broke out, he interrupted his acting to accept a commission as captain in the Twenty-eighth Massachusetts Voluntary Infantry. Soldiering occupied him until the war was over, when he returned to the theatre and played with Edwin Booth at the Winter Garden. During this time, his Cassius in *Julius Caesar* and his mad monarch in *King Lear* were much admired. He progressed from these successes to others as an actor-manager in New Orleans and then as McCullough's California co-star.

Barrett was back in the East again by 1885 and scoring a tremendous hit in *Francesca da Rimini,* a romantic tragedy in blank verse written by G. H. Boker. This play had been unsuccessful for thirty years until Barrett revived it, after which it was generally regarded as the best drama by an American written prior to the twentieth century. Shortly after this success, and after a brief but brilliant English interlude, Barrett rejoined forces with Edwin Booth—Barrett's Othello to Booth's Iago, his Cassius to Booth's Brutus, being invariably applauded. He was perhaps the first American actor to turn his hand to writing biography instead of the more usual volumes of personal memoirs. His *Life of Edwin Forrest* became a standard work on its subject. *Edwin Booth and His Contemporaries* was equally well received.

The brief but glowing career of Mary Anderson shed its light over two of the century's closing decades. Born Marie Antoinette Anderson in Sacramento, California, she received her formal education in a convent and her early stage training under the illustrious sponsorship of Charlotte Cushman. By 1875, when she was still only sixteen, she was considered ready for a dramatic debut as Juliet in Louisville, Kentucky. Her rise thereafter was so rapid that she was asked to star as Rosalind when *As You Like It* opened the Shakespeare Memorial Theatre in Stratford on Avon in 1879—a signal honor for the English theatre to accord so young an American actress. Producer Daniel Frohman described her as "the most beautiful actress that America has ever brought forth."

Mary Anderson's Perdita in *The Winter's Tale* (in which she doubled as Hermione) was acclaimed the finest of its time, taking its place alongside her Rosalind and her Juliet. She was also successful as Meg Merrilies, a role unfitted to one so young and doubtless undertaken out of admiration for her distinguished mentor, Charlotte Cushman. The public probably loved her best of all as Galatea in *Pygmalion and Galatea,* a dramatization of the same Greek legend used years later by George Bernard Shaw as the basis of *Pygmalion,* which in turn gave the twentieth century one of its greatest musical successes, *My Fair Lady.*

Always a sincerely religious young woman, Miss Anderson was deeply wounded when various newspapers hinted that her daily attendance at mass was a mere publicity stunt. This kind of thing prompted her premature withdrawal from the theatre after an active career of only fifteen years. She and her husband, a retired New York lawyer, went to live at Court Farm in Worcestershire, England, where she continued to live even after his death in 1932.

The nineteenth century's nearest approach to a present-day movie idol was doubtless the Jersey Lily. Actually, in 1913, she did make one motion picture for Daniel Frohman—*His Neighbor's Wife*—but this was long past her stage heyday.

The celebrated Mrs. Lily Langtry of the late Victorian Era began life on the Isle of Jersey in the English Channel, and as a church dignitary's daughter. An early marriage plunged her into the gay social life of London, and here she soon became the intimate of such celebrities as Oscar Wilde; the artist, James McNeill Whistler; and the great Shakespearean actor, Sir Henry Irving. Gossips soon whispered that the beautiful Lily was even carrying on a secret romance with the *bon vivant* Prince of Wales, later King Edward VII!

Her husband was supposedly wealthy, heir to a fortune. But the Langtrys lived beyond their means and fell upon difficult days financially. The whispers of scandal about exquisite, chestnut-haired Lily, when added to her reputation as the loveliest woman in London, made her the most talked-about person in the city. This public interest suggested that a stage career might set family money matters straight. Placing herself in the hands of an expert dramatic coach, Lily assailed the stage. New York was as avid as London to see the fabled Mrs. Langtry. Very shortly after her first appearances, she received a lucrative offer to cross the Atlantic. When she sailed in 1882 for her American debut, *As You Like It* was one of the three plays in her repertory.

Critics were unkind enough to suggest that her performance was lacking in every necessary quality except physical beauty; but the public adored her, crowding after her wherever she went, jamming the street outside her suite at the Hotel Albemarle. When Lily visited Wall Street, the Stock Exchange suspended operations as soon as her glamorous presence in the gallery was made known. Carriages turned on the drive in Central Park to follow her own when it passed. Men-about-town were as instantly bewitched in New York as in London. Bands played *The Langtry March* and *The Jersey Lily Waltz*. Langtry fever was the disease of the day.

Five years later—believing it would speed divorce from her husband so that she might marry a wealthy American seven years younger than herself—Lily took out her citizenship papers. This made her, at least technically, an American actress. By then, she had toured the country. America's growing network of railroads had enabled her to appear in theatres from coast to coast. And she was still the "love goddess" of the crowds.

Her subsequent attempts at Shakespeare (Rosalind had remained in her repertory) were not such as to shed much new light on the old roles. But they did attract huge audiences. In England she staged *Antony and Cleopatra,* paying for the production with her American earnings. Her performance as the Egyptian queen was less than fiery, and the play's love scenes are few; but the physical production was elaborate and its opening occasioned much public excitement. Her picture had by then been placed (with other mementos for posterity) in the base of the Egyptian obelisk called "Cleopatra's Needle," when it was erected on the Victoria Embankment overlooking the Thames. A lucky future thus was assured its glimpse of her fabulous loveliness.

When she returned to New York, Shakespeare was again her choice, and she essayed *Macbeth*—playing opposite the seasoned star Charles T. Coghlan, who was more accustomed to acting with such proven talents as Ellen Terry's. Once more the production was sumptuous. And astonishingly, in view of the record, Mrs. Langtry drew respectful notices for her performance. "Admirable," "grand," and "exquisite" were some of the adjectives critics used to describe it. In her sleep-walking scene, she sought to inspire pity for a haunted and dying murderess rather than to chill the blood as most actresses since Mrs. Siddons had done. Mrs. Langtry was no longer playing the pretty social comedy in which she had gained her popularity. Playgoers who had hitherto sniffed at her as an "amateur" now spoke of her seriously. But the general public wanted her in the gay, smartly-gowned roles that were what they expected of their Jersey Lily. She never again undertook Shakespearean tragedy.

A long, long roster of Americans served Will Shakespeare well, from the nineteenth century's beginning to its end. There was pretty Julia Dean, with her delicate Juliet and Beatrice; and Thomas Hamblin, that third Macbeth of the week of the Astor Place Riot, also a popular Coriolanus; and the versatile

James W. Wallack, who could please the public as Mercutio or Benedick, Jaques or Shylock; and venerated Henry Placide, with his Polonius and other Shakespearean "character" impersonations. There was E. L. Davenport, who could always fill the house for his Hamlet or Othello or Benedick; and James Hackett, Lincoln's favorite Falstaff; and Fanny Davenport; and Ada Rehan, so fetching in all the comedies, especially as the Shrew, Viola, or Rosalind when she played them with Augustin Daly's brilliant company.

There was Daly himself, no actor but a critic and a playwright and a theatrical press agent. His Fifth Avenue Theatre was a center for the best the stage could offer from 1870 until his death in 1899. About Daly a stage carpenter once said: "That man thinks theatre, talks theatre, dreams theatre, and would eat theatre if he could." His permanent company of outstanding actors always climaxed each season with a handsomely mounted Shakespearean revival, generally a comedy, and this custom was observed no matter what current hits in the repertory were in popular demand.

There was Anna Cora Mowatt, of New York City's bluest blood, who startled her contemporaries in 1845 by writing the first really successful American comedy, *Fashion*. She then switched to an acting career with immediate acclaim, and was soon touring as an admired Rosalind—the first "lady" to become an actress, and responsible for much of the improvement in the status of stage folk thereafter.

There was James E. Murdoch, whose Petruchio and Faulconbridge were only two of the roles in which he was cheered; and Polish Helena Modjeska, who having played Shakespeare in her native country then came to America to triumph in the same roles here despite her difficult accent; and impressive

Mrs. D. P. Bowers; and scholarly C. W. Couldock, a beloved Wolsey.

All of these—and a long procession more—toiled with devotion and talent during a Golden Age to bring Shakespeare honor in one of his adopted countries. In doing so, they played a great part in shaping the trends all American theatre took in their time. Master Will was indeed well served by his nineteenth century henchmen and handmaidens. They gave to the creations of his matchless imagination "a local habitation and a name" throughout America.

16. Murder Most Foul

To the public of the 1860s, the very name Booth meant Shakespeare. Junius Brutus had been the pre-eminent American star of a still recent day, applauded in all the great roles. His three acting sons had already achieved some distinction in the theatre. Junius Brutus, the younger, was presently starring dependably, and Edwin brilliantly, in Shakespeare. And John Wilkes, with his dark handsomeness, was popular in all the romantic parts that set the ladies swooning.

They were Shakespeare's own, the Booths. In Southern cities particularly, John Wilkes was an adored idol. This adulation fed his innate affection for the Southern cause as war clouds gathered, then as actual civil war broke out. He made no secret about where his loyalties lay. His frequent use of the term "Damn Yankee" endeared him to Secessionist audiences, though it damaged his popularity in the North.

Politics aside, members of his inherited profession made no secret of the high esteem in which they held him. John A. Ellsler, manager of one road theatre where he scored several successes, and a man who much admired Edwin's intellectual and artistic powers, still attributed to John Wilkes "more of the old man's power in one performance than Edwin can show in a year. He has the fire, the dash, the touch of strangeness. . . . Wait a year or two till he gets used to the harness and quiets down a bit, and you will see as great an actor as America can produce!"

But John Wilkes's career was more than a promise. It was an established fact. Already, critics had acclaimed his Romeo as "the most satisfactory of all renderings of that fine character." He had challenged the great Forrest in Philadelphia with a rival production of *Macbeth;* and (although no horror such as the Astor Place Riot resulted) the old lion knew he had been wounded, and hated Wilkes for it. Playing *Richard III* in Washington, in 1863, the young actor had been billed by the management as "The Pride of the American People"; and as "The Youngest Tragedian in the World, who is entitled to be denominated A Star of the First Magnitude." It was agreed by most that John Wilkes Booth would become a truly great actor—once he learned to control both his inherited fiery temper and his untrained voice, which he projected from the throat rather than from the chest cavity in elocutionary scenes.

As a romantic idol, he was constantly pursued by women. Amorous notes were forever flooding his dressing rooms. Rather than risk possible future embarrassment to their indiscreet authoresses, Wilkes would carefully snip the signatures from them and burn them. "Women's folly is no excuse for our knavery," he once said in explanation. "The letters are harmless now. Their sting lies in the tail."

Though he was overweeningly ambitious in his work, driven by visions of personal glory, he was also considerate of the lesser actors with whom he played. During one guest-starring engagement in Cleveland, he appeared as Richard III to the Richmond of an actor named McCollom, the resident company's tall leading man. Throughout rehearsals, Wilkes had repeatedly urged McCollom to make a big thing of the final sword duel between them. In performance, carried away by his efforts to please, McCollom delivered an extra two-handed blow with his sword which the star was not anticipating. Booth's forehead took the brunt of it, one eyebrow being nearly sliced through.

The audience gasped in horror and the luckless McCollom froze with panic. But Booth, suppressing his pain and brushing the spurting blood from his eyes, murmured, "Never mind me, old man! Come on hard and save the fight!" They resumed their parrying, until a stunned manager brought down the curtain. When the house doctor had taken necessary stitches, when ice and compresses had been applied, McCollom steeled himself to approach with an apology. Booth only grinned and set him at ease with a light, "Don't worry, old fellow. You look as if *you* had lost the blood!"

Clara Morris, later to include a much-admired Lady Macbeth among the roles which made her a reigning star of the seventies, was in Civil War days merely a member of the "ballet" (a group of girls hired for bit parts and crowd scenes) in the Ellsler company when John Wilkes Booth starred with it. She wrote of him later that "He was so young, so bright, so gay, so kind . . . like a great elder brother. . . ." And she described how he appeared, a brief few years before gaining his dark immortality:

> Rather lacking in height, but his head and throat, and the manner of its rising from his shoulders, were truly beautiful. His coloring was unusual, the ivory pallor of his skin, the inky blackness of his densely thick hair, the heavy lids of his glowing eyes, were all Oriental, and they gave a touch of mystery to his face when it fell into gravity; but there was generally a flash of white teeth behind his silky mustache, and a laugh in his eyes. . . .

John Wilkes Booth saw the Southern cause to which he was dedicated crumble in defeat. He saw men he regarded as hateful oppressors take over his beloved Dixie. Perhaps even more shattering, he saw the coming end of his own stage career. For the voice he had long abused with improper use had begun to betray him. It was impaired to such an extent that critics repeatedly referred to his increasing hoarseness as a blemish on otherwise brilliant performances in *Richard III, Othello, The Merchant of Venice, Macbeth.* Even in New Orleans, where he could do no wrong, the newspapers lamented this increasing infirmity. Scheduled appearances had to be canceled because of it.

For John Wilkes Booth, still so young, still so ambitious

for public adulation, the handwriting was on the wall, although he still had the almost legendary good looks which, together with his emotional fire, had been his chief stock in trade. On the very morning of the day on which he assassinated the President of the United States and blackened his name forever, an acquaintance who glimpsed his elegant figure strolling up Tenth Street said to a companion, "Here comes the handsomest man in Washington."

Abraham Lincoln, the man with whom John Wilkes Booth was destined to play out a brief, horrifying, real-life drama in a box at John T. Ford's new theatre, had in a very different way felt Shakespeare's influence. Lincoln himself, describing his meager frontier education, once said that it had been "picked up under the pressure of necessity." That Shakespeare was so integral a part of that education from Lincoln's New Salem days onward is a strong indication of how "necessary" Americans of the day considered a familiarity with his plays.

Although he acquainted himself with them by reading them over and over, it has been pointed out that Lincoln's chief approach to the plays was "oral." It was a day of public orators, when rhetoric was an essential part of any rising young lawyer's equipment. Lincoln learned the speeches by repeating them aloud, which was his method in all study. Thus, he *heard* them—as Shakespeare intended them to be heard.

This fondness for reading and reciting Shakespeare aloud was to last Lincoln through the remainder of his life. As late as 1863, his then secretary, John Hay, described in his personal journal an evening when the President "read Shakespeare to me, the end of *Henry VI* and the beginning of *Richard III*, till my eyelids caught his considerate notice and he sent me to bed." After the death of his young son, various friends remembered Lincoln's having recited to them from memory the passage out of *King John* which, to him, summed up his bereavement:

> And, father cardinal, I have heard you say
> That we shall see and know our friends in heaven:
> If that be true, I shall see my boy again. . . .

Indeed, it was Lincoln's lifelong custom of reading and quoting from Shakespeare which furthered the rumor, widely circulated after his death, that he had entertained a premonition of his own murder. Immediately prior to the tragedy, he had taken a two-day trip by the steamer *River Queen*. Twice during it, he had read aloud to companions lines from *Macbeth* which seemed to obsess him and which they later took to indicate a dark foreknowledge. Such reading was only a matter of habit with the President, yet later it was regarded as significant that on this occasion, so close to his end, he had chosen the passage: "Duncan is in his grave; After life's fitful fever he sleeps well. Treason has done his worst. . . ."

Numerous records survive of Lincoln's attendance at Shakespearean performances, both before and after he became President; among these, a performance of *Othello* which opened the new National Theatre in Washington in 1863. Bringing to the theatre his considerable personal knowledge of the plays and his definite opinions as to how the roles should be interpreted, he frequently engaged in spirited arguments on the subject. The eminent Shakespearean star and scholar, James Hackett, whose Falstaff Lincoln greatly admired, was the recipient not only of invitations to several evenings of Shakespearean discussion at the White House but also of letters from the President discussing the plays. Lincoln wrote in one of these: "Some of Shakespeare's plays I have never read, while others I have gone over perhaps as frequently as any other unprofessional reader." It was his opinion that "nothing equals *Macbeth*"—his other expressed favorites being *King Lear, Hamlet, Henry VIII* and the plays in which Falstaff took part, and *Richard III*.

This was the man who, almost at the last moment, made his fateful decision to occupy the Presidential box at Ford's Theatre on Good Friday evening of 1865.

Laura Keene was the star of the evening. In the past, Lincoln had seen her in Shakespearean roles. But tonight's bill was lighter fare—the closing performance of a popular comedy, *Our American Cousin*. An invitation to attend had been extended by the theatre's manager to Mrs. Lincoln only that same morning. In accepting, she had intended that they take with them important visitors to Washington—the idolized war hero, General U. S. Grant, and his wife. But the Grants, already delayed in a personal visit further north, declined and left the city before nightfall. The Lincolns' substitute guests were Miss Clara Harris, daughter of a New York senator, and a Major Rathbone, her fiancé.

John Ford's brother, Harry, manager of the new theatre, prepared during the day for his distinguished guests. A partition between two boxes overlooking the stage from the right was removed to increase the space comfortably. From his own quarters in the building adjoining the theatre, Harry Ford had a special chair brought in to provide the President's long frame additional comfort. The orchestra was ready with *Hail to the Chief,* to be played upon Lincoln's arrival. Special programs had been rushed to the printer.

It is generally assumed that John Wilkes Booth first learned of the evening's guests of honor from gossip around the theatre (where he was in the habit of picking up his mail) on that very afternoon. Therefore, the actual plan to murder Lincoln could have been only a few hours old when it was carried out. But for several months previously, as later evidence was to prove, Booth had been at the heart of a dramatic, glory-dazzled scheme to kidnap the President and deliver him over to a "betrayed" South. A crew of others with equally fanatic notions had joined in developing this plot, and it had been worked out in the most painstaking detail.

Now, however, Booth saw himself cast in a greater role. He could rid the world of the man he regarded as the South's worst foe, and at the same time of the detested General who had brought Lee to his knees at Appomatox! (It was then still believed that the Grants would be accompanying the Lincolns to the theatre.) To the unstable and emotional actor, with his wrought-up hatred of the Union, it must have seemed a heaven-granted opportunity. Drinking brandies at the theatre bar earlier that evening, almost as if in celebration, he is known to have boasted, 'When I leave the stage . . . I will be the most famous man in America."

The kidnaping plot, in those few hours, had to be drastically altered. Meeting in secret with his co-conspirators, Booth agreed with them that he personally would kill both Lincoln and Grant. Each of the others was to dispose simultaneously of one or another of the top government officials, thus disorganizing the Union's affairs—perhaps even giving the fallen South one last desperate chance to wrest victory from unendurable defeat.

Long before curtain time that night, darkness had fallen over Washington. The street upon which Ford's Theatre faced was unpaved at the time, a quagmire on rainy nights. To attract patrons in from busy Pennsylvania Avenue, barrels were set along the way at intervals, each with a blazing tar torch embedded in it. Beside each light, a hired barker bawled "This way to Ford's!" at the passing traffic.

The carriage from the White House arrived well after the first curtain had risen. The Lincoln party were shown to their seats and the plan continued. And downstairs John Wilkes Booth sauntered through the lobby and into the theatre unchallenged. John T. Ford, in common with most theatrical producers then and since, extended to all members of "the profession" in good standing (such as no one could deny the admired Mr. Booth to be) the "privilege of entering any part of the theatre."

In the alley behind the building, Booth had left a small bay mare in charge of one of the stage crew. He had rented her hours earlier from a livery stable, and she was saddled and ready. According to those he passed on his way, he was humming a tune as he climbed the stairs to the darkened balcony.

Naturally, a guard had been posted outside the closed door to the Presidential box. But had the Metropolitan Washington Police been Booth's accomplices, they scarcely could have picked a man more ideal for his intentions than John Parker. Parker had abandoned his post to take an empty seat nearby and enjoy the play. He never glanced up as a quiet figure opened the door, entered the box and shut the door behind him.

Wilkes knew the play. He had only to wait a few moments, undetected in the shadows at the rear of the box, until the actor playing the comedy role of Asa Trenchard reached a line that never failed to draw a roar of laughter from the audience. Under cover of their merriment, the assassin had only to step forward, level his loaded pistol at the back of the President's head, and fire. The shot was not heard. Before anyone else in the box could guess what had happened, Booth dropped the gun, whipped a more dramatic dagger from its sheath, and cried out in his most effective Shakespearean style, *"Sic Semper Tyrannis!"*

Then—slashing the arm of Major Rathbone, who was just turning toward him in bewilderment—Booth was over the flag-draped railing in a dramatic leap to the stage; that leap he was so certain would never be forgotten by those who witnessed it. Actually, one of his favorite Shakespearean roles had been a sort of rehearsal for that action. An athlete who kept himself in prime condition—"he was always training, riding, shooting, at the gymnasium," John Ford said of him— Booth had amazed audiences, during the Witches' scene in *Macbeth,* by springing with ease to center stage from "rocks" considerably higher up than any box in Ford's Theatre. The *Baltimore Sun,* commenting on this bit of business, had belittled it as "gymnastic." But Booth delighted in the sensational effect. He had no worries as to its serving him equally well in this new role of murderer.

The luck to which he was accustomed, however, deserted him. As he cleared the railing, the spur of one riding boot caught in the draped folds of the Treasury Guard flag which, with the Stars and Stripes, decorated the Presidential box. His carefully calculated balance for the fourteen-foot fall was upset. Instead of landing lightly on his feet, he fell down hard upon the stage and a bone in his left ankle splintered.

Above him in the box, Rathbone was shouting, "Stop that man!" And Mrs. Lincoln's horrified screams for a doctor tore through a stunned silence. Booth lurched to his feet, brandishing the dagger to ward off anyone interfering with his flight, and made his last exit from any stage. The man whose grace and presence had enchanted many an audience vanished into the wings like a toad, hopping grotesquely.

The knife he carried, and the frenzy of his livid face, were enough to clear a path for him out into the alley. Then, mounting with what agony only he could know, he was astride the mare and galloping off.

It took his pursuers several days and nights to catch up with him, despite the broken ankle. In the end, he was cornered in a burning barn and shot like some rabid animal. His body was brought secretly back to the gloomy prison in Washington and buried in shame under the floor of an unmarked cell.

But his end was far from being an end of tragedy for those who had shared so many stages with him in the days of his glory. Of all citizens in America, actors suffered most directly as a result of that crazed assassination. Once the populace at large learned that a man of the theatre had destroyed the President, all people of the theatre were targets for their fury.

Several leading actors were forced to flee for their lives to Canada, and remain there for a considerable period until tempers cooled. One of these was John McCullough, made an innocent object of popular indignation because John Wilkes Booth's last appearance before an audience had been in *The Apostate* at a benefit performance honoring McCullough. Other stage people suffered as well. The homes of actors in various cities were attacked by mobs, walls were defaced, windows broken. Theatres closed down. Companies were thrown out of work. Players found it wise not to show themselves in the streets.

Edwin, famous brother of the assassin, suffered most deeply of all. On the night of the murder, this most gifted of all the Booths was playing *The Iron Box* in Boston. (A few early telegraph reports out of Washington named him as the slayer, a mistake quickly corrected.) One of his lines in the play was: "Where is my honor now? Mountains of shame are piled upon me!" He returned to his dressing room after speaking it, to find the first black news awaiting him. But not until next morning did he understand that his own brother was the killer. He at once canceled his Boston engagement and, after a day of rigorous questioning by Federal authorities, was allowed to return in disguise to his home in New York City. There he shut himself away for weeks, looked after by loyal friends who were deeply concerned lest his brooding drive him mad. He announced that he would never again appear upon any stage.

The elder Booth brother, Junius, had to flee his hotel in Cincinnati to evade a street mob bent upon lynching him. He made his way to the home of a sister in Philadelphia, where he gave himself up for questioning to a United States marshal, was transferred to Washington, and spent some time in the Old Capitol Prison before authorities were convinced he had no connection with his brother's crime. Leaving the capital to continue the tour of *Our American Cousin,* Laura Keene and several of her company were arrested and held. It was not a safe time to be closely connected with theatre. And actors as a class felt themselves disgraced.

More than that, those who had known John Wilkes in the past were stricken with a personal grief. "That unhappy boy" was what the actors called him; a far gentler epithet than those bestowed upon him by the rest of his countrymen. Clara Morris might have spoken for almost the entire profession when she wrote: "We can only shiver and turn our thoughts away from the bright light that went out in such utter darkness. Poor, guilty, unhappy John Wilkes Booth!"

17. A Various Frontier

As America's civilization
pushed steadily westward during the nineteenth century, what
had been Far West to an earlier generation became Middle
West to their descendants. What now came to mean the West
were those sweeping plains on the far side of the Mississippi.
As new waves of settlers reached that distant shore and from
there pushed on toward towering mountains and even the

ocean lying beyond, they did what their ancestors had done. They took the theatre—Will Shakespeare's theatre—with them along the trails.

This West they sought was a varying dream. To some, it was the silver of Colorado or the gold of California. To some, it was the cattle range or the sheep graze. To some, it was Northwest farmland or prairies right for wheat. Into each region where the seekers pressed, Shakespeare followed, in understandably different ways.

Arkansas, at the big river's bank, was settled early. A "Thespian Corps" was acting the farce *The Blue Devils* at the Territory's Fort Gibson by 1830. Eight years later, just two years after Arkansas had become the twenty-fifth of the United States of America, a theatrical manager from Tennessee named Sam Waters arrived at the brand new state capital. Permanently settled in 1812 on the site of a former French trading post, Little Rock was now a bustling community. Finding no theatre, Waters improvised one from a vacant warehouse and opened for a season. The public was delighted, and welcomed the enterprise so warmly that Waters decided to remain through the winter. For this purpose he leased the Arcade Building ("hithertofore devoted to drinking and other intellectual amusements") and made it over into a playhouse seating some five hundred customers. The impresario announced that he meant to engage "the most eminent stars, who will appear in rapid succession" and a gala opening was held on January 16, 1839.

The theatre prospered at first, its novelty attracting customers from all the surrounding rural areas. But those visiting stars failed to appear. And soon even the work of the local regulars grew so sloppy as to disgust the audiences. On this still primitive frontier, there was a famine of actresses, as of women in general. Those Waters could hire had to take several parts in one play. Also, his ambition outran his resources. He chose big plays—*Virginius,* some Shakespeare, *Pizarro*—and then could not squeeze their heroic requirements into his theatre. The stage was too small by far to house an adequate *Othello, Macbeth,* or *Richard III*—yet all these works were attempted before the season ended. Warning Waters of his folly, the local critic wrote: "We, in common with a good many others, hope never to see Shakespeare murdered again."

As business faded, Waters sought a desperate remedy. He imported *Mazeppa* with its famous trained horse. The audience surged back and, despite short cuts necessitated by cramped quarters, the production was a solid success. To hold his houses, in April Waters attempted a play by a local Arkansas author, John Field of Hempstead County. *Bill Screamer: or, The Man of the West,* was the work presented. Not even local pride could claim that Field had outclassed even a handicapped Shakespeare. The same honest critic reported that the play "was wretchedly butchered, and if it had any merit we were unable to discover it." Waters could not keep his season going after May, and presently departed. But he at least had achieved the honor of introducing Will Shakespeare to the infant state of Arkansas.

Utah, settled decades later, represented a very different West to the men and women who tamed it. They were Mormons, Latter-day Saints, led by their prophet, Brigham Young; and they were seeking religious refuge after having been violently persecuted in earlier communities back East. Young and his band arrived at the Great Salt Lake Valley in 1847; applied for admission to the Union two years later; and saw

Congress create a Territory of Utah in 1850. Unlike many older sects, Mormons always had approved of theatre. Their founder, Joseph Smith, had organized a dramatic group at Nauvoo, the settlement in Illinois which had been their previous headquarters. And in Utah, Brigham Young, Smith's successor, promptly followed suit after being sustained as president of the church. Plays were produced by the faithful almost as soon as they had driven the last nail into a meeting hall. By 1861 the celebrated Salt Lake Theatre, which Young had erected at a cost of $100,000, was ready for use.

The Mormons supported religiously a return to first principles. And theatre in its earliest classic form had begun as a religious rite. The Mormon leaders felt that moral precepts might best be expounded in an atmosphere of enjoyment; hence the building of a theatre before Utah had even a high school. Brigham Young intended to preach morality from its stage. He intended that the lives of the actors and actresses trained for the theatre's company be models to the whole flock, of good taste, decorous conduct, and proper manners. To this end, as an example, he made his own daughters members of the company.

The exterior of the theatre he built was Doric in design, simple and dignified. Inside, emphasis was placed upon airy simplicity and light—the whole interior being painted white, with touches of gold. Sharply canted upward, so that every seat had a good view of the stage, the pit was far superior to those in most contemporary eastern theatres. Mormon families rented the benches. On play nights the bishops and elders and their wives and children came to relish the drama and to applaud wholeheartedly. In the center of the pit stood Brigham Young's own rocking chair, where he could enjoy himself surrounded by his people. The theatre was built with only two boxes. One of these was for the use of Young if he wished to be alone or to entertain some particular guest. The other was reserved for the ladies of the cast, so that they might observe whatever scenes they took no part in.

A visiting Englishman, soon after the theatre was opened, was much impressed by its tone of orderly pleasure. He wrote:

Neither within the doors nor about them, do you find the riot of our own Lyceum and Drury Lane; no loose women, no pickpockets, no ragged boys and girls, no drunken and blaspheming men. As the Mormon never drinks spirits, and rarely smokes tobacco, the only dissipation in which you find these hundreds of hearty creatures indulging their appetites, is that of sucking a peach. . . . The curtain, which rises at eight, comes down about half-past ten; and as the Mormon fashion is for people to sup before going out, they retire to rest the moment they get home, never suffering their amusements to infringe on the labours of the coming day. Your bell rings for breakfast at six o'clock. . . .

The same writer was also much taken with the excellence of backstage accomodations, remarking almost in awe that, "Every lady, no matter 'how small her part in the play, has a dressingroom to herself."

His theatre erected, Young put it to the most logical of uses. He spared no effort to achieve excellence in the company it housed. Then he went out of his way to attract into it the best of the touring stars. The Salt Lake Theatre quickly became one of the standard stops for prominent actors on their way to the Pacific coast or back. Since the repertory of a majority of these road players was based upon Shakespeare, and since the philosophical and moral values of his works was apparent to all, it was inevitable that Salt Lake City should early enjoy his plays under the very best of auspices. Actors found the theatre far pleasanter than most. Audiences greeted them with respect and enthusiasm. A healthy climate for genuine enjoyment of the Bard was quickly established. Right down to the present day, members of the Mormon faith have been dedicated theatregoers.

In Montana, as in other western areas where Indian hostility was particularly felt, theatre arrived wearing the spurs of the United States Cavalry. By 1870 Fort Shaw had been established in the foothills of the Rockies. The fort commanded the stage route between Fort Benton and Helena, in a good position to protect the settlers from marauding warriors and to safeguard fur and gold shipments headed to Fort Benton from the greed of renegade whites.

The fort's commanding officer in its early days was a General Gibbon. One day, returning from a trip to Helena, his wife paused at a shanty in Prickly Pear Canyon to ask for a drink of water. She discovered that the occupants were a family of six, Boll by name, who had been actors in Europe and had been lured to Montana during the gold rush by overly enthusiastic relatives. Now, their dream of easy millions faded, the Bolls were homesick and unhappy.

Mrs. Gibbon had little difficulty in persuading them to come to Fort Shaw to play a professional season there, replacing the willing but crude performances of military amateurs. The Bolls were delighted to get back into harness. They still had with them their old costume trunk and their dog-eared scripts. Perhaps, too, the prospect of getting within the fort's protective walls appealed to them. Chief Sitting Bull and his allies had at the time begun to make unfriendly rumblings.

Although they had played Shakespeare along with other

"standards" at home in their own language, the Bolls never had acted his works in English. Presumably there were no copies of the original plays to be found at the post, for, while quarters were being prepared for his family, Boll set about translating the foreign language scripts for use by himself and his talented wife, Ida May. Meanwhile, hammers were pounding and saws were whining at the fort. The post theatre was a barnlike structure, with a stage at one end. It was unfloored, quite innocent of paint, crude in the extreme, but at least not open to the weather as had been the playhouses where Shakespeare originally had been enacted. Adjoining this structure, new accommodations for the Bolls went up quickly. These consisted chiefly of a combination living room-kitchen with a door which connected directly to the stage, two steps up. Thus, during performances, the room also became a cast dressing room.

When their new home was ready, the Bolls were sent for and arrived to occupy it. In the adaptable living room, rehearsals were held each evening until tattoo signaled the order for lights out. Stage-struck cavalrymen played the smaller parts and the walk-ons, giving a real flavor to the troop movements frequently required in Shakespearean action. The opening bill, however, was not Shakespeare but *Ingomar the Barbarian*—an old favorite which displayed Ida May to advantage. Word of the event, along with printed handbills, circulated throughout the Territory. On the opening night, rigs and riders poured in from mountains and plains to pack the hall with eager settlers.

That night, as every other when the Bolls played at Fort Shaw, fresh sawdust was sprinkled over the earthen floor for the accommodation of the audience. Kerosene lamps equipped with reflectors lit stage and house alike. Lighting effects were achieved by members of the orchestra, who on cue arose to turn wicks down for a subdued glow or up for a bright gleam. The orchestra being also the post's military band, its music was at least of a professional quality.

Shakespeare has perhaps never before nor since received such a unique tribute as was paid him on one night at Fort Shaw, when Ida May at last felt ready to tackle a translated Desdemona. One member of the audience was an old mountaineer who had never before seen a play. He was so exhilarated by this initial experience that after the performance of *Othello* he insisted that Boll accept his most prized possession —a highly individualistic mule, whom the soldiers promptly christened Ingomar in honor of the company's first performance at the fort.

The Boll family were versatile. With no apparent strain, they could switch from *Othello* to that lachrymose and moral melodrama of the period, *Ten Nights in a Barroom*. On the night they first played this tear-jerker, with little Minnie Boll as the tiny waif who implores her father to abandon his sottish ways and who at last is gathered to the angels, the burly soldiers wept unashamedly. Afterward, virtually the whole audience repaired to the sutler's shop and bought all the bright, cheerful calico he had, to comfort the wronged child. The yardage was sufficient to clothe the entire distaff side of the family in matching dresses and sunbonnets.

Beyond the gentling reach of theatre, meanwhile, Chiefs Sitting Bull, Crazy Horse, and Rain-in-the-Face had been goading their followers to ever-mounting resistance against abuses by white renegades from the gold fields. Replying to provocative incidents, the United States sent Army units against the Sioux. Montana's first acting company was warned that it had better leave while the leaving was good. The Bolls sadly packed their costume trunks for departure to Fort Benton and a safer East. Shakespeare was given his final hour on the Fort Shaw stage. The curtain rang down. The bugles sounded. The troops swung into their saddles and galloped away, leaving a darkened playhouse behind. They arrived at the Little Big Horn River just twenty-four hours too late to reinforce Colonel George A. Custer, and perhaps to prevent that needless massacre of his entire column known to history as Custer's Last Stand.

The state of Hawaii had her own brand of theatre long before she was first discovered by England's Captain James Cook in 1778. In their story-telling hulas, in unwritten chants passed from generation to generation, and in elaborate pageants combining drums and torchlight and flowers and marchers, the early Polynesians who had ruled the islands expressed their history and their elaborate legends. White men arrived in numbers on the heels of Cook, and within mere decades, the arrival of American missionaries and businessmen had transformed Honolulu from a pagan settlement of grass-roofed shacks to a bustling little modern city. A local stock subscription financed construction of the Royal Hawaiian Theatre—a professional house in every detail—in 1848. Here, returning from his Australian tour with Laura Keene in 1854, Edwin Booth laid down virtually his last fifty dollars to rent the theatre for a series of performances intended to remedy the company's strained finances.

Always a temperamental woman (to members of her companies, she was privately known as The Duchess), Miss Keene had a bitter falling-out with her co-star while they were rehearsing *Richard III*. She flounced aboard a ship just ready to sail, and left Booth—then still young and inexperienced as a manager—facing his opening without a Lady Anne.

In this desperate situation, he was told of someone in the city who was "up" in the part. The seemingly providential substitute turned out to be a dwarfish male stagehand, cross-eyed and minus his front teeth, who spoke with a thick Dutch accent. But beggars could not be choosers. The play went on. Manfully, Booth spoke the lines of honeyed flattery: "Divine perfection of a woman . . . fairer than tongue can name thee. . . ." When at last he reached the passionate, "Teach not thy lip such scorn; for it was made for kissing, lady, not for such contempt. . . ." the squat little Dutchman, simpering coyly, revealed wide, toothless gums. Yet Booth's acting was of so high a caliber that from his rapt audience there arose not even the suspicion of a titter.

The star had other matters on his mind that night. There was a royal guest in his theatre; and backstage, too. Young King Kamehameha IV had so recently come to the throne of Hawaii that the Kingdom was still in official mourning for Kauikeaouli, his predecessor. The King had wanted to attend the performance, for earlier travels in England and America had given him a taste for Shakespeare, but he did not think it proper to occupy the royal box. So he was seated in the wings to view the play, a towering Polynesian guard at one elbow, and the French Ambassador to Honolulu at the other. The chair he occupied was also, in the drama, the throne of England. When the coronation scene was reached, His Majesty had to be asked to give up his seat. He watched the rest of the performance standing, taking the violation of protocol with quiet good humor and warmly applauding the star at the final curtain.

Thus royally introduced to Shakespeare, Hawaii became a favorite stopping place for companies traveling to and from the Orient and Australia. During the seventies and eighties, many a reputable Shakespearean star walked that elegant little stage in Honolulu. Other commendable productions were put on by amateur casts on the visiting warships of foreign powers, of which one or more always seemed to lie in harbor.

When the theatrical "road" died early in the twentieth century, the remote islands were left largely to their own dramatic resources. But Shakespeare did not vanish from Hawaiian stages. Instead, he was acted—by the excellent Honolulu Community Theatre and other competent groups— in productions which could be matched nowhere else in the world. Hawaii's sugar industry had been responsible for a great influx of Chinese, Japanese, and other Oriental workers, who lent their own exotic flavor to the community and a typical production of *Julius Caesar* included in its cast *haoles* (Caucasians), Polynesians, Spanish, Koreans, Japanese, Portuguese, Filipinos, Chinese, and a smattering of other nationalities. *Romeo and Juliet* was presented with a Chinese Juliet and a Portuguese Romeo. Handsomely staged in the manner of a Japanese Kabuki drama, yet with not a line of the original text altered, *Coriolanus* was put on with a cast entirely made up of Orientals.

As in Hawaii, the drama's beginnings in Oregon antedated arrival of the white man. Early fur traders in the area, in the 1830s, found their efforts to traffic with the Indians hampered by a marked preference of the red men to trade exclusively among themselves. The tribes sent delegations to great annual fairs held in the Yakima Valley and elsewhere, and often, encampments at these gatherings covered six square miles and housed over three thousand Indians. Archery, horse racing and other sports were mere preludes to the climactic event, which was held within a great circle of squatting drummers beating barbaric rhythms. The most illustrious warriors of the convention gathered inside this arena, while the rest looked on.

The "actors" put on a sham battle with all its ferocious maneuvers. At the circle's center, where a huge fire blazed, the "stars" of the performance went through even more horrendous rituals, flourishing their spears and arrows, howling wildly, waving tomahawks, and pantomiming the scalping of enemies. Props at these events included the mummified hearts of brave foes, sewn into pouches of beaded leather. The last act was always a mass wedding, featuring brides becomingly costumed in beads, feathers, paint, nose quills, and rings for fingers, wrists, and ankles.

The first recorded Oregon performance by white men took place in May 1846, when sailors aboard *H.B.M.S. Modeste,* a ship in the service of the Hudson's Bay Company and anchored at Fort Vancouver, undertook to stage a musical play. It was called *Love in a Village,* and its object was to repay the local settlers for hospitality to the visiting tars. The production on shipboard was complete even to scenery painted by the crew, and to a drop curtain diplomatically featuring a replica of towering Mount Hood.

Oregon became a territory of the United States in 1848, during the administration of President Polk. Professional theatre was waiting to knock at its door. In the early 1850s, the redoubtable Chapman family came up by steamer from gold-rush San Francisco to bring the new Territory a repertory which included its earliest on-stage Shakespeare. And the first literary work ever to be published in Oregon (in 1852) took formal notice of the Swan of Avon on its title page.

This masterpiece was a play, and it was called: "A Melodrame [sic] entitled *Treason, Strategem and Spoils* in Five Acts by BREAKSPEAR." Mr. "Breakspear" was actually W. L. Adams of Oregon City, and the work he had based on Shakespearean models "in rhymes and blank verse" was a political satire which ripped into the Democrats and delighted the Whigs. It was recorded at the time that "Crowds flocked to every postoffice to get a copy and read it, till half the people of Oregon had committed most of it to memory."

A Portland Theatre is referred to in letters written during the same early fifties; but no definite record survives as to where it stood, or what it was like. By 1858, there was a regular playhouse—Stewart's—operating in the city. And Moody's Hall was opening at The Dalles, then a military post. A company headed by one Professor Risley had already played at the fort "in a canvas pavilion," singing songs, doing acrobatic acts, and performing *The Lady of Lyons*. But Shakespeare had to wait for Mr. Moody's new building, and afterward the Bard was frequently on the boards.

By the 1860s, Oregon theatre was flourishing. Touring stars, including such lights as Charles Kean, his wife, Ellen Tree, and Julia Dean, were playing the Shakespearean (and other) roles which had built their reputations in more settled areas. The Dalles, being a stagecoach and pony express stop as well as being served by the river steamboats, early became a favorite goal for such traveling companies. All over Oregon, local opera houses were springing up as centers of community life. Arriving at Portland, players could fan out to Vancouver and

The Dalles by riverboat, or "up the valley" by stage and later by local railroad to play Salem, Eugene, and Oregon City. Even at first, these performances attracted audiences of a certain elegance; for one observer wrote, "The men in their cowhide boots and silk hats are very gallant to their be-mittened and be-bustled ladies."

Will Shakespeare had found himself sympathetic country when the Chapmans got off their steamer in Oregon Territory. The first of the major Shakespeare festivals in the United States was begun in Ashland, Oregon, in 1940. There the Oregon Shakespeare Festival—oldest Elizabethan theatre organization in the Western Hemisphere—has built a handsome replica of the Fortune Theatre stage of sixteenth-century London, where annual summer seasons present selected Shakespearean works in alternating schedules.

Each new section of the West, as it became American territory, thus bade the Swan of Avon welcome in its own particular accent. A measure of his greatness is the ease with which he met each new circumstance on its own terms, and gracefully embraced them all.

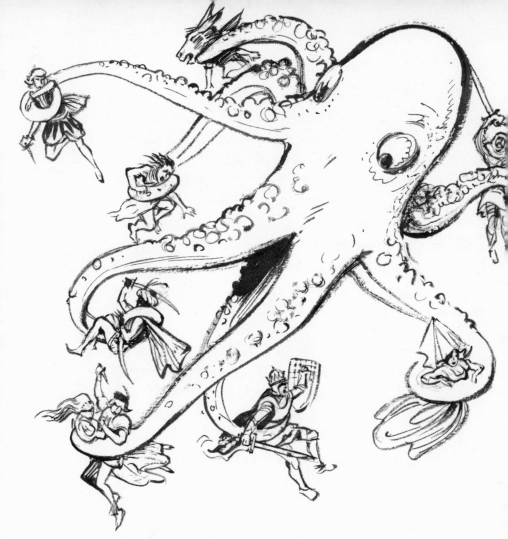

18. Revolution on the Road

The shine of an age of great American performers began to dull for Will Shakespeare only as deepening shadows of big-business theatre fell increasingly across it. And for this, the theatre had largely itself to blame. There was no real villain in the piece. Yet in the end the stage suffered severely.

In the 1890s, almost every community which later operated a movie house was able to boast a legitimate theatre. Throughout the era of the local stock company, gradually taken over by traveling stars, these scattered playhouses were what formed America's "road." As the star system encroached more and more, usurping the prerogative of play production, theatre impresarios (who had once served a creative function) tended to become mere managers of real estate on which they had to show a profit.

As resident companies dwindled, these managers counted on touring road shows—the single play or the repertory company—to fill their seats for them. New York City was the point at which most such tours originated. The managers came to New York each spring to dicker with road producers for the succession of attractions they would need to keep their houses in operation.

At first, such negotiations were handled on an individual basis. But this proved unsatisfactory. Managers found it very difficult to secure suitable offerings for the exact dates when they would be needed to fill out a house schedule. Companies had to crisscross the country, backtracking and taking uncomfortably long jumps between engagements, in order to keep playing. It was natural that booking agencies should arise to handle these problems; filling a theatre's season with a series of plays, and arranging a company's tour with a minimum of lost travel time.

To untangle the booking snarl further, theatre owners tended to combine into sensible units or blocs. Several of them, either near one another or along the same main railroad lines, would join forces so that one company might be booked into a series of houses in sensible succession. Increasingly, the men who headed these combinations (or who owned several theatres) discovered that it was to their definite financial advantage to pool their resources.

In Philadelphia, Sam Nixon and Fred Zimmerman controlled a majority of available stages. In New York, it was Abe Erlanger, Marc Klaw, Al Hayman, and Charles Frohman. In 1895–96, when these men united in what came to be known as the Syndicate, they controlled virtually all theatre in America. They owned or supervised the best houses in every city across the continent. It was therefore their own booking agencies which filled those theatres' schedules. Often, the very productions themselves had been put together by one or another of the Syndicate. Independent theatre owners had to fall in line, or shutter their houses. Actors, even stars, had to accept Syndicate terms or stop touring.

Thus, business ledgers—not great acting in great plays— became the yardstick for success or failure. From its beginnings, with the Hallams and their ilk, America's stage always had been commercial—in the sense that it had to make its own financial way, without noble patrons and without state financing. Where it could not attract a paying audience, it had withered on the vine. Yet each actor-manager, striving to please, had done so by offering his own best earnest efforts at interpretation and stagecraft. In a competitive market place, this is always a healthy situation and tends to encourage excellence. The Syndicate had removed the competition and the risk. Art was leveled out to mediocrity, tidily packaged to serve waiting houses on the road.

In effect, the Syndicate was a powerful trust. Under its sway, business was made as stable as theatre business ever can be. If one came to terms, one was assured of comfortable profits. Theatres were supplied with plays; companies were certain of continuing engagements. But, creatively, the theatre was being choked to death. There was no room in such an arrangement for experimentation, or for the plays with primarily artistic aims. The whole idea was merely to turn out sure-fire attractions to guarantee audiences at a succession of road stops.

For the first decade of the 1900s, the Syndicate ruled America's stages autocratically and there was no place in their arrangements for Will Shakespeare. It was not a matter of dislike. Shakespearean productions required large casts, elaborate costumes, and heavy scenery costly to create, expensive to transport. All this cut into the profits. The ideal play, the yielder of the big financial net, was a small-cast, one-or-two-set affair, tailor-made for the talents of some particular star with a following. And because the repertory which once had trained them was dying, these stars tended to be less and less identified with Shakespearean roles. Drawing room comedy and domestic drama were becoming the standard fare of the road tour.

Another circumstance tending to edge Will Shakespeare out of his position at center stage, at the turn of the century, was a change in the status of native American playwrights. For forty years or so, authors for the theatre had increasingly been paid royalties—or percentages of performance receipts—in exchange for use of their works. But in the days of repertory, where long runs of a single work were not the rule, such financial rewards were small. Often plays were sold outright by hungry scribblers to the stars who accepted them. But by 1880 the royalty system and the extended run were beginning to join hands, to the profit of the writer. The international copyright law of 1891 barred competition from free foreign plays. A writer in America could at last make a decent living at his trade.

New plays by Americans began to appear in quantity, competing in their novelty against Shakespeare's acknowledged but familiar genius. William Gillette wrote and starred in *Secret Service* and then *Sherlock Holmes*. Mrs. Leslie Carter, of Chicago society, was made a star in *The Heart of Maryland*. Clyde Fitch was writing deft comedies on social foibles; among them, *Captain Jinks of the Horse Marines,* which overnight made a star of a young actress named Ethel Barrymore. The enormous spectacle *Ben Hur* packed New York's Broadway Theatre for a full season and triumphed on the road. By 1901 tuneful operettas by Victor Herbert were beguiling the public. Henry Miller and Margaret Anglin were soon co-starring in William Vaughn Moody's *The Great Divide*. Early plays by an opinionated Britisher, George Bernard Shaw, were attracting attention.

Almost alone, at the turn of the new century, English-born actor Richard Mansfield was fighting in America to hew to the old line—to keep repertory and Shakespeare, all but synonymous in the past, alive on America's stages. In October 1900 he opened a production of *Henry V* in New York which was a showcase for all that he was trying to accomplish. Magnificence was the key word for that production. The crowd scenes in which it abounded had never been equaled for color and movement, whether they depicted the streets of London or the Battle of Agincourt. Mansfield's techniques in handling realistic crowd scenes were to be the basis for the work of such later motion picture directors as David W. Griffith and

Cecil B. De Mille. They left nothing further to be accomplished, in that direction, on the living stage.

But Mansfield was struggling against an ebb tide. He was the last of the old-time actor-managers, by now almost entirely superseded by producer czars such as Charles Frohman. In an age where the long run had become a requisite for economic survival, Mansfield tried to play the old repertory—constantly changing his plays and roles. At the age of fifty, he had exhausted himself in the impossible struggle and died.

For almost two decades, the Syndicate ruled supreme. Those who set themselves up against it fought, like Mansfield, against overwhelming odds. On the road, theatres were denied them. They sometimes had to offer their dramatic wares in barns, from which situation was coined the dramatic term "barnstorming" to describe a catch-as-catch-can tour. Let a rugged rebel like David Belasco plan a tour for his successful *Madame Butterfly,* and the Syndicate was a week ahead of him at all his booked stops with a shoddily scrambled together drama about a Japanese geisha which soured the market for another. Competition was not to be tolerated. Still, a very few who found the situation odious continued to fight it.

One of the popular favorites who dared oppose the Syndicate was James O'Neill, with his hit *The Count of Monte Cristo;* a play he acted so long that, paradoxically, he was eventually unable to remember his lines in it. Another was James A. Herne, with his *Shore Acres.* A third was Minnie Maddern Fiske, whose long career had begun when as a child of five she had played Arthur to John McCullough's Faulconbridge in Shakespeare's *King John.* Mrs. Fiske battled the Syndicate doggedly, building her great reputation in Edward Sheldon's *Salvation Nell,* and as Shakespeare's and Ibsen's heroines. Her last tour, in the 1930s, was opposite Otis Skinner in *The Merry Wives of Windsor*.

The blind commercialism of the stage under the Syndicate's grip, however, could not fail to breed a time of wider rebellion. By 1909, a sufficient undercurrent of disgust had developed so that private philanthropists contributed the funds to build a monumental playhouse, called the New Theatre, on New York City's Cental Park West. A visionary and talented young producer of considerable out-of-town achievement, Winthrop Ames, was hired to supervise the project. His aim was the creation of a strong but starless repertory company, appearing in handsomely mounted plays of artistic merit. The enduring status of Will Shakespeare as "the genius of our mother tongue" was testified to by the selection of his *Antony and Cleopatra* for the New Theatre's opening bill.

Almost from the first, the artistic aims of the experiment had to compromise with business realities. In order to attract an audience conditioned by the Syndicate to "name" performers, stars had to be hired—in this case, E. H. Sothern and Julia Marlowe, a moving team in *Romeo and Juliet* but wrong for many of Shakespeare's heavier parts. The auditorium proved to be acoustically faulty; but even this mechanical defect did not disguise the inability of a generation of actors untrained in playing Shakespeare to project his lines properly. The sets were so massive that even a revolving stage could scarcely handle the changes. Moreover, finances demanded that when one entry in the repertory—Maeterlinck's *The Blue Bird*—proved a huge hit with the public, it had to be removed from the roster and transferred to another theatre for a long commercial run.

After two years, the project had to close up shop as a

financial failure. Still, it had inspired tremendous interest in the return of a stage dedicated to something finer than dollar-grubbing. And Will Shakespeare had, not surprisingly, led the way.

19. Our Revels Now Are Ended

The theatre-as-business approach to what once had been an art was a hard blow to Shakespeare in America. But this was only one of the foes arrayed against him as the twentieth century lengthened. Equally effective in the enemy camp were the devotees of the expanding school of stage realism.

These apostles of a new creed had begun to take over the theatre from its heroic and romantic elements as early as 1891, when James A. Herne wrote and produced his markedly realistic drama *Margaret Fleming*. On the heels of Herne, Henrik Ibsen had taken the stage with his even more depths-probing works such as *A Doll's House*. The respected critic William Winter spoke for most American audiences when he wrote of this play as "the most unpleasant of the many unpleasant productions of the Norwegian crank," and went on to call it "odoriferous" and "abominable stuff, both dull and dirty." Still, the realists were clearly on the march—and gaining strength with each new season.

This "realism" now elbowing its way on stage scorned virtually every tradition to which Shakespeare's audiences were accustomed. It cut out the asides to the audience by which characters had conveyed thoughts at variance with their speeches to other characters. Soliloquies, such as Hamlet's immortal ones, were anathema. The kind of forceful physical action that makes Shakespeare's plays so exciting was abandoned in order to concentrate more and more exclusively on inner conflict. At peaks of crisis, pantomime rather than the flowing Shakespearean speech was used to convey anguish. Down-to-earth everyday details were used in abundance to show how like the little lives of little people were to what was happening on stage. And the "big" curtain was avoided in favor of a quiet dribbling away of whatever action had been going on.

The actors cast in these realistic offerings were developing a new style to fit the requirements of their vehicles. Instead of the oratorical and full-voiced emotion of an earlier day, they were struggling to suggest these emotions in relative silence.

Some of the more successful new stars rather specialized in inarticulateness and imperturbability.

The producers (whom the Syndicate's long sway had made more important than either actor or writer) plunged into the new realism with a relish. David Belasco was their high priest, and had soon outstripped all competition. The plays he staged were often trash, but the lengths to which he went to insure verisimilitude in the staging of them were the wonder of his day. Offering red-haired Mrs. Leslie Carter in a play with a stage background, *Zaza,* he showed the audience the backstage operation of a theatre right down to the devices which simulated galloping horses and wild thunder storms. In another play, he set up on stage a working facsimile of a Horn and Hardart Automat restaurant.

Were the demands of Shakespeare's plays to be met in similarly realistic style—as indeed they were in the Mansfield *Henry V*—the costs would have been prohibitive. It was a simpler matter, or so the producers believed, to eliminate Shakespeare.

While the century moved on to a deeper and deeper commitment to stage realism, yet another factor arose to discourage new productions of the Bard. Unions invaded the theatre world. To rid themselves of the iron grip of the managers, the actors struck; and from their long and bitter fight, when they won it, emerged a professional association, known as Actors' Equity, for the protection of actors' rights. Soon, the scene shifters were organized; so were the electricians; so were the theatre ushers, and the musicians, and the set painters, and even the dramatists. An example of how far this new union control could go to hamper Shakespearean production was offered in 1922 when—for the first time since

Edwin Booth's long reign—a really important production of *Hamlet* was put upon the stage in New York City. It starred the rising young actor John Barrymore, and it elicited cheers from the most serious of critics. Yet the musician's union strove to have it classified as a musical comedy, in order to justify their demand that unneeded extra musicians be kept "standing by."

The effect of this dictation by union bosses, this profit-hunger by business-oriented managers, this scorn of the imaginative by the disciples of realism, would doubtless have bewildered Will Shakespeare himself, could he have returned to witness it. In the theatre he had known and loved no one had worried about who got overtime pay, who had the right to move a bench on stage, how many spoken lines required a pay advance over minimum scale, what staggering salary a publicized box-office star might demand, why a play should be staged in the first place if there were no subsequent motion picture rights to be sold, or any of a hundred other production factors which closely concerned the twentieth-century entre-preneur. At the Globe and at Blackfriars, every man simply had pitched in and done his best to make the play go. It had been a happier time for the theatre.

Faced by all the new forces in theatre arrayed against him, it would have been understandable if Shakespeare had van-ished, at least temporarily, from the American stage and taken a shadowy place among other eminent but half-forgotten Elizabethans.

And during the first quarter of the century, Master Will's place in the professional theatre in America was indeed precarious. Only when one of a decreasing number of aging old-time stars ventured a pallid revival of some once favorite role did he briefly reappear from limbo. It was a time when Eugene O'Neill was emerging as a vital theatre force with his *The Hairy Ape,* his *Desire Under the Elms.* It was a time when a realistic "dour little play" like *John Ferguson* was well enough received to save the infant Theatre Guild from dying in its cradle; and when the first Pulitzer Prize for drama was being awarded to an unmemorable little comedy of divorce called *Why Marry?;* and when a world war and shoddy productions and spiraling transportation costs had killed "the road," turning professional theatre back upon the cramped island of Manhattan.

Had Shakespeare himself been able to gauge the currents of these times as the active managers were gauging them, he might well have glanced sadly back to brighter days and said with Prospero: "Our revels now are ended. These our actors, As I foretold you, were all spirits and Are melted into air, into thin air."

Shakespeare, however, once again proved himself indestructable. Instead of being swept away by the times' trends, his works reversed the trends. As early as 1904, Sir Sidney Lee, prominent Shakespearean biographer, wrote: "The history of Shakespeare's fame is indeed that of a flowing tide; the ebbing was never long enough sustained to give it genuine importance; the forward march was never seriously impeded, and is from start to finish the commanding feature. . . ."

Repertory theatre and "the road," Shakespeare's unfailing supporters, were things of the past. But the newer "long-run" tradition was turned to his uses. This same half-century in which Shakespeare's eclipse was so frequently proclaimed also accorded one after another of his plays its longest run of all time.

Thus, the John Barrymore *Hamlet* (1922) was acted 101 times, to overshadow even Edwin Booth's staying power in the role. Jane Cowl's *Romeo and Juliet* (in 1923, while *Hamlet* was still running) scored for that play an unprecedented 157 performances. David Warfield (still in 1923, a vintage year for the Bard) made new history for *The Merchant of Venice* by appearing as Shylock for 92 consecutive times. John Gielgud's *Hamlet* of the 1936–37 season (partially qualifying as American, in that Lillian Gish was the Ophelia) topped Barrymore's version by playing 132 performances. In the same season, Maurice Evans (now an American citizen) played 133 performances in *Richard II,* and Lynn Fontanne and Alfred Lunt played *The Taming of the Shrew* for 129, each a new record of endurance. In 1942 Maurice Evans triumphed again, with Judith Anderson, in topping all old scores for *Macbeth* with a new one of 131 performances. And the Margaret Webster–Paul Robeson *Othello* of 1943–44, by ringing up its curtain 276 times, both topped the previous record for that play and registered the greatest number of consecutive performances for *any* Shakespearean play in America.

These successes handsomely disproved the previous claims made by experts in show business that Shakespeare could no longer attract an audience unless he were played in constantly changing repertory. An even more interesting thing was happening. Shakespeare's plays had been edged off the stage because the profits to be made from producing them in the "realistic" manner were highly dubious. But now Shakespeare had begun to reverse the trend of realism in the American theatre. More and more, as the century advances, it is realism that has become "old hat," and Shakespeare who has become "avant-garde." Still continuing, this trend reversal rather suggests that no vogue in theatre unable to make room for the Swan of Avon will very long survive.

An early foretaste of things to come was offered by the Barrymore *Hamlet,* mounted by Robert Edmond Jones, in 1922. Startled critics found the stage set and the actors costumed with no such magnificence as Mansfield had brought to Shakespeare; no such authentic detail as had been supplied by Edwin Booth. Instead, there was "a rhythm of images, of light and shade innate to the moment," which in the end held "a quality of excitement in it like that of music; it seems not so much a setting as the rich shadow of thought behind the play's events."

Within a very few years, the schism between suggestion and realism widened considerably further. Gordon Craig had been creating much excitement in Europe with his architectural, expressionistic stagings; and before the twenties were over, New York had a first view of his work in a *Macbeth* which featured its designer even above its well-regarded players. The producers had intended to star Margaret Anglin as Lady Macbeth, with Lyn Harding in the title role and William Farnum as Banquo. But the Craig scheme for the production, massive as a brooding granite mountain, left the role of the bloodstained queen too minimized. Even an Anglin could not assert herself over the Craig design. After several weeks of rehearsals, she withdrew from the cast and was replaced by Florence Reed. The production when it opened inspired a mixed reaction in a public not yet ready for such lengths of un-realism. But it pointed the way in which Shakespeare would move in the future. And this way was no downward path into obscurity!

Beginning in 1926, actress Eva Le Gallienne tried to reverse the trend away from repertory theatre, when she founded her Civic Repertory Theatre in an ancient playhouse on New York's Fourteenth Street. For six valiant seasons, she kept this enterprise alive—presenting a repertory of thirty-four "un-commercial" classics which included *Twelfth Night* and *Romeo and Juliet*. While the noble gesture ultimately failed financially, it showed a whole new generation of playgoers what repertory of the highest standards might be. And it was to be remembered by those of still a later generation who would urge the creation of a National Theatre along similar lines.

By the time the Depression struck, Shakespeare was back with a vengeance. One of the top playwrights of the time, Maxwell Anderson, when offering his *Winterset* in 1935, did not attempt to deny that it was very much a modern-dress rewriting of *Romeo and Juliet,* even though he had based it upon the Sacco-Vanzetti trial in Boston. Said one reviewer: "Shakesperian? Precisely, patently—and successfully. . . . Shakespeare in shirt-sleeves, and not a jot incongruous be-cause of that undress." Anderson had used the sordid slum materials of realistic theatre at its drabbest, but he had turned them to Shakespeare's uses, making soaring blank verse of them.

Theatregoers in 1937 were startled and delighted when, in the face of the theatre's now-established need for a run suf-ficiently long to "make it pay," actor Maurice Evans had the courage to stage a new production, not of one of Shakespeare's more popular works, but of the seldom produced *Richard II*. Coming from England, he had played Romeo to Katharine Cornell's Juliet two years earlier, but otherwise was not widely known in this country. The critics hailed his new production, brilliantly staged by Margaret Webster, as "A fine theatre-going adventure" and marveled that so absorbing a play had not been acted more often. Its setting was a simple combination of draperies with skeleton forms and sparse furnishings. This very simplicity, it was felt, added to the play's effectiveness.

But it remained for the newly formed Mercury Theatre, two seasons later, to strip down modern Shakespeare staging to stark essentials. Young Orson Welles took Shakespeare's *Julius Caesar* and made of it what its author had not—an antidictator play, aimed at the hateful figures of Hitler and Mussolini who at the time seemed to be striding the world in seven-league boots. The actors wore Fascist uniforms instead of Roman togas; the set was the bare stage, with its blank brick rear wall in full view. Only a brilliant shifting of lights to underscore the action served as scenery. The acclaim won by this production proved to the last doubter that elaborate staging of Shakespeare was unnecessary. "Something to stand up and cheer about," pronounced the *New York Herald Tribune*'s critic; and added, "It is perhaps a chastening thought that the theatre had to go back to your old friend, the late Mr. Shakespeare, to arrange this new miracle." The way toward repertory festivals of his works was clearly indicated.

Old-style Shakespearean productions have not, of course, completely vanished from our stages during the years since World War II. Some of them have competed triumphantly with the normal "run" productions of Broadway. Maurice Evans appeared in a succesful *Macbeth* with Judith Anderson; then a well-attended *Twelfth Night* with Helen Hayes. Sir Laurence Olivier and Vivien Leigh offered a memorable

Antony and Cleopatra, and Katharine Cornell another. But "on-Broadway" Shakespeare has largely, if perhaps temporarily, become the sphere of visiting English stars, rather than an American effort.

One brave attempt to revive the repertory system commercially was made in New York in 1946, when Eva Le Gallienne, Margaret Webster, and Cheryl Crawford organized the American Repertory Theatre. It opened with a beautifully staged *Henry VIII,* Miss Le Gallienne appearing as Shakespeare's Queen Katharine and Walter Hampden as the wily Cardinal Wolsey. Despite a well-patronized season, the economics of modern Broadway—in this case, particularly the stagehands' and musicians' unions, who refused to make concessions to the lowered profits of a repertory season—doomed the project to failure. At the end of a single year, the dedicated trio had to admit defeat.

The defeat, however, was not Will Shakespeare's. All over America, as the new symbolic set and even experimental returns to the bare Elizabethan stage made production of Shakespeare once more a financial possibility, the "festival" approach to repertories of his plays began making headway. The revels were not ended, for Master Will. He was about to reach a far wider American audience than ever before.

20. Lights! Cameras! Shakespeare!

Any veteran actor at the time of the First World War (or a little earlier) could have told a questioner exactly why America's theatre was in the doldrums. Worsening conditions in Europe hadn't a thing to do with it. The woes the Syndicate had wrought for theatre on the road were only a minor contributory factor. No, what was hurting the theatre was the competition of those moving pictures Mr. Thomas A. Edison had invented only the day before yesterday. Audiences were swarming to the movies. They were forsaking the legitimate theatre which had served them so long—that's what the trouble was.

One wonders what Will Shakespeare, with his acute theatrical instinct, would have made of motion pictures. Surviving records clearly indicate what motion pictures shortly attempted to make of him!

Will's first brush with a crude new entertainment form destined to rocket swiftly to unheard-of popularity seems to have taken place not in America but France, and in 1907. In that year the Frenchman, Georges Melies, took to experimenting with the purely technical aspects of picture animation. He produced a short film which he called *Le Rêve de Shakespeare.* The English version of the picture was titled, more prosaically, *Shakespeare Writing "Julius Caesar."* In one corner of the screen sat M. Melies himself, garbed as the Bard with quill in hand. Above him on a cramped platform, other actors wearing somewhat makeshift togas went through the business of the assassination scene. Subtitles to explain action or indicate dialogue were still unknown. One had to possess at least a rudimentary knowledge of the event to guess what the hacking and stabbing were all about.

Where France led, America was not slow to follow. By 1908 several homegrown companies were in hot competition and producing films hand over fist all over the New York City area. One of these, Vitagraph, undertook what for those days was a full-scale treatment of *Romeo and Juliet.* Since advertising budgets were small, it was deemed permissable to display the Vitagraph trademark prominently on the wall over Juliet's bed. Production costs, too, had to be watched. The Bathesda Fountain in Central Park served admirably for that "public place in Verona" where Tybalt and Mercutio cross swords. Since pictures that moved had first been used to tell a story only in 1903, with a pioneer epic called *The Great Train Robbery,* the Bard was well served. The production was no cruder of its kind than was many an early frontier performance of "live" Shakespeare in a tavern bar or a one-room school-house.

Perhaps encouraged by success with its first Shakespearean offering, Vitagraph tried again the following year. On December 25, 1909, it made America a Christmas present of a full-length *A Midsummer Night's Dream.* Surviving reviews do not even mention the players, but confine themselves to outlining the complex plot. Scenarios still were sufficiently clumsy to make it a good idea for a viewer to have a libretto at hand.

Meanwhile California was getting ready for a second dive into the entertainment world—one which would leave the gold-rush boom of the 1850s pale by comparison.

A respected citizen of Los Angeles, which by the late 1880s was a bustling city of 25,000 souls, had purchased a ranch seven miles beyond the city limits. On it, he intended to grow citrus fruit, apricots, and figs. His name was H. H. Wilcox, and he had a wife who loved to travel. On one of her frequent trips, Mrs. Wilcox struck up a train-passengers' acquaintance-ship with a wealthy easterner who frequently referred to her country place, Hollywood. The name so appealed to Mrs. Wilcox that upon her return to California she bestowed it upon her husband's rural acres.

With the passing of time, the ranch was subdivided into building lots. By the turn of the century, Hollywood had a population of five hundred. Ten years later, the pioneer movie producers discovered it. The first real studio built there was for the Nestor Company in 1911. And the rest is history.

Not until 1912 was the new dabbling with pictures that moved formally recognized as an art form. In that year, the aging Sarah Bernhardt made a film of *Queen Elizabeth,* and intellectuals who had never before entered a nickelodeon crowded to see her. "This is my one chance at immortality," she said, well aware of the ephemeral nature of the actor's art. It was posterity's loss that sound had not yet been coupled with motion in the studios. The famous *voix d'or* which so thrilled her audiences could not be preserved along with the shadow of a wooden-legged woman, no longer young but still a commanding actress, whose American tours had included performances of Cordelia in *King Lear* and of "the melancholy Dane" himself in a French version of *Hamlet.*

American audiences once having been forced by *Queen Elizabeth* to take the movies seriously, Adolph Zukor promptly and shrewdly began developing his idea for presenting picture versions of "famous players in famous plays"—an idea of which Paramount Pictures became the end result. The stage idol Minnie Maddern Fiske made her *Tess of the D'Urbervilles* for him. Geraldine Farrar made *Carmen.* And no one could scoff at the movies as before.

Once the medium had achieved this status, Will Shakespeare did not loiter long outside the studio gates. The romantic team of their day, Beverly Bayne and Francis X. Bushman, did a longer and more ambitious *Romeo and Juliet* in 1916. In competition, another prominent studio (Fox) filmed a second version of the play in the same year, incongruously offering their voluptuous "vampire," Theda Bara, as Shakespeare's fourteen-year-old heroine. The rivalry between the two films could not be whipped up, even by earnest press agents, into anything faintly approaching that of the Macready and Forrest Macbeths. Still, it was sufficient to establish the Bard as a Hollywood writer to be reckoned with.

Of all Shakespeare's plays, *Romeo and Juliet* has since proven cinematically the most popular. Although never attempting a full-scale Shakespearean film, Cecil B. De Mille in his 1924 picture *Triumph* did include a long "cutback" sequence with Rod La Rocque and Leatrice Joy as the star-crossed lovers. Well after the advent of sound, Irving Thalberg mounted an elaborate version for which he sent crews of researchers to Verona to authenticate every physical detail of his production, and in which he starred his wife, Norma Shearer, along with Leslie Howard, John Barrymore, and Basil Rathbone.

Shakespeare's early gains in Hollywood were counterbalanced at least in one instance by Shakespeare's loss on the stage. A rugged young Shakespearean leading man, who had appeared opposite such solid road stars of the day as Julia Arthur and Helena Modjeska, was persuaded in 1914 to quit his involvement with Macbeth, Othello, and Antony in favor of a career in films. However, his mission was not to repeat his classic roles on celluloid but to pioneer a new and instantly popular folk hero—the American cowboy. Hollywood's first great star of "horse operas," William S. Hart, never thereafter played a scene from Shakespeare. But he created a hero-type which still endures, and he made his own name a household synonym for the Great Open Spaces.

The richness of Shakespeare as a source for picture material made it all but inevitable that Hollywood luminaries not in the least suited to his roles should aspire to "get in on the act." In a 1922 film titled *Day Dreams,* concerned with an early-day Walter Mitty, the frozen-faced comedian Buster Keaton in one sequence portrayed a Hamlet such as was never seen before or since. Two of Hollywood's most enduring stars of the silent era, Mary Pickford and Douglas Fairbanks, attempted a version of *The Taming of the Shrew* which was a wide enough departure from Fairbanks's athletic adventure roles and Miss Pickford's previous versions of America's Sweetheart to prove a professional mistake for both.

In the late 1920s, the picture industry was turned upside down by the introduction into it of a new element—sound. Established stars whose voices could not match their looks faded overnight. New people, many of them from the stage, were rushed before the cameras. Within the two years following the 1927 release of Al Jolson's *The Jazz Singer*—the first full-length feature sound movie—the revolution was complete. Subtitles no longer flashed the essence of dialogue across the screen. Pianos in darkened orchestra pits no longer pounded stirringly as the hero rode to the rescue, or tinkled sentimentally as the baby died. The screen had surrendered itself, for good or ill, to talk.

In the case of Shakespeare, whose language had for centuries been the proudest jewel of English literature, the change was all for the good. Or almost all, for there were exceptions. Max Reinhardt's 1935 all-star production of *A Midsummer Night's Dream* proved "no masterpiece, but a brave, beautiful and interesting effort"—perhaps best summed up by the fact that the clowns, notably Joe E. Brown as Flute, "took the notices" from the players in the bigger roles. And in 1948 perhaps the most pretentious Shakespearean film ever made by Americans was a notable failure both with the critics and at the box office.

This ill-starred enterprise was the Orson Welles *Macbeth.* Welles had behind him a considerable reputation in the theatre and at least two outstandingly original motion pictures. His spokesmen announced that his new production would be "archaeologically correct" to life in ninth-century Scotland. Apparently, every effort was expended to make good on this claim. Since the actual Macbeth succeeded Duncan I as King of Scotland in 1040 and ruled until 1057, a mere decade before the Norman Conquest, exactly why the ninth century should have been so honored seemed something of a mystery. But it was not the only mystery posed by the production.

Welles introduced a priest into the action, thus improving upon Shakespeare, because Scotland's thanes of the period he was depicting were illiterate and Macbeth could not write. Macbeth dutifully dictated his fateful letter to his wife, but Milady had no trouble whatever in reading it. Welles dressed his king in shaggy furs and grotesque horns. Glamis Castle, a proud edifice in actuality, became a series of evil caverns, some with underground water trickling down their rough walls —an establishment King Duncan could not conceivably have termed a "pleasant seat" with "delicate" air. Worst of all, the characters addressed one another in absolutely authentic Highland accents! The studio for which Welles had produced the masterpiece hastily dubbed in a new sound track in intelligible English, but nothing could save the other unfortunate aspects of the film. It failed wretchedly with the public and (at least temporarily) ended its star's career in Hollywood.

On at least one occasion Hollywood has made splendid use of Shakespeare without actually filming a Shakespearean work. In a Ronald Colman picture called *A Double Life* the leading role was that of an actor gradually going insane. During the action, he gave three supposed performances of the strangling scene from *Othello:* one while the actor playing it was still normal, one after immersion in the role had begun to unsettle his reason, and a third in which he was unbalanced enough to intend Desdemona's actual death on stage. While the demands of the surrounding plot naturally altered the values of the famous scene as part of the play Shakespeare had imagined, the scene itself was superb material for an effective tour de force. There have also been straightforward Hollywood productions of Shakespeare which have shown considerable merit—for instance, the 1953 *Julius Caesar,* with Marlon Brando as its Antony.

It remained for an Englishman, however, to teach American picture audiences what filmed Shakespeare might be at its very best. Sir Laurence Olivier has made motion pictures of three plays which have been both brilliant artistically and enormous successes at the box office. In 1943, before the invasion of Normandy, he made *Henry V,* which provided an inspiring reminder of England's strength in a beleaguered hour. He produced, directed, and played the leading roles in *Hamlet* (1948) and *Richard III* (1955).

For the first time, a whole new audience in this country was shown the Shakespeare who had spoken so familiarly to their ancestors from the stages of a hundred years earlier. Here was a Shakespeare stripped of "snob appeal" and pomposity, of all the dreary overtones of assigned school homework. Here were intepretations of the originals, brilliantly mounted and sensitively acted. They were given the sweep and pace of the excellent, exciting stories which audiences had once known them to be. As one newspaper commentator put it: "By daring to believe Shakespeare could be popular, Sir Laurence raised the movie business to new dignity and won a unique place for himself in the history of modern art."

Naturally, the filming of such works presented its own special problems, often quite different from those of stage production. As star, producer, and director, Sir Laurence should be allowed to speak of them in his own words:

> Film technique is primarily visual. I felt it would be a safish rule to follow to imagine I was *illustrating* Shakespeare. The audience thus sees things that are only talked about in the play [*Richard III*] —the murder of the little princes, the drowning of Clarence in a barrel. . . .
>
> On the stage, the approach to Shakespeare is all in the music of it, the poetry. Shakespeare is something to hit the audience's *ear*. But the movie technique, aiming at the visual, has to be followed with great care and tact so that Shakespeare is not robbed of his essential virtue—his poetry. . . .
>
> It's right and proper to give [theatre audiences] Shakespeare pretty nearly in the full. But for a new movie audience . . . you must deal with the shape of the plot and the progress of the picture in a new way. By editing and transposing . . . you have to get the story flowing. . . .

The unquestionable soundness of Laurence Olivier's "safish rule" has been demonstrated in his three magnificent productions. They offer to movie-makers everywhere a shining example of how excellently Shakespeare may be put onto film, and of how genuinely, by the least highbrow of audiences, he may be enjoyed.

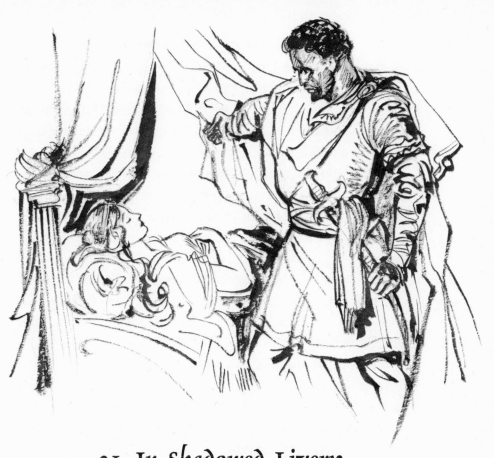

21. In Shadowed Livery

Little evidence survives that, in his lifetime, Will Shakespeare understood the members of the Negro race even so superficially as he understood the American Indian.

In writing his Moor of Venice, he seems to have recognized no ethnic differences between the Moors and other peoples out of Africa. He apparently considered Othello to be a Negro. Yet definitely there is no hint of bigotry in his attitude toward one of his most outstanding heroes. And when another of his darker-skinned characters, the Prince of Morocco, begs Portia in *The Merchant of Venice,* "Mislike me not for my complexion, The shadowed livery of the burnish'd sun," he might be phrasing—and eloquently—the basic plea of those working for American civil rights four centuries later.

That Negro interpreters of Shakespearean roles were late in appearing upon the American stage is not surprising. So long as Negroes were chattels even in the northern states they could have little opportunity to become familiar with theatre at all, let alone with its greatest classics. It is true that shortly after the Revolution, "an African boy" was known to have acted the role of a Capulet page in *Romeo and Juliet* (whether in New York or in Philadelphia is a disputed point). If he had talent, the brevity of this appearance failed to reveal it, and he was not heard from again.

Nor were any of his fellow American Negroes to be heard from in the theatre until the arrival in this country of the English actor Edmund Kean. In 1820, Kean crossed the Atlantic bringing his virtuosity in Shakespeare roles to awe and delight America's young cities. One setting for his initial American success was the Chatham Theatre in New York City, and there, as a result of an accidental backstage encounter, the greatest star of his day came face to face with Ira Frederick Aldridge.

Young Ira was still in his teens then, tall and husky, and he was working as a temporary stagehand at the Chatham. He was the son of a Negro freedman, who was preacher of a small church on Green Street. Ira himself was intended for the ministry, and was already entered at Schenectady College after a diligent course of studies at the African Free School. But once exposed to the stage, the young man recognized his only true love. The dedication, the untried talent, the emotional fire in him, must have revealed themselves to Kean where lesser eyes had failed to detect them. At any rate, the star had soon taken on the boy as a sort of apprentice.

Kean left New York to continue his tour and young Ira went with him, performing the duties of a body servant to pay his way while studying the incredible wonders the star could reveal to him. Any future as a missionary was forever forgotten. Even the grief of his parents could not deter him. Having met his destiny head on, he was both honest enough and intelligent enough not to betray it. With each engagement played by the company—in Boston, in Philadelphia, in Baltimore—Ira grew more and more into the world of the theatre; which, since it was the theatre of Edmund Kean, was also the theatre of Shakespeare.

When Kean returned to England in 1821, Ira still followed. For the next several years, preparing himself to be an actor, the young American had the great Kean as his tutor. It was at once the toughest and the most rewarding sort of training any neophyte could undergo. Kean's standards were exacting and would accept nothing less than excellence. This rugged apprenticeship was interrupted only once, for eighteen months, while Ira attended the University of Glasgow and won a medal for superior achievement in Latin. With the advantage of such training, no pupil possessed of his innate talent could have failed to make impressive strides toward his goal.

Talent Ira Frederick Aldridge unquestionably possessed. He had also been endowed by nature with a striking physique, an expressive grace of movement, a true dramatic instinct, and a voice which lent itself readily to the music and thunder of the Shakespearean phrase. By January 1827, his mentor considered him ready to face the public. Ira Aldridge played in *Othello* at London's Royalty Theatre, and his fame soared like a skyrocket. A successful engagement in Coburg was followed by another at Covent Garden, both in the role of the Moor. But Kean had trained him in the other great parts as well. When he took to the provinces on tour, young Aldridge gave them King Lear and Shylock for contrast. Nor was his repertoire exclusively Shakespeare. Kotzebue's then-standard *Pizarro* and other popular hits were included. One of his great successes was in a comedy role, as Mungo in *The Padlock.*

During the next decade he became a reigning favorite in virtually every capital of Europe—in Paris, Stockholm, Madrid, Berlin, and most especially in St. Petersburg. It was in Russia that the French poet-novelist, Théophile Gautier, saw his *Othello* and wrote of it: "His entrance on the stage was magnificent. It was Othello himself as Shakespeare had created him, with eyes half-closed as if dazzled from the African suns . . . and that . . . air that no European can imitate."

Aldridge partially repaid his debt to Shakespeare by reviving the all-but-forgotten *Titus Andronicus,* which had not been acted for a hundred years—and making a hit of it. Only Ireland was reluctant, at first, to accept him. But he played in Belfast (Othello to the Iago of Charles Kean, and Aboan to the same star's title role in Thomas Southerne's melodramatic *Oroonoko*) and the Irish soon were at his feet along with England and the Continent.

Such success could scarcely have failed to breed jealousy among actors less enthusiastically received. One of these, in a rash effort to remove competition, circulated a false rumor of Aldridge's death. It was widely reported that, while returning home from the country estate of a friend near Llandille,

Aldridge's carriage horses had become so frightened by the blazing glare of some ironworks near the road that they had bolted and plunged over a cliff, dragging carriage and driver with them. The news was a brief sensation. Newspapers published his obituaries, and an astonished Aldridge read them. His living presence of course refuted the tale, and it cannot greatly have benefited the envious rival who had invented it.

Aldridge was billed more frequently than under his given name as "The African Rosicus." As such, he was unquestionably one of the outstanding stars of his generation. Twice during his career, he was married; first to an English woman, and after her death to a Swedish baroness. This second alliance gave him a title, and in Continental society (although not in the theatre) he became known as Baron Aldridge. He and his second wife had three children. One daughter, Amanda, was musically gifted and in her youth studied under the great Jenny Lind. Toward the end of her long life, she was a distinguished teacher of music whose pupils included such American artists of her father's race as Marian Anderson and that Othello of a later generation, Paul Robeson. When he died, in 1867, Ira Aldridge had won public honors such as few of his profession could claim. The Czar of Russia had decorated him on numerous occasions; Prussia had bestowed upon him its seldom-awarded Medal of Arts and Sciences; in Austria, he had received the Grand Cross of Leopold.

The one flat failure of Ira Aldridge's professional life had been an attempt to repeat European successes in his native America. Some four years after his much-cheered London debut, and when Europe already had amply acknowledged his talent, he re-crossed the Atlantic for a reunion with his parents. It was his intention to act in some of the "good theatre towns" along the seaboard and show his countrymen what he had learned. Unfortunately, his countrymen were not interested. He played to small, unappreciative houses and to financial disaster. When he returned to Europe it was with the realization that his future as an actor would bloom only on foreign stages. In all the years of triumph which lay ahead, he did not come "home" again. Nor during the nineteenth century did American theatre welcome any other Negro performer with the enthusiasm Aldridge had aroused abroad.

By mid-century, *Uncle Tom's Cabin* had begun its long career as a supreme stage hit. But in all the "Tom shows" touring the nation, the beloved Uncle Tom and the hound-pursued Eliza were depicted by white actors in makeup. Along the Mississippi, showboats developed the minstrel show based directly upon Negro music and Negro humor. But white men with burnt cork on their faces plunked the banjos and answered to the calls for "Mr. Bones." Shakespeare had his place in all of this pseudo-Negro theatre, although he would scarcely have been overjoyed at the form it took. From early in the century on through the 1870s, a spate of parodies of his plays appeared as parts of several series of published "Ethiopian dramas," put out primarily for amateur production.

Hamlet was the chief victim. One winces to think how many audiences in America's small towns witnessed productions of *Hamlet the Dainty*. *The Case of Dr. Macbeth* also had its hours on stage, as did kindred burnt-cork versions, supposedly hilarious, of Shylock's misfortunes and *A Comedy of Errors*. Sometimes, these burlesques carried political overtones, as when in San Francisco in 1876 *The Hamlet Travestie* hooted at Samuel Tilden, Ulysses Grant, and Roscoe Conkling, all then in the public eye. Sometimes, they had social or professional implications—as in another *Hamlet* parody in Philadelphia, in the 1830s, which took off the quack medical practices of that day.

There is an implied compliment to Will Shakespeare in the fact that wide public knowledge of his works had to be assumed, otherwise how was the public expected to get the point of all this jollity? But the parodies show no link between his talent and that of the true Negroes. They were white man's fun, white-written and white-acted.

The increase of realism and experimentation in the theatre which began in the early 1900s actually brought American Negroes into their own in the theatre. When a playwright like Eugene O'Neill created *The Great God Brown,* when *The Green Pastures* became the hit of its season, when *Anna Lucasta, Mamba's Daughters,* and other plays of their kind gave Negro actors a chance to show what they could do with serious modern drama, and when a successful musical like *Show Boat* with its immortal "Ol' Man River" gave Negro stars opportunity to shine, then the Negro performer did begin to come into his own as an integral part of our theatre.

It was not yet time, however, for Shakespeare's plays to become a part of this forward surge. The classic roles had for too long appeared to offer an insurmountable stumbling block in the matter of color. Generations to whom Ira Frederick Aldridge was no longer even a remembered name regarded the casting of Negroes in these roles as impossible. But in the end, Shakespeare's universality overcame this obstacle.

Modestly, the advance began with Little Theatre groups across the country—of which several excellent ones were Negro organizations. The drama students at Negro colleges began to undertake productions of Shakespeare, and to do well with them. In the late 1920s in Hartford, Connecticut, an organization called the Charles Gilpin Dramatic Club, after the distinguished Negro actor, staged successful readings of *The Merchant of Venice.* Most members of the group worked hard at regular jobs during the day, but there was no compromise with quality in the devoted work they gave to their stage activities at night. Shakespeare awed them no more than had O'Neill and Ibsen. They were interested in the best,. and here it was.

The commercial theatre, as so often happens, lagged behind. But in July 1936, at New York's Adelphi Theatre, the recently organized Federal Theatre did an all-Negro *Macbeth,* with a company of 150 actors and 25 musicians, which created a theatrical furor. The physical background of the play was shifted from Scotland to Haiti, and its historic period changed from King Duncan's day to Napoleon's. Its costuming was lavish enough to satisfy the Empress Josephine herself, and the adaptation of Highland moors to tropical jungle, of witchcraft to voodoo, seemed not at all incongruous with Shakespeare's lines and dramatic intent.

At almost the same time, *Othello* was being played to Broadway audiences with a Negro Othello for the first time since Aldridge's day. Paul Robeson was the Moor, Uta Hagen the Desdemona, José Ferrer the Iago. Margaret Webster, responsible for the production, ruefully records in her book *Shakespeare Without Tears* that it took five years to get this production on stage. But it was more than merely "accepted" by the public. It broke the record of number of performances for any Shakespearean play ever staged in America.

A Shakespearean experiment of the early 1960s was a two-actor production called *The Worlds of Shakespeare,* with a pair of experienced Negro performers, Earle Hyman and Vinnie Burrows. Marchette Chute, distinguished for her writing about the Bard, wove this sampler together from his plays primarily for a tour of colleges, but it played a limited New York engagement with Miss Burrows appearing as Rosalind, as the shy Katherine from *Henry V,* as a chilling Lady Macbeth, and as Cressida of the seldom-acted *Troilus and Cressida.* Mr. Hyman's roles included Othello as well as the opposite numbers to all Miss Burrows' ladies. Although *The New York Times* observed that the production "suffers from the ills that compendiums are heir to," the critics were enthusiastic. They noted that the two performers were "poised, attractive and spirited" and that "at the best, they soar brilliantly with throbbing exchanges" and act "with uncommon skill and taste."

Surely one of the least orthodox performances of Shakespeare in history has been the unique contribution of one of his American Negro interpreters, the actor Ted Butler. A Broadway veteran, Butler learned through experience the frequent economic uncertainties of his chosen profession. To support his family, he took on a second job with the New York Transit Authority. After the final curtain of a current show, he would remove his makeup, hurry home to Brooklyn to change into his subway conductor's uniform and be ready by 1:30 A.M. for duty on the "A" train. From then until 9:30, when he returned home to sleep until theatre time, passengers in his sparsely filled cars could listen in at will while Butler unconcernedly rehearsed Shakespearean roles. His excellent trained voice rose clearly above the clacking of wheels on rails. Not in the least abashed by the amazement of his audience— many of them regulars who came to expect and enjoy his "performances"—Butler explained calmly, "First time I tried it, the riders thought I was crazy. You see a lot of unusual things on the subway at that hour of the morning. But how often does a conductor recite poetry?"

22. Temple to a Titan

The ways in which Americans have arrived at a feeling of kinship with William Shakespeare have been almost as varied as the Americans themselves. Lincoln came to know him through reading his works aloud in a frontier cabin; Washington through seeing the plays performed amid the social pleasures of Colonial Virginia; John Adams through study in a New England gentleman's library; Solomon Smith through being carried on stage in a property coffin. The start of Henry Clay Folger's lifelong dedication to the Bard was a result of one teacher's revelations in one specific place. The teacher was Ralph Waldo Emerson, visiting lecturer; the time was 1878; and the place was the campus of Amherst College in Massachusetts.

Directly upon his graduation, young Folger went into the oil business—he was friend and classmate to a son of one of John D. Rockefeller's original partners in this field. Presently, in his off hours, he was working toward a law degree at Columbia University. In 1885 he married a Vassar graduate, Miss Emily Jordan, who fully shared the enthusiasm for Shakespeare which had never dimmed in Folger since that Emerson lecture. Modestly at first, they began building together a collection of Shakespeare materials.

The first Folger purchase—for $1.75—was a facsimile reproduction (1876) of the Roberts Folio. This humble item started its young owners on a career as Shakespearean students, collectors and bibliographers which years later would see them add the original Roberts Folio to a library already including many rarities of even greater distinction.

Their avocation was to last Emily and Henry Folger half a century. It widely increased in scope as Folger mounted the financial ladder to an ultimate presidency and board chairmanship of the Standard Oil Company of New York.

Childless, the Folgers lived unostentatiously. They centered their full attention upon the development of what very soon began to be a truly important collection. They, and their agents, combed Europe for available material by Shakespeare and about him. Gradually, the collection widened to include material on other Elizabethan literary figures—Christopher Marlowe, Ben Jonson, Francis Bacon—and on the period itself, the golden era in which this man who was their central interest had worked and lived.

As treasures were uncovered and purchased, they were crated and shipped to America, here to be stored away in bank vaults and warehouses, out of reach even of the Folgers themselves. Almost from the first, their ambition had been to build a proper repository for their treasures; a temple in America, as it were, to the Titan of English literature. The ultimate aim of the collection, as Henry Folger himself described it, was "to help make the United States a center for literary study and progress."

Mr. Folger was an American businessman, one of a breed too often sneered at by intellectual snobs, caricatured in fiction, depicted as blind worshipers of the Almighty Dollar. This fact made all the more significant his dedication to the unmaterial goal he had set himself. He brought to his labors, of course, the techniques of an excellent business training. Until he was ready to put them into action, he was careful never to reveal his plans to possible competitors. Having uncovered some Shakespeare rarity, he and Mrs. Folger would move with quiet discretion to acquire it. Very few men in America, even among Shakespearean scholars, had any idea of the true magnitude of the task the Folgers were performing.

As their purchases reached this country and were stored away in safekeeping, the Folgers kept a complete record of them in a manuscript notebook. Otherwise, not even they themselves could have kept accurate track of their collection —the early editions of plays and poems; the plays wrongfully attributed to Shakespeare by sixteenth- and seventeenth-century publishers greedy to profit from his popularity; the rare works of other Elizabethan and Jacobean authors; the priceless manuscript materials; the autograph letters from famous writers, down through the intervening centuries, who had commented upon Shakespeare; the prompt books used by great actors of the roles; the playbills; the programs; the portraits; the costumes; the stage properties with special significance; the statues and prints and drawings; the models of old stages; the scrapbooks. With the single exception of the Henry E. Huntington Library founded at San Marino, California, in 1919, no such effort to assemble Shakespeareana even had been attempted in the United States, until the Folgers began their labors.

Not until the 1920s did they consider their collection ready for the quarters they always had planned would one day house it. What they envisioned was a place where the wealth of materials they had amassed would be available; where those scholars best equipped to make use of it might enrich American culture. For nine years, moving with their usual quiet purposefulness, the Folgers acquired title to piece after piece of the land in Washington, D.C., which lay adjacent to the Library of Congress, within a brief walk of the Capitol, and nearby the Supreme Court. And here in 1932—on the anniversary of Shakespeare's birth and in the presence of President Herbert Hoover, his Cabinet, and other dignitaries—was finally dedicated the building to house the great collection which Mr. Folger had called a "fine kit of tools for the proper study of Shakespeare." Folger himself did not live to see the dedication day. But he had participated with his wife in the laying of the cornerstone, almost two years earlier.

Henry Folger's will still further advanced his dream of providing a proper place for the study of Shakespeare in the United States. He made certain that his library would not degenerate into a dusty mausoleum or a mere storage facility, by naming the trustees of Amherst College to administer the project. His reasoning was that his cherished life work would best be carried on and expanded by a body of men who valued education and who were already giving their time and skills to advance American scholarship. He provided that in return for its services the college should receive approximately one quarter of the annual income from the Shakespeare Fund he had established. Thus he made sure that men truly concerned with the spread of learning, and who genuinely appreciated Shakespeare's literary genius, would be in charge.

The Folger Library, designed by Paul Philippe Cret, is a bold architectural concept. Its exterior is of marble, classic and pure, blending well with its governmental neighbors. It features nine panel-reliefs picturing various great scenes in the Shakespeare plays. But the interior design is completely Elizabethan, its tone set by the main reading room, built to resemble the great hall of an Elizabethan manor. Around this are ranged vaults for the storage of rarities, library stacks, individual study rooms, staff offices, a photographic laboratory, and a room for the binding and repairing of treasures in imperfect condition. There is also an exhibition gallery, intended for displays of material interesting to the general public. A final important component is a complete theatre constructed after the plans of those in Shakespeare's own day, where concerts and lectures and even full-length plays may be given.

Into this handsome building, the priceless Folger collection was moved by truck from the vaults and warehouses where it had awaited completion of its permanent home. Well over two thousand wooden boxes were transported in a six-months-long "moving day." Nine more months were required to open the boxes and appraise their varied contents. Years were to pass before a precise catalog would be available. But by the time the library opened on a limited basis for the use of accredited scholars, in January 1933, it was already recognized that one of our world's most important and exhaustive collections of material on Shakespeare and his world had been assembled.

As a research center for work on the man and his period, the Folger possibly outranks even the great British Museum in London. England's respected *Manchester Guardian* described the library as "a positive powerhouse." A highly trained staff can produce from its files any requested document in, generally speaking, the remarkably brief time of five minutes. Since Folger's own death, and Mrs. Folger's in 1936, the library has kept on in the way they showed—constantly alert to broaden and enrich its already fabulous resources. Several years ago, it announced as one of its objectives the acquisition of a copy of every book printed in England before the year 1700.

Many of the volumes already in the Folger Library's possession are the only known copies of works, or of particular editions, to have survived. One example is the sole existing copy of the 1594 *Titus Andronicus,* first of all Shakespeare's plays to be set in print. Another is a First Folio copy inscribed by its printer, William Jaggard, to Augustine Vincent, the herald who had obtained the grant of Shakespeare's coat-of-arms. A third is the only full set of the 1619 Jaggard-Pavier quartos to have survived in seventeenth-century binding. A full listing would require its own fat volumes.

The predominating object of the lifetime Henry and Emily Folger invested in their collection was, of course, to make their treasures available for serious study. To accomplish this, a three-fold program was early begun at the library. The research center proper was functioning even before the Folger's formal opening. Two further means of carrying out the original purpose were soon added.

A publications program made it possible that the "Folger Booklets on Tudor and Stuart Civilization" might be written, published, and distributed. Each of these booklets, researched by a competent authority from the Folger's own riches of materials, covers some specific phase of the indicated period. Their titles to date range from *Schools in Tudor England,* through *English Dress in the Age of Shakespeare,* to *The Bible in English, 1525–1611,* and *The Art of War and Renaissance England.* A second series, "Folger Documents of Tudor and Stuart Civilization," reprints rare original books and manuscripts, among them Henry Peacham's *The Art of Living in London* and Richard Eburne's *Plain Pathway to Plantations.*

The second means of accomplishing the basic objective of the library is a studied campaign to attract qualified scholars to the Folger's doors. The rise of its financial resources had enabled it to make grants to promising research fellows, both from America and abroad. By financing travel and other necessities, it has drawn a steady procession of scholarly specialists to study rooms where its treasures can be put to use.

Not only scholars but the general public as well have been made welcome at the Folger Library. In its Elizabethan theatre, a continuing schedule of allied events—lectures, readings, concerts—has been offered. In its gallery, visitors may view ever-changing exhibits culled from the collections. Its paperback editions of Shakespeare's plays, and its program of public information, have served school classes across the nation.

The expansion of this huge Shakespeare collection still continues. To a certain extent, the Folger's entire staff share in the hunt, but Eleanor Pitcher, the chief purchaser of new materials, is the foremost expert. A world authority on the period, she spends months abroad on her searches. One great advantage she possesses is the Folger system of payment for purchases, another benefit of its founder's business experience. Whereas most museums and libraries must consult boards or committees and submit invoices to complex financial departments, the Folger's representative can render a decision and a payment within a week. This is an obvious advantage where dealers must often pay high bank interest on the funds invested in their merchandise.

Thus, the wedding of practical business methods to ideals of the highest scholarship have produced for America a Shakespearean "headquarters" second to no other in the world. Henry and Emily Folger and the devoted men and women who now carry on for them have given to their country a priceless cultural treasure; and to Will of Stratford, a New World home befitting his bright genius.

23. Three Times Stratford

By the three-hundredth anniversary of his birth—on April 23, 1864—the little Warwickshire town of Stratford-on-Avon was well aware of the enduring quality of the world's homage to its most distinguished son. Through the years, reverent demonstrations had been staged there to honor Will Shakespeare; notably, one in 1769 presided over by the great David Garrick. But in 1864 it was decided to hold a mammoth Shakespeare Tercentenary Festival.

It lasted a week and more, with the town decked in bunting and banners, the visitors pouring in by uncounted thousands, formal balls and banquets, performances of the plays with brilliant guest players, and a fancy-dress gala where dancing continued until five in the morning. A monster fireworks display climaxed in a set piece called *The Vision of Shakespeare,* which showed the Swan's portrait "*formed of many thousand lights, and gigantic Transparent Effects.*" A pageant featured a Grand Military Band and a Grand Triumphal Car on which Shakespeare rode at the apex of a living pyramid of his famous characters. The crowds were enthusiastic, but at the end of it all, the committee in charge discovered that the great event had lost two thousand pounds for its backers!

This sobering financial fact bred modesty in attempts to honor the Bard thereafter. Not until 1879 was the first Shakespeare Memorial Theatre built in Stratford, replacing a Royal Shakespearean Theatre which had been torn down in 1872. The new structure was erected with funds raised by a national appeal, on a marshy two-acre riverfront site donated by an enthusiastic townsman. It was completed in 1884, with seats for seven hundred people, and its initial ten-day season— featuring *Much Ado about Nothing, Hamlet,* and *As You Like It*—was a reasonable success. Stratford was then just coming into its own, with the birthplace lately rescued from Mr. Barnum's predatory schemes and safely presented to the nation.

For several Aprils thereafter, an annual "festival" of plays continued in modest style beside the English Avon. But between 1885 and 1919 (when the project was headed by a vigorous actor named Francis Robert Benson) its fortunes flourished. Benson sometimes managed to set as many as twenty different plays upon the theatre's stage in a single festival. A Silver Jubilee in 1904 stretched the season to three weeks, and in 1910 a summer season was added for the tourist trade. Even during World War I, Benson managed to keep the festival going, and in 1916 was knighted for his achievements.

By the mid-twenties, the Festival Company had toured Canada, the United States, and South Africa, had played before British royalty, and had been invited to act in Oslo's State Theatre before the Norwegian King and Queen. The first Memorial Theatre (George Bernard Shaw had dubbed it a "Victorian atrocity") was destroyed by fire in 1926, and was replaced by a new structure financed by subscription and opened by the Prince of Wales on April 23, 1932. Contributions from Americans alone accounted for almost two-thirds of the full sum raised, an impressive tribute indeed to an adopted son of the New World.

Since the opening of the new building, the festival's progress has been more spectacular. A continuous season from April to September became a reality in 1935. During World War II, even though audiences were required to carry gas masks to performances, attendance figures steadily increased. Mounting receipts, coupled with mounting prestige and the acquisition of two London theatres in which to offer winter runs of its productions, have established the Shakespeare Memorial Theatre as an assured fixture of the English stage.

This example was the inspiration for two almost simultaneous projects to achieve similar homes for Shakespeare on American soil. Both Canada and the United States saw the launching, quite independently, of drives to achieve what already had been achieved for Master Will in Warwickshire. It was the Canadian project which first succeeded in ringing up its curtain.

In the Province of Ontario's wide southern farmland, a small railroad shop city of some sixteen thousand population bore the name of Stratford. It even boasted a small stream meandering through it, called the Avon. And only five miles distant on Route Eight lay the village of Shakespeare. None of these names had been bestowed because of any theatrical or literary connection, but were simply survivals of a somewhat flowery real estate scheme of the nineteenth century. Still, one energetic and visionary young businessman of the city began to imagine the potential success—the boost to local prestige— of a Shakespeare festival.

When he had committed his project to paper, it became clear that at least $150,000 would be needed to make it an actuality. He set about communicating his own enthusiasm to others, and did this so successfully that Stratford sources alone provided $70,000 of the required sum. As news of the project spread, so did the enthusiasm. Some eighty Canadian actors signed up to participate in the first season. Local Sea Scouts volunteered to provide the drums for parade scenes. And problems mounted along with the public zest: Stratford was a hundred miles from any theatre center, and costumes and properties would have to be manufactured in shops with no theatrical experience; housing for all those arriving to work on the undertaking must be arranged; and transportaion must be organized.

It was early decided that the festival would run five weeks and that the theatre to house it would be a tent in one of Stratford's pretty parks. Work on the tent was in itself a staggering undertaking. It was to seat an audience of fourteen hundred. Its stage was to have no proscenium, but a narrow apron projecting into the audience, a layout on which could be constructed a permanent formalized setting of steps and wooden columns with a balcony level above. The arrangement was not unlike that of London playhouses in the Bard's own day.

If the stage was to be Elizabethan, the lighting most certainly was not. It was to be high-powered and modern, so that its use could account for many scene changes. The rest of the scenic effects would be achieved through use of magnificent costumes and properties, from which the productions would derive their color. The opening plan, *Richard III,* demonstrated how successful this plan could be by literally filling the stage during a typical scene with King Richard's magnificent scarlet coronation robe.

Stratford dedicated itself to its undertaking with a sort of community frenzy. The first festival season was to include, in addition to *Richard III,* a production of *All's Well That Ends Well.* It was agreed from the first that top leading actors and a top director would be needed. Alec Guinness was persuaded to star, with Irene Worth as his Queen Margaret and his Helena. Tyrone Guthrie the English actor-producer, seemed ideal as director; and on being asked by trans-Atlantic telephone if he would consider the position, Guthrie became so imbued with Stratford's enthusiasm that he agreed to accept. But during the conversation a temporary break in the connection occurred while his salary was under discussion.

He arrived in Canada ready to work but without the slightest idea what he was to be paid for his services!

Opening night for that first festival was July 13, 1953. As the appointed hour arrived and the park filled with an expectant audience, all the factory whistles in the city blew and all the church bells rang. A flourish of trumpets summoned the spectators to their seats. At 8:15 P.M. exactly, a rocket gun was fired, spraying the sky over Stratford with synthetic stars —and the play was on. Nothing could dampen the enormous elation of all those who had toiled to bring the infant festival into being, not even the incessant hooting of engines from the many rail lines converging on the city. Guinness is reported to have said, next day, "The only train in Canada that didn't whistle was the one I wore in Act III."

Richard III was a rousing success with audiences and critics alike. It was followed in due course by the second festival play, *All's Well That Ends Well,* done in a sort of modern-Edwardian style, very elegant and sophisticated, with Guinness as the French King. The whole complex operation of planning, preparing, rehearsing, and performing had been recorded by motion picture cameras, and from this footage a film called *The Stratford Adventure* was assembled and widely distributed —forming excellent publicity for what already had been decided upon as a continuing effort.

The second festival, in 1954, ran nine weeks instead of five. This time, James Mason with his great screen following was the visiting star. The plays were *Measure for Measure, The Taming of the Shrew* and a non-Shakespearean third, the *Oedipus Rex* of Sophocles. In addition, an exhibition tracing the history of theatre was put on view, and a short drama course was offered. In 1955, with a "no-star" policy decided upon but with Tyrone Guthrie still directing, a Stratford Music Festival was organized to supplement the plays—*Julius Caesar, The Merchant of Venice,* and a revived *Oedipus Rex.*

By 1956, the Stratford festival was a proven venture and its permanence a matter of concern both to Canadians and to theatre folk elsewhere. In this season, the model for a permanent home to replace the canvas tent was on display, and a drive to raise the necessary $984,000 was under way. Tentative a few years back, the Ontario Provincial Government now proudly involved itself to the extent of a $100,000 appropriation. Foundations and individuals and business concerns and cultural organizations carried the drive forward. In this same year, the festival invaded New York City with Christopher Marlowe's *Tamburlaine the Great,* the first time in the 350 years since its debut that this maiden work of another great Elizabethan dramatist had achieved production on the North American continent.

The strikingly original permanent theatre was up and ready for the 1957 festival. Much the same stage arrangement as before had been retained, but the handsome house afforded a much increased seating capacity, including a balcony, and lavish backstage areas. *Hamlet* and *Twelfth Night* were the attractions; and the season also included opera, jazz, and a film festival. Continuing success and experimentation in each season since suggests that eventually almost every play that Shakespeare wrote will "strut its hour" upon Canada's Stratford on Avon stage.

Meanwhile, to the south and east, others had been dreaming much the same dream. The chief dreamer, in this case, was a man already a lifetime deep in theatre. Lawrence Langner, out of Wales and then England, came to the United States as a young man. He bowed to his family's wishes in the matter of his career just long enough to establish here one of the most important patent law firms in the world. Having thus satisfied their professional hopes for him, he turned to his real enthusiasm—the stage.

By 1914, he was founding the Washington Square Players, an experimental group from which emerged much of the vital new theatre talent of its day. From there he went on to organize the famous Theatre Guild, which became American producer for George Bernard Shaw, Eugene O'Neill, and other respected playwrights. It was Langner who, among other hits, set *Oklahoma!* on the stage. In Connecticut, he became owner and operator of the Westport Country Playhouse, one of the first and best of American summer theatres; and was the author of numerous plays and books concerned with the drama.

Langner's dream, crystalizing into a determination, was to create in the United States a center where Shakespeare could be performed and Shakespearean actors could be trained in techniques far different from those of the "realistic" commercial stage. In 1952, a year before Canada's Stratford Festival was launched, he had made his idea into at least a corporate reality. Connecticut's State Legislature had passed an act chartering The American Shakespeare Festival Theatre and Academy.

Enthusiasm for the project was widespread, but costs were high. It took several years to gather in sufficient private contributions, foundation and corporation grants, and gifts from interested organizations, to pay the initial expenses. But a site was chosen early. Naturally, it was at Stratford—this time, Stratford, Connecticut. The river that met Long Island Sound at the point where the building would rise was not another Avon, however, but the Housatonic.

By July 1955, the theatre was standing where Langner had envisioned it and its doors were opening. *Julius Caesar,* with Raymond Massey, Jack Palance, Christopher Plummer, Hurd Hatfield, and Roddy McDowell, and *The Tempest* with the same players, were the first season's attractions, followed in 1956 by *King John, Measure for Measure* and *The Taming of the Shrew;* and in 1957 by *Othello, The Merchant of Venice* and *Much Ado about Nothing,* with the company headed by Katharine Hepburn and Alfred Drake. His project now was well launched, yet Langner's aims for the Festival were still far from being realized. To him, an American center for Shakespeare required more than an annual season of productions, however well received. One project of equal importance, right from the beginning, was the establishment of an academy where novice actors could learn their craft; where professional entertainers from other fields could do advanced work in classic acting. Jack Landau, the director of the school, explaining its aims in its first season, said: "Shakespeare is the bible, although we teach other fundamental texts and techniques, too." And: "The expressive verse and the style of Shakepeare's plays demand acting of great virtuosity, a controlled body, voice and imagination, and an appreciation of period and cultural background."

Students at the summer sessions of the academy, taking up residence at Stratford, were instructed by professionals acting with the festival company and in a few cases were invited to join the company themselves. Others won opportunities to understudy roles in festival productions, or to appear as extras in the plays. Training courses also were offered to hopeful directors and stage technicians. A school fencing master instructed in the art of swordplay so essential to Shakespeare's dramas.

Winter and spring terms for the academy were soon established at quarters in New York City and still continue. Here, advanced students explore the "color of words" to aid them in developing the full-bodied speech required for reading Shakespeare's lines. Speech taught at the academy, however, is American, not British, in keeping with the project's over-all purpose of establishing a truly American Shakespeare center. Body movement as well as vocal interpretation is stressed in the curriculum, as are singing, dancing, and verse-reading. There are even class sessions in such phases of the art as the wearing of elaborate period costumes with ease and authority. This last line of instruction was found to be advisable when the festival's *King John* costumes were issued to the cast. Three noblemen and seven soldiers fainted at the dress parade, under the bulk and weight of their heavily padded armor. Special ventilation had to be introduced into their helmets and boots.

Its own academy apprentices are not the only students in whom the festival takes an interest. In order to familiarize young scholars in general with on-stage Shakespeare, it has instituted a Student Audience Program. Busloads of undergraduates from schools and colleges scattered thoughout the ten eastern states most easily accessible to Stratford have been brought in, spring and fall, to attend major Shakespearean productions at reduced student prices. Study materials are sent out to them in advance by the festival, and opportunities provided at Stratford for informal question-and-answer sessions with the actors. This system has proven an excellent antidote to the traditional dry techniques of the classroom, and has inspired wide enthusiasm for the plays. Some seventy thousand students, in 1962, saw the spring production of *Henry IV,* Part I; while an additional sixty thousand visited Stratford in the fall for performances of *Richard II.* By the end of the program's fourth season, an estimated half-million students had been thus exposed to the Bard in living terms. A Shakespeare Student Guild, joined by many young visitors, sustains the enthusiasm through the year by means of a newsletter and other publications.

In keeping with its aim to establish an American classic theatre which would be truly national, and to train new acting talent for it, the festival in 1960 undertook its first countrywide tour, taking its production of *A Midsummer Night's Dream*— which featured Bert Lahr as the clown, Bottom—to thirteen cities from Boston to San Francisco. In October 1961, Shakespeare was formally acted for the first time in the White House at Washington when President and Mrs. John F. Kennedy invited the festival to play an evening of scenes from its productions in the East Room. A special stage was erected for the event and the audience was one of national officials.

Encouraged by this accolade, the festival promptly announced its hope of presenting Will Shakespeare with a Four Hundredth Birthday present in his quadricentennial year of 1964. It was to be a new Student Center at Stratford on Housatonic, joined to the existing playhouse by gardens and an arcade, which would contain lecture and classroom facilities, a costume workshop, and a gallery for the display of the festival's excellent art collection on Shakespeare—representations in sculpture and on canvas of great actors of the past in their most famous Shakespearean roles.

Thus, in two Stratfords on this continent, the basic purposes of the original festival in Warwickshire have been adapted to varying circumstances and then carried forward. Will's good friend, Ben Jonson, wrote of him that he was "not of an age, but for all time." In Stratford, Connecticut, and Stratford, Canada, his continuing role in an Atomic Age is being insured.

24. The Poet in the Park

Will Shakespeare got his first clear look at New York City's Central Park (much later to become his home in a particular sense) in 1872.

This was the year when the pensive statue of him wrought by John Quincy Adams Ward was set up facing a Mall then only recently come into existence. A dedicated sculptor, who in his raw Ohio youth had cried, "I want to see every statue that has even been made!" Ward was already represented in the Park by his celebrated bronze, *Indian Hunter*. New Yorkers had known him even earlier. As brilliant young pupil to Henry Kirke Brown, he had assisted with Brown's famed equestrian statue of George Washington in Union Square— once saying, "I spent more days inside that horse than Jonah did inside the whale!" Ward's Shakespeare was a work of patient love, a work for which Edwin Booth was his consulting expert in such matters as the arrangement of the Bard's garments.

The statue had been a favorite project with theatre folk for nearly ten years. Edwin Booth had acted to assist it in more than an advisory capacity. As early as the spring of 1864, he had put on a performance of *Romeo and Juliet* at the Winter Garden for the benefit of the statue fund. And on November 24, 1864, he made an even greater Booth contribution. All three of the Grand Old Man's actor sons on that night appeared together, for the one and only time in their entire careers, in a benefit performance of *Julius Caesar*. The younger Junius played Cassius with a perfect aristocratic dignity. Edwin cast himself as Brutus, and his younger brother John Wilkes as the fiery, rabble-rousing Antony, a role for which Wilkes was ideally suited. The program for this dramatic event, which packed the Winter Garden to its rafters, declared that the evening's purpose on the part of the brilliant triumvirate was "to do honor to the immortal bard from whose works the genius of their father caught its inspiration, and of many of whose greatest creations he was the best and noblest illustrator the stage has ever seen." From a stage box, the old star's widow, Mary Ann, watched with pride as her three sons made their first entrance side by side to a deafening ovation.

At each curtain, the crowd went wild. Many of its two thousand members would be shouting for Booth blood four short months later, after President Lincoln's murder in Ford's Theatre. But this night was all glory.

Eight years in creation, the statue for which the Booths and many another of the profession had worked so hard finally stood in its place. It was dedicated before a crowd of six thousand people on May 23, 1872. William Cullen Bryant delivered an oration, standing before a pavilion gay with the wind-stirred flags of thirty-nine nations.

Almost half a century was to pass before another obeisance to Will of Stratford was made in Central Park. The three hundred fiftieth anniversary of the poet's birth was widely celebrated in 1916; and nowhere more elaborately than in the city of New York. A "community masque" titled *Caliban by the Yellow Sands* was planned for the celebration—"the largest dramatic spectacle ever given in New York." Citywide enthusiasm was tremendous. A "little army" of volunteers from "all classes of society . . . labored faithfully to achieve a common purpose."

Starred in the role of Shakespeare himself was the stage favorite John Drew. The chief characters of the allegory were those of *The Tempest*—Caliban, Prospero, Ariel, and Miranda. Prospero first made a prisoner of Caliban, the archetype of brutishness, and then lifted him to the level of civilized humanity by displaying before his astonished eyes a pageant of ennobling scenes from Shakespeare. Stars acting in the scenes (without pay) included Robert Mantell, Emanuel and Hedwig Reich, E. F. Mackay, Margaret Wycherly, and Edith Wynne Matthison—all noted interpreters of Shakespearean roles.

The stadium of the College of the City of New York was reconstructed for the event into a giant open-air auditorium in which there was room for seventeen thousand spectators. On the immense three-fold stage, two thousand performers could appear at once. Over the proscenium of the inner stage was accommodation for a full symphony orchestra, plus a large chorus of singers. Boxes were sold at auction for substantial sums, and advertisements mentioned "miles of seats."

Unfortunately, the gigantic effort in many ways fell short of expectations. The lines of the play were inaudible to most of the occupants of those "miles of seats." As theatre, critics could only treat it with regretful candor: "There is no humor, no suspense, no excitement, no sensuousness, no grotesqueness in the entire composition." Worse still, it was difficult for an audience in that particular year—when the very real brutishness of war was sweeping over Europe—to accept the masque's premise with much seriousness.

Caliban was by no means the only fare provided by a Shakespeare Tercentenary Celebration Committee headed by Mayor John P. Mitchel himself. A series of special Shakespeare supplements appeared week after week in *The New York Times*. For the benefit of Armenian and Syrian war victims, *Hamlet* was presented in Arabic. The German-language press of the city lauded the Bard himself, even while bitterly denouncing his homeland. And in Central Park, a Shakespeare Garden was planted under the guidance of Shakespearean scholar and naturalist Edmond Bronk Southwick.

Two rocky hillside acres on the western side of the park were dedicated to the project. It was calculated that 180 trees, flowers, and shrubs had been mentioned throughout the poet's works. A worldwide search was undertaken to secure specimens of as many of these as possible. A bust of Shakespeare in marble was set up in the garden, donated by the city's Shakespeare Club. Henry Clay Folger made a large gift to finance the garden's maintenance. As botanical specimens arrived, the project took form. Stratford oaks were transplanted from the banks of the Avon. Rue, balm, mint, ash, rhubarb, wild thyme, lavender, yew, the red rose of Lancaster, the white rose of York, bittersweet, flax, savory, eglantine, woodbine, primrose, cowslip, columbine—an earnest effort was made not to overlook the humblest or the most exotic.

The city's populace was enthusiastic about the undertaking, but the uncertain climate of the region was not cooperative. Almost immediately, soot and bitter winters began to take their toll of many of the more delicate specimens. Chill winds did their worst with the orange and lemon trees. Others of the tenderer growths shriveled and disappeared. And, as is likely to be the case with sentimental understakings, public interest soon shifted elsewhere. The city's Park Commission grew indifferent. The garden's list of Shakespearean plants diminished sharply, so that today only a fraction of its original entries survive. And even these have been corrupted by the introduction of fancy chrysanthemums, Dorothy Perkins roses, and other intruders of which Will never heard. When some vandal chipped the nose off the marble bust, the authorities did not see fit to replace it.

The only memorial truly befitting a living genius is a living memorial; one, in Shakespeare's instance, involving the human audiences for which his plays were written. For this sort of testimonial to his enduring participation in the life of New York, Will Shakespeare waited eighty-odd years after his first arrival in Central Park. But when it came at last—in the form of the altogether unique New York Shakespeare Festival—it proved worth waiting for.

The man with the arresting idea for this venture was a young television stage manager named Joseph Papp. Wholehearted personal involvement with theatre had convinced him that the sort of productions Broadway had arrived at, by 1954, were both beyond the means of the Bard's potential audience and too formalized for it. Himself a New Yorker, Papp dreamed of bringing free Shakespeare to the citizens of his city; Shakespeare plays stripped, as originally they had been, of all unnecessary trappings. To this end, he first organized a Shakespeare Workshop with headquarters in a church basement on the Lower East Side. A talented young director named Stuart Vaughn soon joined with him to stage the plays. Actors were willing to appear with him without salary. His original financing totaled two hundred dollars. His stage lights were salvaged from a defunct movie theatre in the Bronx. And from so humble a springboard, New York's Summer Shakespeare Festival launched itself.

Those first basement audiences, admitted without charge, convinced Papp by the quality of their response that he could never abandon his project. Even he had not, until then, quite recognized what their response could be to honestly presented Shakespeare. Some of them, to be sure, were seasoned Shakespeare lovers. But hundreds more never had seen a play of any sort; and old people as well as children sat wide-eyed with delight.

By the summer of 1956, the fame of Papp's undertaking had spread sufficiently to persuade the city of New York to offer its East River Park Amphitheatre for his use. Early summer found the unorthodox unit offering productions of *Julius*

Caesar and *The Taming of the Shrew* which evoked instant praise not only from nightly free audiences of two thousand but also from first-string drama critics. Comment took note of the fact that while the performances were robust and lively they did not "condescend to the sort of mixed crowd likely to gather in a city park in the evening." Papp never relaxed his personal standards of excellence. Night after night, week after week, the amphitheatre was crowded.

Working conditions for the dedicated little company were almost prohibitively difficult. Planes roared across the metropolitan sky overhead, the hum and rumble of traffic never stilled on the nearby East River Drive, tug boats hooted on the river, diesel engines sputtered. And open-air performances, even under ideal circumstances, are trying for actors. Amplifiers can almost never be placed so that every section of the acting area receives uniform pick-up, and delivery of speeches becomes uneven, often distorted.

Costs for that two-months' park season were a modest two thousand dollars. Contributions from friends of the undertaking made up for every dollar of it, since admission was free (or "cuffo," as the theatrical paper *Variety* reported). Three weeks before they closed, the company discovered itself to be several hundred dollars in debt—largely for amplifying equipment. The enterprise seemed doomed. But when a newspaper's dramatic column reported gloomily that the festival's assets might be attached, a check to cover the deficit was instantly forthcoming from the producer of one of Broadway's smash musical comedy hits.

Papp was already nursing more ambitious plans for a second summer. He announced that he hoped to raise $25,000 dollars to finance free Shakespeare in several other city parks.

More private contributions rolled in. Foundations were persuaded to award small grants. Early summer of 1957 found the company touring the town with a stage mounted on a truck base, offering (still without charge) a production of *Romeo and Juliet* which drew the same enthusiastic capacity audiences and moved critics to the same warm reception. All boroughs of the city had their opportunities to attend free Shakespeare, and everywhere grateful citizens took full advantage of them. Before the truck-stage took up a "permanent" stand in Central Park for the closing half of the season (featuring fine productions of *The Two Gentlemen of Verona* and *Macbeth*) thousands of erstwhile non-theatregoers—a whole vast untapped audience—had enjoyed the attraction.

But the city-wide tour had proven a strain, both technically and economically. Eighteen hours were required for setting up the portable stage by amateur technicians. Money for advance publicity was lacking, so that people often missed performances through ignorance of the scheduling. Papp now announced a new objective—the establishment of a permanent free Shakespeare theatre in Central Park. Civil Defense authorities were contributing a generator for his lighting there; television colleagues were solving his sound problems without charge; actors were working for Equity's $40 weekly minimum salary, or even less. Despite financial deficits, Papp still refused to compromise his underlying aim by resorting to any sort of an admission charge.

The festival's third summer season—its second in Central Park—opened early in July with *Othello*. Despite two successful winter productions in the Heckscher Theatre nearby on Fifth Avenue, only approximately a third of the backing necessary to stage the planned program was in hand. The

actors scheduled to play Othello and Iago were both summoned suddenly to Hollywood, and could not assume the
financial loss of refusing to go. Still, there was reason for
optimism. The Department of Parks was erecting a new multi-
leveled stage on the site where the truck-stage had parked in
the previous season, with the reservoir and the picturesque
Belvedere Tower for a backdrop. The departing stars were
replaced with seasoned substitutes. And Philadelphia had been
so impressed with the company's quality as to sign it for a
pre-season June engagement, which helped pay rehearsal
and costume costs. A conflicting offer from Boston had been
regretfully refused. Once again, money came in from well-
wishers to stave off curtailment of the season. It was not
enough to leave a surplus, but enough to make possible the
planning of yet another summer's Shakespearean fare.

Then an unexpected blow was struck in the early spring
of 1959 by the most unexpected of hands. Erstwhile supporter
of the project though he was, the city's frequently autocratic
Commissioner of Parks suddenly announced that there would
be no more free Shakespeare in New York. Mr. Papp would
charge a suitable admission, he was advised, or his people
would not perform. The public, insisted the Commissioner,
was ruining the grass, and its replacement must be paid for.

Papp firmly rejected the order to establish box-office prices.
The Commissioner announced that Shakespeare in the Park
was at an end. Public reaction was instant and outraged. Newspapers protested editorially; civic organizations presented
formal demands for the project's reinstatement; thousands of
high-school students petitioned City Hall; strong theatre organizations registered their condemnation of the edict. The
Commissioner announced over the radio that, "It is a closed

incident"—and then wisely withdrew himself beyond the reach of telephones and interviewers, while the storm beat higher. When Papp's views on the matter were sought by the press, he would say only, "I have a feeling that Shakespeare will be presented in Central Park this summer in spite of the enormous power of the Commissioner of Parks."

He was correct. Public indignation had blown up the dispute into a full-scale political issue. A "We Want Will" committee established Fifth Avenue headquarters. A State Supreme Court Justice offered to mediate the dispute. The Commissioner circulated an unsigned letter referring darkly to Papp's "socialist background." As a result of his determination to "fight City Hall," Papp temporarily lost his bread-and-butter television employment, but was presently reinstated. Lawsuits were instigated and met by counterappeals. High civic officials scurried for cover, prudently removing themselves from the line of fire. And in the end, New Yorkers had their summer Shakespeare in the Park—free, as before. Very soon, and perhaps coincidentally, they also had a new Commissioner of Parks.

In spite of the need to prove itself financially and politically, New York's Shakespeare Festival has never been under attack in the matter of artistic integrity. It had established itself as an essential before the city undertook to construct a 2500 seat permanent open-air amphitheatre to house the free Summer Festivals. But this project seemed doomed when actual construction costs bid fair to exceed by $145,820 the appropriation passed by the City Council.

In the crisis, publisher-philanthropist George T. Delacorte, Jr., stepped forward with a check that more than made up the difference. Mr. Delacorte was no stranger either to Central

Park or to Shakespeare. His publishing company's Laurel Editions of the plays were standard for study in almost two thousand schools and colleges across the nation. A statue of Alice in Wonderland, a memorial to his first wife, had stood for several years beside the Park's Conservatory Lake. Now he united two enthusiasms in making the amphitheatre possible. Soon an accomplished reality, it was given his name. In the Delacorte Theatre's first summer, an estimated 135,000 people saw the plays presented, with thousands more unable to be accommodated.

In anticipation of a tenth Festival, with Shakespeare's *Hamlet, Othello,* and Sophocles' *Electra* announced for presentation in the Park, Mr. Delacorte again stepped forward with a gift. This was to pay for a mobile stage on a forty-foot trailer —to carry its own lights and generator, and to be towed by a Department of Sanitation truck—which could tour outlying city areas as Papp had done in his second season. A production of *A Midsummer Night's Dream* thus could be brought to New York audiences everywhere.

Acquisition of its new physical plant enabled the company both to offer notably more ambitious productions and greatly to enlarge the size of its audience. A televised performance of its *The Merchant of Venice* in the summer of 1962 proved so popular that this was followed in the next seasons by a televised *Antony and Cleopatra,* and a televised *Hamlet.* Although the annual budget by now had risen to $300,000, new and hard-working friends capable of securing the sum were on hand to raise it. The 1963 festival season was preceded by a gala fund-raising dinner dance for four hundred guests in the Imperial Ballroom of the new Hotel Americana, a far cry indeed from the humble church basement of only a few years earlier! And none of those who danced in celebration of Joseph Papp's unprecedented dream had the slightest doubt that Will Shakespeare had come to stay—free of charge—among his beloved "groundlings" in Central Park.

25. Mr. Shakespeare, I Presume?

One of the most engaging aspects of America's long, long friendship with Will Shakespeare has been the predictability with which he has turned up in the most unpredictable places. Backwaters and byways where a classic dramatist would seem to have no proper business often have been his special habitats.

For example, Will Shakespeare shared in originating what became a prize attendance-boosting gimmick at our American theatre box offices where business was slow. The legend FREE DISHES TONIGHT! has not infrequently appeared on motion picture marquees in letters bigger than the title of a feature attraction. This began in the 1860s when John T. Ford, owner of Ford's Theatre in Washington, took steps to bolster attendance at his traditional two weeks of Shakespeare in nearby Baltimore. This April engagement, with which Ford closed his season each year, was invariably a money-loser. Baltimore needed stronger inducement to enter the theatre than a routine road company in plays the audience already knew by heart. So Ford concocted the scheme of presenting each purchaser of an opening night ticket with a gift. The most popular of several he tried proved to be a small china pitcher, made in England, one side of which pictured Shakespeare and the other his birthplace at Stratford. Antique shops of the present day offer these pitchers as valuable rarities, but even when they were cheap and plentiful the first such premiums had value as business-getters, and established the popularity of "give-away china."

One would think that the most enduring genius in all English literature could have no possible connection with modern comic books. Yet in 1950 intrepid souls were devoting their efforts to making Will Shakespeare a staff writer for the comics. Pointing out that over forty million so-called comic magazines were purchased by the nation's youth each month, publishers of some of them countered hostile criticism by bringing out titles "of real cultural worth." One of the very earliest of these was *Macbeth*. Others of Shakespeare's dramas soon suffered the same absurd fate—were stripped of their poetry and nobility, reduced to flat captions under crude polychrome drawings, and (according to the cover blurb on *Macbeth*) "adapted from the Original Text for Easy and Enjoyable Reading." Though the whole process was regrettable, it also was proof of Shakespeare's startling ability to pop up in the least likely American corners.

Another unlikely place to find Shakespeare's work is among the rhymes and jingles which have come down to us as Mother Goose. But as early as 1786, a Boston publisher, Isaiah Thomas, printed an American edition of the time-honored rhymes, calling it *Mother Goose's Melody* and including an entire group of songs respectfully listed as "Those of that Sweet Songster and Nurse of Wit and Humor, Master William Shakespeare." Announcements described the section as "embellished with cuts and illustrated with notes and maxims, Historical, Philosophical and Critical," indicating that Master Will's debut as a nursery entertainer was taken by Thomas very seriously indeed.

Shakespeare wrote his plays, of course, to be performed by the adult acting favorites of his day—Burbage and the rest. Americans found no difficulty in twisting this purpose in whatever bizarre direction the fashions of the moment might dictate. The great public enthusiasm for the performances of the little Bateman sisters in Shakespearean roles during Gold-Rush days in California, was an acceptance of Shakespeare's being reduced to freak proportions. In this, the audiences perhaps merely imported England's earlier acceptance of Edmund Kean as "a celebrated theatrical child" when he played scenes from *Hamlet* and *Richard III* in 1801, at the age of fourteen, having made his debut in *The Merry Wives of Windsor* even five years earlier. Phineas Barnum found it proper to offer Shakespeare acted by midgets. Female stars of the nineteenth century for some reason felt an irresistible challenge in Shakespeare's male roles, and audiences applauded Charlotte Cushman as Romeo and Hamlet and as Cardinal Wolsey in *Henry VIII;* Sarah Bernhardt as Hamlet; even Adah Isaacs Menken as Richmond in *Richard III.* There seemed to be no distortion of casting so wild that the public would boo it off the stage.

As with unorthodox casting, so with unorthodox productions. As recently as 1959, an American *A Midsummer Night's Dream* exported to England set the play in a Texas version of Never-Never Land, complete with lariat twirlers, ten-gallon Stetsons, whooping cowboys, and an Indian princess. The plays have been offered in modern dress, made to represent the condition of a present day (such as the Orson Welles *Julius Caesar,* commenting on the Nazi evil); and in the costumes of virtually every period between today's and those originally intended by the author—as with Sir John Gielgud's New York *Hamlet* in Stuart Restoration guise, the Federal Theatre's Napoleonic voodoo *Macbeth,* and Stratford on Housatonic's conceit of linking *Troilus and Cressida* with the American Civil War. Yet no matter how periods and settings for the plays have been altered, the plays themselves have remained Shakespeare—and have attracted audiences.

Idolized though he has been in this country, Shakespeare certainly never intended himself to be set up as a god. At least one American, however, undertook even this. Robert Green Ingersoll, known popularly as "the great agnostic" during the height of his lecturing and writing career in the late 1800s, maintained that the Bible could be destroyed with no loss to the human race so long as the works of Shakespeare

survived; that "nothing would so raise the intellectual standards of mankind," along with providing the world with all
the moral guidance it needed.

Conversely, there have been those Americans who have
treated Shakespeare not as a replacement for the Bible but
as an integral part of it. One of these was Charles B. Parsons,
who combined two careers in the early days of Louisville,
Kentucky, by being both a local Methodist preacher and the
acting manager of the city's theatre. As an actor, his contemporary Sol Smith wrote of Parsons that he "played
Hamlet, Brutus . . . and pale-face-hating aboriginal characters
[Noble Indians] 'written expressly for him', much to his own
satisfaction. . . ." Smith also attended the church where Parsons presided, and set it down that he gave "copious extracts
from the speeches of Hamlet in the pulpit, without having the
candor to acknowledge the name of the poet whose words he
was transplanting into his sermons." Parsons ended his career
as a preacher only, apparently finding nothing reprehensible
in this literary larceny.

America's amusement world, during the first third of the
twentieth century, leaned heavily on vaudeville. In theatres
strung across the country, full variety bills were popular; and
Five Big Acts, Five! were a standard accompaniment to the
unreeling of feature motion pictures. Shakespeare was never
the backbone of such entertainment, which ran more to
stand-up comedians, animal acts, acrobats, blues singers, and
straw-hatted hoofers who could perform a soft shoe or a tap
and then shuffle off to Buffalo. Yet even in this unlikely
company Master Will was far from being a stranger. Every
so often, a "class" act would offer him—or scraps of him—to
audiences unaccustomed to such material. The legitimate star

Julia Arthur played a capsule version of *Hamlet* in vaudeville houses during the 1920s, and her appearance was far from an isolated instance.

Or consider the Bard as a fairgrounds attraction—something to catch the fancy of a holiday crowd between the cotton candy vendor's stall and the Ferris wheel, something to detour the fun-seekers on their way from the freak show to the hot dog stand. The New York World's Fair of 1939 discovered that Shakespeare could be popular even under such alien circumstances. On a midway replica of the old Globe's Elizabethan stage, a company of actors offered compressed versions of *A Midsummer Night's Dream* and *A Comedy of Errors* at frequent intervals. Many among their audiences found this reminder of the rich world of yesterday curiously comforting, in contrast to the fair's much-vaunted mechanical and scientific miracles of the World of Tomorrow.

Music of their own the lines of Master Will's plays certainly have in abundance. Yet they proved themselves graciously adaptable to a different set of musical demands when, largely during the nineteenth century, grand opera composers went on the hunt for likely librettists. Music-lovers who seldom attended the legitimate theatre thus encountered his plays in operatically altered versions. Giuseppe Verdi's *Macbeth* was first heard in New York in 1848; his *Otello* reached America forty years later; and his *Falstaff* was originally sung at the Metropolitan Opera House in 1895. Charles Gounod's *Romeo and Juliet* crossed the Atlantic in 1868, and the *Hamlet* of Ambroise Thomas followed it as an 1872 hit at New York's Academy of Music. *Macbeth* has always been the most challenging of the plays to the operatic minded, and various versions of it—with music by Chelard, Taubert,

André, and Reichart—were sung in Europe during the century. And even in the century of Shakespeare's own death, two separate operatic *Macbeths,* one by Davenant and one by Eccles, were sung in London at the Drury Lane. A modern operatic *Twelfth Night,* with a score by David Amram, was planned for a 1964 offering at the Delacorte Theatre in Central Park, but was later cancelled. And where the musical intention has been less serious than opera, Shakespeare has been almost as popular as a "book" writer for musical comedy. *The Boys from Syracuse,* "freely adapted" from *A Comedy of Errors,* with music by Richard Rodgers and Lorenz Hart, has had great popularity since it was first performed in 1938. Cole Porter's *Kiss Me, Kate* is indebted for its plot to *The Taming of the Shrew,* and *Romeo and Juliet* provided the basic structure for Leonard Bernstein's *West Side Story.*

Just as Will Shakespeare has proved himself adaptable to music, so have his words proved themselves suitable to modern methods of reproduction. In the record stores of America, Shakespeare has become a big item. As early as 1958, disc versions of *Twelfth Night* and *As You Like It,* joyously performed by actors of the Dublin Gate Theatre and embellished with songs and the incidental music of harp and tabor and recorder, were released in the United States and Canada. By 1964, the year of Will's quadricentennial, at least half his plays were available on records, all achieving or approaching excellence. A recording company in New York City had established a special division called the Shakespeare Recording Society for the production of play albums, starring the foremost stage performers of the roles, and operating the project in the manner of popular book clubs.

Many companies make Shakespeare recordings in both

monophonic and stereophonic versions to accommodate all types of playing equipment. Printed texts are provided with many of the albums, so that a listener may follow the spoken words, and a recording provides at least the aural equivalent of attendance at a stage production. The plays are not the only Shakespeare thus available. Sir John Gielgud has made American recordings of the *Sonnets,* and of his two famous Shakespeare potpourri programs, *Ages of Man* and *One Man in His Time,* which are in themselves beautifully organized dramatic entities. Shakespeare-inspired music, such as that by Mendelssohn for *A Midsummer Night's Dream,* are of course also on the record counters.

With the single egotistical exception of George Bernard Shaw (who wrote, "I despise Shakespeare when I measure my mind against his"), there have been few professional writers since Will's own day who would not have trembled at the thought of co-authoring a work with the Master. Yet for some reason this awe has not always extended to American amateurs. The optimistic talent of Americans for rushing in where angels fear to tread is amply proven by their frequent willingness to improve upon Shakespearean originals. The rash of burlesques on the plays which peppered our nineteenth-century stage is a group example. A recent individual one was furnished in 1959 by the enterprising Mayor Frank Zeidler of Milwaukee, Wisconsin.

On the theory that high-school students, his own children among them, were as often mystified as enlightened by the language of the Bard, the Mayor set about "translating" *Macbeth* into terms comprehensible to contemporary youth. "The merciless Macdonwald . . . from the Western Isles Of kerns and gallowglasses is supplied" became "The merciless

Macdonwald . . . is from the Western Isles with Irish light-armed soldiery supplied"; and " 'Aroint thee, witch!' the rump-fed ronyon cries" emerged as " 'Get on, you witch!' the fat old slattern cries." When Mayor Zeidler's new version was completed, it was staged by the Milwaukee Players for a run of six performances, and much applauded. Such "collaborations" between Shakespeare and Americans have not been infrequent down through the years. Some of them have not even been entirely infelicitous. And all of them have illustrated the warm informality with which the Yankee has accepted Master Will as equal and fellow worker.

Perhaps the American foible most difficult for even a soaring genius to rise above is our avid quest for "culture," revived from Victorian days. Since the Second World War, this old hunger has caused us to be taken in by all manner of pomposities. Part and parcel of this curious drive have been the earnest attempts to "interpret" Shakespeare—whose lusty dramas have excited red-blooded audiences through the centuries—in a sort of "potted palm" atmosphere. Typical of such efforts was the attempt made in New York by the celebrated English poet, Dame Edith Sitwell to "give a poet's conception of Shakespeare's dramatic verse." *Macbeth* was the subject for the Dame's lecture on obscure poetic techniques combined with a dramatic reading. The audience was impressed, but the critic John Mason Brown observed that he suspected "such highfalutin talk would have caused Shakespeare to outlaugh Little Audrey." He summed up the pompous performance by saying that "Shakespeare was murdered along with Duncan and Banquo."

But Shakespeare, even in lecture-hall platform guise, is happy in the hands of the professional actors for whom he originally wrote, for his scenes and characters belong to those who have been trained to play them. Thus, New York City's opening event in its celebration of the Four Hundredth Anniversary Year was an *Homage to Shakespeare* in which Sir John Gielgud, Dame Edith Evans and Margaret Leighton participated. With only three chairs, three lecterns, and two small tables on stage, the trio ranged through scenes from *The Winter's Tale, King Lear, Henry VIII,* and others of the plays. English all of them, they nevertheless made an American evening to remember of their joint appearance at Lincoln Center's new Philharmonic Hall. Actors, who know him best, have the good sense to let Shakespeare speak for himself.

It would be impossible to list the full range of unexpected side-roles Will of Stratford has played, and still plays, among Americans. We come upon him repeatedly outside the theatres for which he intended his works and the libraries where they are available and the classrooms where they are studied. Perhaps this sampling may indicate how often, in our daily round, we are likely to recognize his familiar influence in places where we least anticipated it; how often, taken quite by surprise by his presence, we may find ourselves silently exclaiming: "Mr. Shakespeare, I presume?"—in parody of the newspaperman Henry Morton Stanley when he finally located the missing Dr. Livingston in Africa.

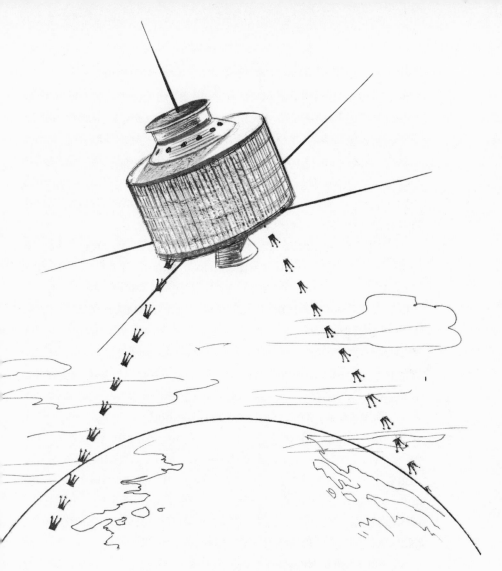

26. A Thing Ensky'd

Ralph Waldo Emerson once
made a prediction that when and if mankind ever made
contact with the denizens of other planets, it would be discovered that Outer Space knew our own star not as Earth but
as Shakespeare. The extent of his belief that such contact

might one day be actually achieved is, of course, a matter for conjecture. But one remembers that Emerson was roughly the contemporary of Jules Verne, whose often uncannily accurate scientific prophecies were wonders of the times. It seems likely that he would not be too surprised, if he could return to Earth, to discover how close humanity has come to being able to test his theory.

Having conquered his own planet, all Master Will required to carry him still further was a means of transportation; a space equivalent of those sailing ships which first carried him across the Atlantic to a new home in America. With the discovery and rapid advance of modern electronics, the vehicle was at hand.

Even in the early 1920s, the new wonder called radio had emerged from the crystal sets and the headphones of its early days. Almost as soon as it had established itself as a means of communication, Shakespeare's plays were being sent out over its air waves. By the mid-thirties, sophisticated radio productions of the plays—generally cut to fit themselves into the commercially allotted span of a single hour—were being tuned in all across America. The Radio Guild, in 1936, offered its listeners Shakespeare's entire historical cycle. In the following year, a sort of Shakespeare summer festival of the air presented the top stage stars of the day—John Barrymore, Orson Welles, Walter Huston, Tallulah Bankhead, many others—in a series of excellent Shakespeare hours. The Bard found little difficulty in taking his place among the soap operas and crooners and newscasters, and in commanding an audience.

America emerged from her war years in the mid-forties to face the presence of a lusty new electronic infant on her doorstep. Television had developed from wild dream to practical reality, and soon the "idiot box" was a fixture in millions of American living rooms.

How this development, enabling picture as well as sound to be transmitted through the air, would affect Will Shakespeare was amply indicated in 1956 when Sir Laurence Olivier's film *Richard III* was shown in a single three-hour telecast. Polls taken to determine the extent of its audience produced an estimate of somewhere in the neighborhood of 25,000,000 viewers. If such an estimate is reliable at all, that one performance was witnessed by more people than had seen the play in all the theatres of the world where it had been acted since it first took the stage in 1593.

Maurice Evans and Judith Anderson played a television *Macbeth* in 1954 which won Miss Anderson the year's "Emmy" for her performance. The televised *The Taming of the Shrew* in 1956 reached an estimated audience of 19,000,-000; and 1957's *Twelfth Night,* 16,000,000. *Hamlet* (14,720,-000 viewers saw it) and *The Tempest* (21,000,000) were both telecast as "spectacular" in 1856, each performance being considered a highlight of the television season. *The Tempest,* in fact, made the Top Ten list in the year's Neilsen ratings, prompting the theatrical paper *Variety* to run a boxed article headed "Shakespeare Makes the Grade." In the sense that he never before had reached such audiences—and that the soaring viewer figures year after year proved beyond doubt Master Will's television popularity—*Variety* was right.

Something new in televised Shakespeare was decided upon when a two-hour color "remake" of the Evans-Anderson *Macbeth* was announced for the 1960–61 season as the seventh Shakespearean production in the Hall of Fame series. The sponsors sent their company to film exterior scenes among the bleak Highland crags where the story was actually set. Hermitage Castle in the Cheviot Hills, and then Glamis Castle itself, were the chief settings. While filming still continued, Judith Anderson, the female star, was honored by being created a Dame Commander of the British Empire by Queen Elizabeth II—whose sister, Princess Margaret, was born at Glamis. The delighted cast gave Miss Anderson a torchlit celebration party within the ancient walls of the castle, and she is reported to have told the film's director, George Schaefer, that she aspired to make the deepest curtsy of her career before the Queen. "And," she added, "I certainly hope I do it right on the first take."

The Evans-Anderson-Schaefer *Macbeth* was a notable pioneering effort in several ways. As an artistic achievement, it spoke for itself. As a business venture, it opened new vistas for the industry. Whereas only a black-and-white "kine" (a record on film of a television show) survived of the earlier production, in this case a full-color film suitable for release in motion picture theatres resulted. Actually, the film was released as a theatre feature everywhere in the world except in the United States and Canada. Thus, it justified to business-minded backers the fact that it was the most expensive television show ever staged—costs ran close to $1,200,000, including fees for prime air time, even with the two high-priced stars working for percentages rather than for their usual salaries.

Maurice Evans, the male star of the televised *Twelfth Night* as well as of *Macbeth,* and probably present-day America's most eminent interpreter of Shakespeare, granted an interview at the time of *Twelfth Night*'s telecasting which contained considerable expert analysis of Shakespeare on our living room screens. Television, he claimed, brought "the play into the same sort of focus that Shakespeare had in mind. This play especially was intended for theatre-in-the-round. TV can achieve that intimacy, very effectively. The cameras can probe, and bring in the actor as close as makeup will permit. Shakespeare would be delighted, I'm sure." But he added: "I wouldn't want to do TV Shakespeare on a repertory basis. Shakespeare is best suited to TV when it's cast with new faces for each play. Also, it has to be spaced out, spotted strategically, so the appetite is whetted, not sated."

Television cameras invaded New York City's Central Park in behalf of Master Will for the first time in 1962, to bring viewers a performance of *The Merchant of Venice* from the open-air Delacorte Theatre. Although most technical difficulties on that evening were successfully surmounted, a helicopter flying south of the park cut across the signals being relayed from the theatre to the Chrysler Tower at midtown and created some confusion. Also, the production was being picketed by a group protesting against *The Merchant*'s being played at all—and a certain amount of sound unsuited to Venice's Rialto was unavoidably picked up by the microphones. However, neither of these circumstances discouraged the network from telecasting the subsequent season's *Antony and Cleopatra* as an unsponsored public service program.

The technical arrangements for the *Antony and Cleopatra* telecast were interesting as a sample of the problem inherent in putting Shakespeare into America's living rooms. The play had to be committed to tape at one of its final rehearsals, since the bulky cameras, extra lights, and crew activity would have been disruptive to a regular performance. Bad weather was a hazard that could not be eliminated; fortunately, this emergency did not arise. New York Airways, operators of the shuttle helicopters which were the only aircraft likely to be passing overhead, agreed to re-route their craft during the vital hours. To prevent risk of any other sound interference, signals were not again relayed across town but were fed directly into tape recorders in a mobile unit parked nearby.

Heavy equipment, brought in well ahead of the performance, included a mobile generator, four dynabeam lights, a control truck, four "machine gun" microphones, and the same number of cameras. Three of the cameras were set up in the aisles, the fourth on the roof of the control booth behind the amphitheatre. The long microphones were placed in the front row of the orchestra, each manned by a technician who could "aim" it at the actors as occasion required; and each was equipped with a foam rubber screen which would prevent chance wind currents from being picked up as sound. Special lights, not necessary if the production were to be viewed "live," had to follow the actors as they moved about the stage. The cameras were fitted with Zoomar lenses, making it possible to cut in for quick close-ups where desired—another factor alien to the production as park audiences would see it. And since there was little time for rehearsal with the cast, the studio crew had to treat their assignment almost as if they were covering a sporting event. They "winged it"—a theatrical term applicable to an actor unfamiliar with his lines, who must study them in the wings between appearances on stage.

Productions of the full plays, however elaborately filmed or expertly taped, have not been television's only use of Will Shakespeare. In 1961, a British-filmed series called *An Age of Kings* garnered much praise when it was shown on American home screens; the fifteen segments of the venture sketching deftly the running story of Shakespeare's cycle of histories. In

1962, a quite unique "spectacular" called *Shakespeare: Soul of an Age* resulted from the filming of scenes where Shakespeare had lived and scenes where high moments of his plays actually had taken place. The aim of this effort was "to show what remains on earth that recalls Shakespeare's life." Thus, cameras visited the Guildhall in Stratford where John Shakespeare held sway as high bailiff, and Ann Hathaway's cottage, and Clopton Bridge which Will crossed on his first trip to London. They also sought out the spot beside the wild Irish Sea where King Richard II landed; Birnam Wood, of such ill omen to Macbeth; every other location possible to pinpoint in the plays, and still surviving. At a small French village near Agincourt, authorities were persuaded to clear away the vines and rubble of centuries to reveal for the camera what was left of a wall that Henry V had stormed. Eminent stage performers served as narrators and readers on the sound track. But as *The New York Times* reported: "The big star of the telecast is unquestionably a former actor named Shakespeare."

Electronics had thus far made it possible for both the sounds and the scenes of Shakespeare to "fly through the air with the greatest of ease." Yet until July 1962, he was still earthbound in the sense that the beams he rode were sent modestly close to the planet's surface by relay towers stationed thirty miles apart. There had been no substantial indication that the prediction of Ralph Waldo Emerson might be even close to realization.

But in Andover, Maine, by that July, a project long in the making was ready to be tested. A twenty-story concrete radome had been constructed to house, among other complex equipment, the world's largest television antennae horns. The horns worked rather like old-fashioned ear trumpets. Their

3600 square feet of opening could scoop up even an extremely weak signal and feed it to a powerful amplifying device called a maser. Fabricated of steel, each mammoth horn weighed 380 tons and was so designed that its receiving and transmitting antennae were able to operate simultaneously.

On the morning of July 10, a satellite christened *Telstar* was sent aloft from its American launching pad—to orbit the earth in space at a speed of more than eleven thousand miles an hour. It was not of this man-made moon that Will Shakespeare had written, in *Measure for Measure,* the words "I hold you as a thing ensky'd." Still, the phrase would have fit—had even he been able to foresee the unforeseeable.

Technicians and scientists at Andover, on that July day, were eagerly standing by. On the satellite's sixth orbit they were ready for a sneak preview of what it could accomplish; the intention being to establish a direct television relay between Europe and America, which until then had been impossible because of the intervening curve of the earth's surface. Andover began transmitting sound and television signals, shooting them to the hurtling *Telstar*—which then, it was hoped, would boost the signals to ten billion times their received strength and direct them back to earth. Materials held ready for the trials included remarks by the then Vice-President of the United States, Lyndon B. Johnson. It was at once reported that the first trial was an encouraging success. Both England and France, to which countries the signals were beamed, reported picking them up clearly.

July 23 was the date arranged for a public demonstration of the new miracle. In preparation for the event, fifty television cameras—divided among the country's three major networks—had been deployed across America to film the material from which final telecast selections would be made. A panoramic view of the continent was the aim of the program. Everything from a baseball game to the Statue of Liberty, from a United Nations session to the Seattle World's Fair, from the majestic likenesses of four dead United States Presidents carved on the heights of Mount Rushmore to the Washington news conference of the living President in office—everything that might present a cross section of America to Europe was included. Not surprisingly, the cameras visited the Shakespeare Festival at Stratford on Avon in Canada.

Macbeth was the current attraction that summer, with Christopher Plummer as the thane and Kate Reid as his lady. In preparation was a production of *Cyrano de Bergerac,* in the Brian Hooker adaptation of that Rostand classic. The original intention had been to film a glimpse of the rehearsal of the new play, in order to show Europe how a Festival attraction was put together. But almost at the last moment the international copyright laws reared forbidding heads. The rights to Hooker's version (he was an American) were owned by his widow and not copyrighted abroad. International film rights, vested in the producer of a previous motion-picture version, might be infringed. In the resultant tangle, it became clear that *Cyrano* could not be telecast outside Canada.

The Swan of an older Avon stepped in to the rescue. His *Macbeth* had been playing since June 18 and therefore could scarcely be considered to be in rehearsal. But Plummer and Miss Reid played the dramatic "I could not say amen" scene with such distinction that there was no question their film footage would be part of the eventual history-making show. The scene that had taken two days of feverish work to make ready was flung into space for a mere forty seconds.

And so Will Shakespeare, so often first during four earth-bound centuries, became the first mortal playwright to make not merely "all the world" but the universe his stage. If citizens of other planets by chance tuned in on that eventful first official utilization of *Telstar,* they very well may have proven Emerson entirely correct.

Hurled from Andover to the far-distant satellite, and back again to Goonhilly Downs in Cornwall and to Pleumeur-Bobdou in Britanny, Master Will that night "opened" simultaneously on two continents. Three hours later, Europe responded to the American telecast with her own. Americans crowding around their parlor screens were allowed to glimpse the art treasures of the Louvre; a production of *Tosca* going on in Rome; the face of London's Big Ben as it struck the hour; and a herd of grazing Lapland reindeer fifty miles from the Arctic Circle. It is doubtful that many Americans who looked on felt a need to apologize for their own New World offering in terms of artistic excellence. America might not have been able to show the watchers in sixteen European countries anything to compare with the venerable products of their ancient culture, but she had shown them how thoroughly and completely Will Shakespeare, the giant of human ages, had been made her own.

Index

Index

303